LONG GONE LONESOME BLUES

THE TEXAS BRANDS
BOOK FOUR

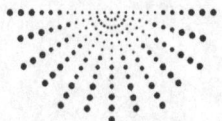

MAGGIE SHAYNE

All rights reserved.

No part of this publication may be sold, copied, distributed, reproduced or transmitted in any form or by any means, mechanical or digital, including photocopying and recording or by any information storage and retrieval system without the prior written permission of both the publisher, Oliver Heber Books and the author, Maggie Shayne, except in the case of brief quotations embodied in critical articles and reviews.

PUBLISHER'S NOTE: This is a work of fiction. Names, characters, places, and incidents either are the product of the author's imagination or are used fictitiously. Any resemblance to actual persons, living or dead, business establishments, events, or locales is entirely coincidental.

Previously titled: The Husband She Couldn't Remember

First Published 1998

Copyright © 2014 by Maggie Shayne

Published by Oliver-Heber Books

0 9 8 7 6 5 4 3 2 1

❦ Created with Vellum

THE TEXAS BRANDS

The Littlest Cowboy
The Baddest Virgin in Texas
Badlands, Bad Boy
Long Gone Lonesome Blues
The Lone Cowboy
Lone Star Lonely
The Outlaw Bride
Texas Angel
Texas Homecoming

CHAPTER ONE

*H*e'd dreamed about his wife again.
Ben lay still in bed, wide eyes staring up into the darkness as he waited for the chill in his blood to fade. A warm, dry breeze made the curtains dance in the open window, and brought in the sounds of a west Texas night. Cicadas whirred and coyotes yipped like brokenhearted lovers. In the dream Penny had been in trouble. And like she always did when she got herself into trouble, she'd been calling to him for help.

It wasn't like her to ask for help openly. Oh, but it was *just* like her to get herself into a mess and then come running to him, scared witless and too proud to admit it. He'd always known when she needed him, though, whether she admitted it or not.

It was later that she'd changed, become quiet and scared and timid. Much later. After Doc told her she was gonna die slow, and there wasn't a thing he could do about it. Seemed like just knowing that had killed her spirit. The most vibrant part of Penny had died before the illness even began to show its cruel symptoms.

In the dream, though, she hadn't been that broken woman

he'd married. She'd been the hell-on-wheels amateur sleuth he'd fallen in love with, crying, but in anger and frustration more than fear. And not so much asking him to help her as demanding he get his ass in gear. Like she used to do, before it all went to hell.

But in the dream he couldn't reach her. Couldn't get to her.

It didn't take a shrink to tell Ben it was guilt. He hadn't been with Penny at the end. And he should have been, dammit. But her death hadn't come quite the way they'd both expected it to. Not slow like Doc had said it would be. As things turned out, it happened all at once, out of the blue. Penny had died alone, despite Ben's promise that he'd be at her side, holding her tight in his arms when the end came. She'd died without him, and that was something he still hadn't managed to forget. It ate at him, the guilt.

A cow bellowed from outside, and her calf bawled back at her. Ben shook himself and slid out of bed, grateful to have something to do besides lie there and dream of Penny, or think back on all the things he should have done and hadn't. He pushed the billowing curtains aside and leaned his hands on the sill to look out over the lawn toward the barns and the pastures beyond.

A lopsided half-moon spilled yellow light over the flat, wide expanse that was the Texas Brand. It bathed lush, fence-post-lined meadows and gleamed on the barn roof. Ben scanned the pasture in search of the noisy cow and calf, just to be sure they were all right. But something caught his eye and dragged his gaze along the worn driveway to the road at its dusty mouth, where the words Texas

Brand rose in a hewed wooden arch that had been there for as long as any of them could remember.

A woman stood there, underneath that arch. Staring up at it. And there was something familiar about her stance and the tilt of her head.

Ben stiffened, then forced himself to close his eyes. "Not again, dammit," he whispered. "She's gone, Ben. And if you don't get hold of yourself, you're gonna have the whole damned family thinking your sanity went with her."

He opened his eyes again. She was still there. Her hair moved with the wind, lifting away from her face. But it was dark where she stood in the shadow of the arch. The half-moon didn't illuminate her features. He couldn't even tell what she was wearing. But there was something about her….

"She's not Penny. She's probably not even real," Ben told himself, even as he wondered why every cell in his body was responding as if she was. He couldn't even see enough to know what color her hair might be. But she didn't vanish when he looked away, rubbed his eyes and looked back again. At least he wasn't imagining things this time, like the other day when he thought he spotted his wife outside the dojo in the middle of his preschool karate class. She'd been staring through the window at him. Of course, there had been no one there. This time there was definitely someone there—just not Penny.

He reached for the jeans on his bedpost, tugged them on without taking his eyes from the spot where the woman stood. He didn't bother with the button or the zipper, ignored the boots standing at the foot of his bed, didn't even consider grabbing a shirt. He just looked out there one last time to assure himself she wasn't going to disappear like the last mystery woman had, and then he ran. Into the hall, down the stairs, through the house and out the door onto the wide front porch. He looked toward the place where she'd been…but there was no one. Nothing. The wind blew a little. Dust devils rose like ghosts in the driveway, and the porch swing creaked as it moved back and forth.

Ben scanned the area as far as he could see, but found no sign of her. It was as if she'd never been there. Just like the woman at the dojo.

Moving like a sleepwalker, he scuffed barefoot down the driveway toward the big wooden arch, ignoring the lights coming on in the house behind him, and the footsteps, and the familiar squawk and bang of the screen door. His brothers, of course, worrying about him like always. They wanted to fix this for him. The problem was, they couldn't. Losing Penny was like losing his own soul. And he was beginning to think he'd never get over it. He was beginning to think he hadn't yet realized the half of just how deeply it had affected him.

"Ben, what the hell's going on?" Garrett's booming, big-brother voice rolled on the night, breaking the gloom. Even the coyotes shut up when he spoke.

Ben just shook his head and kept walking. He stopped beneath the arch, looking for footprints in the dark, and seeing none.

"Ben, are you okay?" Elliot called. He sounded scared. He was the youngest. It must shake his sense of security to see one of his big brothers apparently falling apart at the seams.

"I'm okay." Ben said it softly, but his voice, like Garrett's, was as big as his frame, and carried. "I thought...I thought I saw someone out here, is all."

He heard booted feet tapping down the porch steps, and then a deep, firm voice saying, "I'll go."

Adam, of course. Ben had always been closest to Adam. That tie had been strained when Adam took off for the East Coast and his executive job there. He was only home now on a month-long leave of absence he still hadn't explained, except to say he'd been missing the Texas Brand and just needed to be home for a while.

Ben suspected Adam had come back because of him. The family seemed to think he'd been mourning too long. They probably figured if anyone could help him through this, it would be Adam.

Ben straightened as his brother drew near, but when he

inhaled, his heart tripped over itself. He smelled lilacs. Penny had always smelled of lilacs.

"So what did you see out here, big brother?" Adam asked, crossing his arms and leaning back against the pole that supported one side of the arch.

The guy looked like a GQ cover, even when he was rousted out of bed in the wee hours. Black designer shirt with its Nehru collar all buttoned up, and shirttail tucked into his black designer jeans. His boots gleamed. Not a scuff mark or a manure stain on 'em. He hadn't been home long enough yet.

Ben shrugged. "Do you smell anything out here?"

Adam frowned, but sniffed. "Yeah. Cows."

"Anything else?"

Tilting his head, Adam sniffed again. "Horses?"

"Never mind."

Adam studied Ben's face. "What did you smell?"

"Nothing."

"Well, what did you see?"

"Someone, just standing here. Doesn't matter now, I suppose."

"Maybe it does and maybe it doesn't," Adam said. "Did you think you saw a man or woman?"

"What difference does it make?" Ben straightened and started back for the house.

Adam's hand on his shoulder stopped him. "Woman, then. C'mon, Ben, be straight with me here. Did you think you saw Penny again, just now?"

Ben stiffened a little, but said nothing.

"That's it, isn't it?" Adam came around so he could see his brother's face. "I'm worried about you, Ben."

"Don't be. Look, I wish the whole damned family would just ease up. I'm going on without her. I set up the dojo, didn't I? Started a new life. I don't see what more you guys expect from me."

"A business isn't a life, Ben. And what we expect from you is that you pull yourself out of this. Stop mourning her with every breath you take. We want you to be happy again."

Ben met his brother's eyes. Darkest blue, and fringed in black, and filled right now with concern. "That's not gonna happen, Adam."

"It's not impossible, Ben. Other people do it."

Hell, he wasn't "other people." When would his family get that? His temper bubbled over, and he didn't bother trying to keep a lid on it. "Like you, right, little brother? Like the way you got over Kirsten Armstrong never showing up on your wedding day—by running off to New York City and never looking back? Like the way you refuse to go into town whenever you come home, for fear of running into her and the rich old geezer she married?"

Adam lifted his chin, anger and moonlight flashing in his eyes, though he fought it visibly. "I'll forgive that, Ben. Once. Because I know you're hurting."

"So are you," Ben said. "You just take a minute to think how much worse it would be if Kirsten died on you, instead of eloping with another man. You think about that, and then you tell me I should be over it, Adam."

Adam lowered his head, shook it slowly. "You're being obtuse. I'm not comparing my history with K—with her—to your loss. And I'm not still hurting over her betrayal. Hell, I hate her lousy guts."

"So much you can't even say her name," Ben said. Then he sighed. He was a jerk to throw Kirsten in Adam's face. His brother's wounds were still too raw. Ben tipped his head back and stared up at the moon for a long moment. "Sorry I ripped into you, Adam. That was hittin' below the belt. I know you're just being such a pain in the backside because you're worried about me."

"I am."

Ben nodded, lowering his head. "So'm I, to be honest."

"Then what are we gonna do about it?" Adam asked him.

Ben shook his head slowly. "Just don't tell me to get over Penny the way the rest of 'em keep doing, okay? There is no such thing as over Penny. Not for me."

"All right," Adam said. "I'll lay off."

Ben looked Adam in the eyes. Then, satisfied his brother meant what he said, he slapped him on the shoulder and they walked together back to the house. "So what do you do, sleep in them fancy duds of yours?"

Adam slanted him an irritated glance, so Ben shut up.

He didn't sleep again after that. There was only an hour till dawn anyway, so he put on his spotless white gi, knotted his black belt at the waist and went barefoot into the backyard to face the eastern horizon.

As the sun rose, he pressed his palms together in front of him, bowed deeply, and then began the slow, flowing moves of tai chi. He went through the yang short form, the long form and the short form again before the familiar feeling of peace began to settle over him. His nerves calmed and his muscles relaxed. The tension drained, and he lost himself in what he was doing, focusing only on that and nothing else. His entire being concentrated on each movement. He'd found it was the only time he could stop mourning the death of his young wife.

But even then, as focused as he was, he kept getting the odd sensation that someone was watching him.

She'd found an address, the name of a ranch in Quinn, Texas, and nothing else. She'd discovered the slip of paper in the lining of her jacket one day—after they'd let her start wearing regular clothes again, and walking outside in the fenced yard on occasion. It seemed to have slipped through a hole in the pocket and worked its way into the lining. She'd felt it there as she dressed, and her natural curiosity made her eager to retrieve it.

Okay, she'd had to tear the lining apart to retrieve it. So maybe her "natural" curiosity was a bit...overblown. Mutant, even. So what?

The Texas Brand. She'd had nowhere else to go when things began to look...less than just right at the clinic. Something was going on there. They were keeping things from her; she knew it. And when she'd mentioned leaving...well, they'd acted so strangely.

Somewhere in her mind there was a vague notion that she sometimes jumped to conclusions. Someone—she wished she could remember who—used to tease her about having more conspiracy theories than Oliver Stone. Maybe she was wrong in being so suspicious of Dr. Barlow.

But she didn't think so. The man had shifty eyes, and he never looked directly into hers when she asked questions. She sensed he was a liar.

Besides, he kept telling her she had no one. That she'd come to this clinic alone and desperate, and had told him herself that she had no family to turn to. And she knew that was a lie.

There was this feeling inside her. A huge, welling emotion that got so big sometimes it nearly overwhelmed her. It was like...like a longing. A craving...for someone. She knew it was some*one* and not some*thing*. And she knew it was someone real...someone lost in the vast black hole that had swallowed up her memory.

He'd loved her, though. She knew that. Because she dreamed about him. And she could never remember the dreams when she woke up again, but they left her feeling good all over. Warm and safe and so loved it was beyond comprehension. At least, she'd feel that way when she first awoke. Then, as reality set in, she'd be left with nothing but an aching sense of loss. Even though she wasn't sure just who it was she was missing so much.

Oh, she had someone, all right. And she would find him if it was the last thing she did. Even if Dr. Barlow did insist this man of her dreams didn't exist.

There were other things that didn't add up. Things that made her realize she wasn't being told all they knew about her. For example, she was American. It was obvious from her voice and her accent. Slightly Southern, with perhaps a bit of a twang. Right in line with the slip of paper and the Texas address. How the hell had she managed to get all the way to England in the first place? And why? Had she known someone there?

If she had, she didn't any longer. She knew no one when she finally clawed her way out of the coma. Not even herself. But some gut instinct had told her to get her rear end to Texas to find the answers. And so she had.

She stood now in the shelter of a large oak tree, her body shielded from sight by its broad trunk, watching him. And every nerve ending vibrated with awareness and a jolting feeling of familiarity. Was he the man in her dreams, the man whose face she could never remember?

Or was she just filling that emptiness with the first likely candidate she came across? It didn't feel as if she was. But damn, how could she believe it without evidence? She couldn't go by just this gut feeling that had hit her so powerfully the first time she'd set eyes on him.

He was a beautiful man. At first glance she'd have pegged him as awkward and clumsy. She'd have never believed he could move the way he was moving now, because he was very large. Tall, and broad as a lumber-jack or a weight lifter. Tanned from hours in the Texas sun.

Watching him move, hands floating as his body turned, she realized he was as graceful as a dancer.

He stood facing the orange sunrise. She watched from

behind, so the fiery sphere cast him in silhouette, turning the baggy white clothing he wore into gleaming red. He was barefoot as he moved his hands and body in slow, synchronized beauty. A slight breeze fingered his shaggy golden hair, despite the fact that he'd pulled it back with a band.

She'd come here because she had no clue where else to go. And this wasn't the first time she'd watched this golden-haired Brand from a distance.

But she'd stopped short of walking up and knocking on the front door of his gym or dojo or whatever he called it. And she couldn't bring herself to just go up and knock at the door of his house, either. She wanted to know what she was getting into first, and so some reconnaissance was in order. Who were these Brands of Texas? Would they be glad to see her, or even know her at all? What had they been to her? And why...why did looking at this man make her stomach tie itself in knots and bring an odd tightness to her throat?

That arched sign above the driveway had captured her gaze for a long, long time when she'd first set eyes on it. And she'd stood there like a fool, staring up and willing the memory to come. It was there, tickling at the edges of her consciousness, but slipping away each time she tried to grasp it. She'd been so immersed in the niggling sensation that she'd nearly been caught when the big blond cowboy came rushing out of the house. And she should have left right then. It was totally unlike her to get caught while on surveillance—she sensed that somewhere deep inside. As if she'd done this kind of thing before. As if she knew how.

But something about the big man drew her. Was still drawing her. She wanted to slip up behind him, right now, to touch him. To see the look in his eyes when he turned and looked into hers. She found it impossible to look away, though she knew she ought to leave before someone spotted her lurking in the shadows like a criminal.

And then he stopped moving in the midst of his practice, and just stood there, staring out into the distant sunrise. His big shoulders began to shake. His shaggy head lowered slowly, and then he sank to the ground as if his legs just couldn't hold him up any longer. She heard his deep, shuddering sigh and the name he whispered as he knelt there. "Penny."

And for some reason her throat tightened up, and tears burned her own eyes, as well.

Swallowing hard, she withdrew and quietly made her way back to the road, and down it to the spot where she'd left the "borrowed" car. Then she drove slowly back through the town called Quinn and on to her hotel in El Paso. But all the way there she couldn't stop thinking about that big man, and the terrible pain he seemed to be in.

At least, she didn't stop thinking about him until she parked the car in the lot behind the Boot-Scoot Inn and started for the lobby. Just outside glass doors with a big golden cowboy boot etched on them, she went still, because there were two lanky Texas Rangers standing at the front desk. It looked as if they were grilling the clerk, and she had a pretty good idea who it was they were grilling him about. She eased to one side of the door, back to the outer wall, and pulled the door open just a little, sticking her toe in to keep it that way, so she could hear them.

"And you don't know where she's gone?" one Ranger asked.

"No. She left sometime last night, but she didn't check out. I'm sure she'll be back."

"Yeah," the other cop muttered. "People who use stolen credit cards are real sticklers about details like checking out before leaving."

"Some of her things are still in her room."

Right, she thought. What few things she had. A change of clothes, a hairbrush and a bag of slightly stale nachos, half of which had been last night's dinner.

"Can you describe her?"

The clerk nodded and then went into excruciating detail about her appearance, making her wish she'd worn the dark glasses and ridiculously large hat she'd swiped from her nurse during her getaway. His description was quite complimentary, though. "Sleek mink colored hair to her shoulders, and the biggest brown eyes you ever did see."

"And did you notice what she was driving?" One of the rangers asked.

"Tough not to," the man said. "It was a beater. A rusted-out Toyota hatchback—blue, I think. In places, anyway. Sounded like the muffler was missing."

"Gee, Luke, isn't there a rusty blue Toyota on the hot list?" one cop asked the other.

She moaned under her breath.

"Looks like the credit card isn't the only thing she stole."

She'd heard enough. With a hungry stab of longing for that bag of stale nachos, she let the door close and slipped back toward the car only to hear the clerk shout, "There she is!" followed quickly by the sounds of Texas boot steps pounding toward her.

She leaped into the car, locked the doors, turned the key hard.

A sickly grunt was the only response from the starter. "Great timing, you junker," she whispered.

A beefy hand tapped on her window. "Step out of the car, ma'am."

She set her jaw, shook her head and turned the key again. It growled with a bit more enthusiasm.

The Ranger tapped the window again—with the barrel of his handgun this time. "C'mon, ma'am, nobody wants you to get hurt over this, now."

Still wrenching on the key, she rolled the window down just

a crack. "I didn't steal this damned car," she told him. Pumped the gas pedal, turned the key again. It coughed.

"Now, ma'am, we have an auto dealer in Horizon City who says otherwise. Claims you took it for a test drive and never brought it back."

"He was going to sucker some poor slob out of eight hundred bucks for this wreck!" she told him. "I did Horizon City a favor by borrowing it. And I swear, I have every intention of returning it and paying that sleaze a fair rental fee, just as soon as I can."

"An' how 'bout that credit card belonging to one Miz Michele Kudrow of London, England, ma'am? You gonna return that, too?"

She dug into the pocket of her jeans and pulled out the card. "Here," she said, sticking it through the window. "I only used it once. I had no choice, and she knows it. You tell her I'll pay her back."

"Well, now, that's gonna be kinda hard to do, ma'am, seeing as how she disappeared right after she reported it stolen yesterday."

She froze and a cold chill raced down her spine.

"You wouldn't know anything about that, would you?" the Ranger asked as he took the card from her and looked it over with a keen eye.

Swallowing hard, she said, "I've been here for three days, Officer. You can ask the hotel clerk."

"I'm afraid you're still gonna have to step outta the car, ma'am. Now, come on. Don't make this harder on yourself than it has to be."

She twisted hard on the key, and the motor wheezed and snorted and hiccuped. God almighty, she should have borrowed a newer one. But her conscience had pricked her enough just taking this piece of garbage.

"What's your name, ma'am? At least tell me your name, so we can talk about this."

She met the Ranger's eyes and felt her own get wet. "I'd be glad to tell you," she said as the engine finally choked to life, "if I knew it myself."

He frowned at her. She prayed she was guessing right when she guessed these two wouldn't shoot at her over one airline ticket and a junk car, crossed her fingers and popped the clutch. The car lurched forward and she gunned the gas, glancing in her rearview. She saw one Ranger lift his gun, look at the other, then shake his head and lower the weapon again. The two of them jogged to their own car, around the front hotel lot she guessed since she hadn't spotted it in the back lot. She wouldn't have much time once they got on their radio.

She sped through El Paso, found a parking garage and drove inside the blessed darkness of the cave-like place. She caught herself ducking her head as the car passed beneath the low beams in the ceiling, and almost smiled at the silliness of doing that. She parked the car in a crowded section. Then she got out, leaving the ticket on the dash and keys in the ignition, but taking Michele Kudrow's Mata Hari hat and sunglasses with her.

Then she stepped out into the sunlight, hat and glasses in place, and watched the police cars go screaming past.

"I don't know where I learned it," she muttered, "but damn, I'm good."

Ben sat very still, legs crossed in the cool green grass beside Penny's headstone. Since he'd come back home, he sat this way, in this spot, every day. He'd thought... hell, he'd thought he might be able to feel her...connect to her again somehow. But he hadn't. Not yet. Maybe not ever.

A soft, female hand closed on his shoulder. "Folks around here never saw no Brand sitting like a yogi before, Ben. You're turning heads and causing tongues to wag. You know that, don't you?"

He opened his eyes, his concentration broken. But he remained as he was, sitting with his hands resting lightly upon his crossed legs, thumb and middle finger touching. He didn't turn his head. "The tongues have been wagging ever since I came back and opened up the dojo, Jessi. Don't tell me you're worried about my reputation now."

"No. I think teaching martial arts to the local kids is good for you. Next to marrying Penny, opening that place is the best thing you ever did. It's your broken heart I'm worried about."

She circled around and sat down in front of him. Eyes round and concerned and spilling over with love. Married now, with a baby of her own, she was still his baby sister. He hated that he was the cause of her worrying.

"You okay, Ben?"

He pursed his lips, shook his head, changed the subject. "I'm going into El Paso this afternoon. Gonna pick out something nice for Garrett and Chelsea's anniversary. You want to come along?"

"I have a clinic to run. Two dogs, four horses and a first-calf heifer to check out today. And I didn't ask you what your plans for the day were, Ben, I asked if you're okay. Tell me the truth. Are you?"

Sighing deeply, he gave up. "Nope. You'd think I would be by now, wouldn't you?"

"It's been more than two years." She tilted her head. "But if I lost Lash like you lost Penny, I doubt I'd be over it in ten—or even twenty. Besides, it has to be even harder on you than usual today."

Ben met his sister's eyes. "She'd like that you remembered, Jess."

"How could I forget? She was always going on about her birthday being the same as Nancy Drew's, remember?"

He smiled, but it hurt. "She thought she was Nancy Drew when she was a kid."

Soft laughter, sad eyes. "Remember that time Mrs. Murphy went out of town for a few days? Penny was just sure Mr. Murphy had done away with her and buried her in the backyard somewhere. He was none too amused to find her peeking through his windows late one night. Surveillance, she called it." Jessi's smile faded slowly. "When he hollered at her, she ran right to you, Ben. She always ran right to you when she got into trouble. And you were always there for her."

"Not always," he said. "Not at the end."

Reaching out a delicate hand, Jessi pushed a long strand of his hair behind his ear, caressing his cheek as she did so. "You can talk to me, you know, I'm not a baby anymore. Besides, I loved her, too. We all did."

Ben shrugged and said nothing.

"What's going on with you, Ben?"

Sighing, he talked. Wouldn't do any good to try to hold out. Not with Jessi. She could talk blood from solid granite if she set her mind to it, and the whole family knew the granite would give up long before Jessi ever would. Nobody ever kept anything from her for long.

"Bad dreams," he said. "That's all."

"About the accident?" .

He nodded. "I found out some things after she died, Jess. Things that just won't let me alone."

Jessi's brows crinkled. "Like what kinds of things?"

"Like...she wouldn't have died easy. She never told me the prognosis. I mean, we both knew she was terminal even before we got married, but she never told me how—" Ben had to pause, swallow and clear his throat before he could go on "—how bad it was going to be."

Her voice a whole lot softer than before, Jessi asked, "How bad?"

Ben shook his head. "Long, drawn out. You don't want to hear details, little sister. But trust me, from what Doc said, it was going to be hell for the both of us."

"And you think...." She didn't finish the thought. Maybe she couldn't.

"I keep going over it all, you know? She'd been taking turns for the worse almost daily for a month before that accident. And the day it happened...there was no reason in hell for her to have been driving the car."

"Ben, tell me you're not thinking she drove into that gorge deliberately."

Ben met his sister's eyes. "How can I not wonder? And how can I not think that if she did, she did it for me? To save me going through the end with her."

"No." Jessi shook her head firmly. "No, I won't believe it. She didn't kill herself, Ben. She wanted to squeeze every minute she could get out of life. She wouldn't just give up like that. Not Penny."

She couldn't bear the thought; he could see it in Jessi's eyes. "Yeah," he said. "You're right, she did. But she changed, Jessi. Once Doc told her she was dying...she changed. Dropped out of that PI 101 class she was taking. Quit reading old Mickey Spillane novels...hell, she even stopped spying on the neighbors."

"I know," Jessi said softly. "But I always hoped we'd get the old Penny back again. You know, once she got over the shock of it all. And I still think she was in there somewhere. Even with all the changes she went through, Ben, I can't believe Penny would take her own life. I won't believe it. And neither should you."

Ben nodded. But he couldn't get the nightmarish memories to leave him alone. The charred, smoking wreckage, the blackened shape he'd glimpsed inside before his brothers had physically moved him away from the scene. Then later, the cops showing him her wedding band, asking him to identify it as hers. They didn't need to tell him it was the only thing still recognizable about his wife.

If she'd done that to herself deliberately—God, the thought tormented him. He'd isolated himself in the hills of Tennessee to grieve. He'd taken up meditation and martial arts to try to ease the pain. But it remained with him like some new organ he'd grown. He'd loved her. He'd loved the woman she'd been, and he'd loved the woman she had become. He would never love another. But even with that, he thought he might be able to find some kind of peace, some kind of acceptance—if only he knew the truth.

The problem was, there was only one person who could answer the questions burning in Ben's mind. And she was dead. And today was her birthday. And he could have sworn he'd seen her again last night. Ben wondered how a man could hurt as much as he was hurting and still be alive.

But he buried that hurt down deep, and managed to keep his voice from breaking as he reached for his gym bag, unzipped it and pulled out a bottle of root beer. Lifting the bottle, staring at Penny's headstone, he muttered, "Happy birthday, Nancy Drew." And in his mind, he could almost hear Penny, laughter in her voice as she said it with him. Her eyes always sparkled when they drank their annual root-beer toast to Nancy. Toward the end it was duller, that sparkle, and her smile was sad but there all the same.

"Damn," he muttered. "Damn, I miss you, Penny."

He had to avert his eyes when his little sister sniffled.

CHAPTER TWO

"I know where she is, Dr. Barlow."

Gregory Barlow turned sharply, startled out of the state he'd slipped into as he sat in the bedside chair in his patient's room at the Kathryn Barlow Memorial Hospice in London. He'd been staring at the empty bed, feeling everything he'd worked for these past ten years crumbling to dust. The clinic would have to be closed down now. He'd have to move the entire operation, use a new name. Again.

He met the nurse's eyes. Michele Kudrow was his most trusted employee, but even she didn't know the whole truth. Even the bit she did know was too much.

"Go on," he said softly.

Nodding, Michele cleared her throat. "They found my credit card in the States. I called my apartment to check my messages and—"

"I told you not to use the telephone." Michele went a bit pale. So he eased the anger from his voice before he went on. "For your own protection, Michele."

"I still don't understand why," she whispered. She was

scared. It was plain on her face. "Gregory, what have you done that's so wrong?"

He shook his head. "Nothing. But if they should find you, question you…. Just trust me, Michele. For the good of our work, you have to remain out of touch. You shouldn't even be here. Were you seen?"

"No."

He nodded. "You're safe at my place…just until things calm down." He touched her hand. "You do trust me, don't you, Michele?"

She nodded slowly. She was in love with him, and dedicated to his work. She would do as he said. For now. But if it looked as if things were becoming too dangerous, she'd have to be silenced. Permanently.

"Good." He made his expression as warm as his voice, better to keep her trust. "Since you did make that call, why don't you tell me what you learned?"

"The message was brief. Just that they'd found her, but that she'd got away."

Good for her, Gregory thought. He needed her back here, but not by way of the authorities. "Where?" he asked.

"Gregory…perhaps we ought to let her be. After all, she truly was well enough to leave the clinic. I don't blame her for feeling a bit stir-crazy, though I can't imagine why she'd go all the way to Texas."

He couldn't either. The files were locked and hadn't been disturbed. And there was no way she could have remembered. He nearly smiled at her ingenuity, though it could cost him everything. Taking Michele's hat and sun-glasses had been ingenious. Her purse and car keys, even more so. Leaving Michele alive, and conscious—though locked in a linen closet—had nearly been a disastrous mistake. If Gregory had been in her place, he'd have clubbed the pretty nurse over the head, at the very least, but he didn't suppose Jane Doe Ninety-eight was quite as ruthless as he was.

Then again, he had to be.

Ninety-eight was clever; he'd give her that. But he had to get her back here. Soon. Before she talked to anyone. Before she remembered anything—if she could still remember. He hadn't thought it possible, but now he wondered.

He kept his thoughts to himself, though, and said only, "Where in Texas?"

"El Paso," Michele told him.

He nodded slowly. "Book me a flight, then. I'll leave as soon as possible."

Lowering her head, Michele whispered, "You can't make her come back if she doesn't want to, you know."

She was wrong, of course. He had no choice about that. But he knew with a sickening sense of dread that it might very well be too late. His life's work was in this patient's hands. She had no idea how easily she could destroy him.

"She needs care, Michele. She's been so sick for so very long. I only want to make sure she's all right. Please, go and book the flight—but use my name, not your own. Get the first possible flight out, all right?"

"All right," she said, and she backed out of the empty room, then paused in the hallway. "The police said I should call them back—"

"Absolutely not."

She licked her lips, but nodded and closed the door.

Gregory tipped his head skyward. "I'll find her, Mother. I promise you that. I won't give up now, not when we're so close. I swear it to you."

From somewhere far beyond the room, he heard the soft, familiar voice. *That's my good boy.*

No car. No money. Basically all she had right now were the big hat and huge sunglasses, and they'd probably saved her butt, so she should be grateful.

She walked along the sidewalk, and smelled the tantalizing aroma of a deep fryer somewhere. The scent hung low in the oppressive heat. Her mouth watered. She couldn't remember when she'd last eaten, but if the pangs in her stomach were any indication, it had been a while. But it didn't matter. Food, she could do without.

There was a bigger emptiness than the one gnawing at her belly. She was lonely. Achingly lonely. She felt like crying, and she hated feeling like that. Melodramatic wimp! Good thing she wore the sunglasses. At least the strangers passing by—all of them walking with purpose and none wandering as she was—wouldn't see the weakness in her eyes.

Hell, even back at the clinic she'd had Dr. Barlow, liar that he was, dancing attendance. And Michele, her favorite nurse, bending over backward to keep her happy. But there had been a wall between them. A boundary they never crossed. She couldn't have called them her friends even if they hadn't been involved in some secret conspiracy to keep her in their clutches. And of course, since they had been, and since she'd known it almost from the moment the coma-induced fog blew out of her brain, she hadn't even tried to think of those people as her friends.

She must have had friends once. But it was as if she never had, because she couldn't remember a thing before the coma, and she certainly hadn't had a chance to get close to anyone since coming out of it.

Not even herself, because she didn't know who she was. Who she had been—or who she was now.

This lonesome feeling had been like a big black hole inside her since the day she'd opened her eyes in the clinic to find herself surrounded by strangers with lead crystal smiles. And now she didn't even have strangers for company.

She was running out of options. She'd have to quit hiding out and spying on the Brands soon, and just face them with her questions about her past and whether or not they had been a part of it. But the thought of doing that, of looking into their eyes, all her expectations boiling over, and seeing only blankness there, scared her senseless. What if they didn't know who she was any more than she did? What would she do then? What could she do?

She'd half convinced herself the big blond cowboy had been closer to her than anyone in the world. But that theory, delicious as it felt when she lay alone in the dark and dreamed about it, really didn't make a lot of sense. After all, if they'd been close, wouldn't he have known where she was? Wouldn't he have come to visit her or checked in on her at the clinic? And if he knew her, and he hadn't bothered to check on her—then maybe it was simply because he hadn't wanted to. Maybe he didn't care.

Her belly growled loudly, and she reminded herself of the task at hand. She had to get back to that small town of Quinn, and she no longer had transportation. It wasn't more than ten miles from here, and she supposed she could walk it—if she had some food in her belly. She'd never make it that far otherwise. Her head was beginning to ache again, as it did periodically for reasons Dr. Barlow had been unable—or unwilling— to explain to her.

The scent of greasy, nutrition-free food wafted past her nostrils again. Okay, food then. Without two dimes in her pocket it was going to be a challenge, and an added burden piled atop her already guilty conscience. But she didn't have a choice here.

The diner emitting all the temptingly unhealthy aromas was just ahead, and the big sign in the window promised great food at bargain prices. No sense piling up debts she'd be unable to repay. Might as well keep it simple. She started toward the front door, but as she passed the alley between the diner and the liquor store beside it, she heard a man cussing, and then a low, halfhearted woof.

Frowning, she stood back a bit, shielded by the brick corner of the liquor store, and peered into the alley. A trash can lay on its side, contents spilled all over the place, and a stubby-legged, barrel-chested, grime-covered little dog stood in what looked like a fighter's stance, front legs wide apart. His bottom teeth showed, lower canines pointing upward as if the animal was thrusting his jaw out. And the alley was filled with a low and ferocious-sounding growl that seemed far too big to be coming from such a little dog. The animal was so dirty, she couldn't even tell what color it was.

The man, on the other hand, was still swearing at the animal for spilling the garbage. He was a big fellow, wearing a spotless white apron over a belly that resembled an overly inflated beach ball. He took a step forward and, without warning, aimed a kick at the dog's head. The little dog ducked it, but stopped growling. The poor thing was shaking now, eyeing the man and then the garbage, licking his lips and funny, smushed-up nose.

"Hey, wait just a minute," she said, and she stepped into the alley. The bully glared at her. She glared right back, hands going to her hips, feet spreading to shoulder width. Fighter's stance, like the dog, she figured. "Just what do you think you're doing, kicking that dog?"

The man looked at her and tilted his head. The dog did likewise, but looked cuter doing it, and when she saw the expression on the animal's face, something in her heart got mushy.

"What business is it of yours?" the bully shouted.

Her gaze slid back to the man's again. "I was just wondering how you're gonna like it when I come over there and kick you."

His eyes widened, then narrowed. Then he shook his head.

"What're you, one of them animal-rights activists? This mutt tears into my garbage every day, and if he keeps it up I'll do more than kick him, I can promise you that."

"Yeah. If you were real bright, you might try feeding him."

"Then he'd never leave."

"But he'd never tear into your garbage, either, Einstein."

The dog walked toward her, turned to face Mr. Meanie and sat down at her side. She had to bite her lip to keep from smiling down at the little runt.

"So this is your restaurant?"

"Damned straight it is, and I don't appreciate strangers comin' around and stickin' their noses in—"

"I'm not a stranger, I'm a customer." She suddenly didn't feel so bad about scamming a meal from the jerk. Any SOB who'd try to kick a dog as cute as this one deserved to be scammed. But she didn't tell him that. "And I'm starved," she added for good measure.

The dog barked softly, as if to say "Me, too." She had to bend down to pet the animal's head, and immediately had her hand bathed as a reward. "I'll bring you something," she whispered. "Promise."

The dog looked up at her with brown eyes that seemed to know exactly what she was saying. The man just grunted at her and went back inside. Shrugging, she turned to go in the front way. The dog trotted along at her side, keeping pace, and when she went in, he sat down and stared at her through the glass door. The look of disappointment was almost heartbreaking. She sat at a small booth very near the door, so the dog could see she hadn't gone far.

God, it smelled good in here. French fries and onion rings. She could hear the fryer sizzling in the back. A few patrons glanced her way as she entered, then looked away, uninterested. She reached up to take off the hat, then saw the police officer nursing a cup of coffee at the counter, and thought better of it.

"Can I help you?" a waitress with big hair asked.

"Yeah. Gimme a burger—" she glanced back at the dog "—make that two burgers, an order of fries, a large coffee and, uh, a bowl of water."

"S'cuse me?"

"A bowl of water," she repeated.

The waitress stuck her pencil into her hair, put one hand on her hip and tilted her head. "I don't think I got that."

"You got bowls?" she asked the waitress, who nodded. "You got water?" The waitress nodded again. "Combine them," she said.

Big Hair shook her head, but fished out the pencil—no small task—finished scribbling on her pad and walked away, shoes clicking.

A few minutes later a hot, juicy burger was beginning to quell the hunger pangs, but she heard a little woof and looked up to see the dog, leaning forward until his squashed nose touched the glass, damp brown eyes focused on the food. Smiling, she took the second burger and the bowl of water to the door, and set them outside, away from the glass so no one would yell at her for feeding the stray. Somehow she didn't think the owner would thank her for it. Poor thing looked as hungry as she was, though.

Then she returned to the table to finish her meal. When she was done, she ordered apple pie with ice cream for dessert, and managed to sneak a tiny sampling of that out to the dog, as well. Not enough to make the runt sick. Just a little, since he'd apparently swallowed the burger whole and had returned to his post by the door.

Finally satisfied, she got up and wandered to the counter, took a book of matches from the bowlful sitting there in the smoking section, and then headed to the ladies' room. She waited until the one person in there finished her business and left, and then stood underneath the fire alarm and lit a match.

She touched the flame to the others, and the entire book flared to life. A thin spiral of smoke wafted upward, and in a second the alarm was shrieking. She tossed the blazing matchbook into the sink, cranked the faucet on and then hurried to join the crowd of diners rapidly exiting the building, and smiled to herself.

The others stood outside, looking back at the building, talking and asking each other questions. She didn't join them. Instead, she made her way through the crowd, and just kept on walking.

Until she heard a familiar grouchy voice yelling, "Hey, you!"

She started to run, glancing over her shoulder to see the owner in hot pursuit. But then the little grubby dog appeared beside him, grabbed hold of his pant leg and held on for a few staggering steps, snarling and shaking his head. The big guy toppled like a giant oak, and the dog ran on, catching up with her before she made it to the end of the block and ducked around a corner.

She crouched down and rubbed the wrinkly face with both hands. "I owe you one, pal," she said.

The dog closed his eyes as if in ecstasy.

"I have to go. You go on, find yourself another garbage can to raid." She rose and started walking, but the dog was right by her side. Frowning, she crouched again. "Look, I can barely take care of myself, to say nothing about a dog." But as she said it, her heart gave a little twist. And inside her, someone—someone she didn't know—whispered, *I've always wanted a dog.*

Where did that come from? She blinked and rubbed her temples, and her head began to throb. She didn't know where the knowledge came from, but it was there. Real. Authentic and undeniable. She *had* always wanted a dog, but she'd never had one. She'd had a cat instead. An independent cat who could get along just fine without her.

But that was before...must have been before, because she

didn't really remember it. Just knew it somehow. She couldn't have guessed the cat's name or imagine what it looked like. It had to have been before the coma.

The dog whined.

Her heart softened a little more. "You don't have anybody either, do you?" she asked. Then she shrugged. "I guess it won't hurt anything if you wanna hang out with me for a while."

One grubby paw rose and settled atop her knee.

"Well c'mon, then. We'd best move along. Old Mr. Meanie back there will be on his way, and he'll probably bring that cop with him."

"Woof!"

She stood up and started forward, only to run smack into a solid chest. And when she jerked her head up in surprise, it was to come face-to-face with the big blond cowboy she'd been spying on...and dreaming about.

∽

Ben had come into El Paso between his morning and afternoon martial-arts classes to visit the jewelry stores. His brother Garrett's anniversary was coming up, and Ben wanted to get him and Chelsea something special. The last thing he expected was what he saw.

He'd heard the commotion coming from the diner, and headed that way out of curiosity and to see if he could help when a mite of a woman with the strangest-looking dog he'd ever seen ran smack into him. But when she backed away a step and glanced up at him, Ben's breath left him in a rush.

Penny!

Her hair was shorter than before, but just as dark as sable and smooth as satin. Her eyes were just as huge and round and velvety brown, but there were shadows underneath them. She was just as tiny as before, but thinner now. And she looked scared.

He just gaped at her, speechless, mouth working but no words coming out. He gripped her shoulders, too hard maybe—and perhaps that was because he half expected her to dissolve when he touched her. An illusion. "My God," he managed to whisper.

Her eyes widened, and she jerked free of his grip. She opened her mouth, shook her head as she backed away from him. Then she just muttered, "I'm sorry," and she turned and ran away.

"Penny, wait!" Ben raced after her, his heart pounding, so shocked his vision blurred. She vanished into the crowd before he could even get close to her.

He kept trying, of course. Pushing past people, desperately scanning the faces. But she'd vanished. Again.

And he stood there, alone in a crowd, not even sure if he was sleeping and this was all a dream, or if he was awake and it was real. Or if, maybe, the grief had finally driven him insane.

He spent the next several hours wandering the streets of El Paso, searching every face, calling her name again and again. But he didn't find her. His heart pounded like a jackhammer, and his pulse was skittering all over the charts. He was sweating.

This was no ghost, dammit, and no glimpse of a shadowy form in the darkness. It was Penny. He'd touched her. He'd know her anywhere. He wasn't crazy and he wasn't imagining things.

Somehow, some way, his wife was alive.

And for the first time in two long years, despite the confusion and the shock and the disbelief...Ben felt as if he was alive, as well.

Making his family believe him was going to be a challenge,

he realized. But he had to get to the bottom of this, had to find her. Now. Immediately.

"God, Penny, come back to me," he whispered. And then he went to the first pay phone he found and called the Quinn Sheriffs Office to talk to his brother.

∽

Why didn't I just talk to him? Why did I bolt like that? Isn't this why I came all this way?

He'd known her. That big blond man she'd spied on, the one who stirred something inside her. He'd looked right into her eyes and he'd known exactly who she was. And yet she hadn't asked. Because he'd seemed so shocked and horrified and overwhelmed it had scared the daylights out of her. So she'd run, like a coward. She'd ducked into the doorway of a building with a For Rent sign and hugged the filthy little dog close, and she'd cried. She had no idea, though, what it was she was crying about. Or whether she was more afraid of never knowing herself, or of learning things she didn't want to know.

The dog licked her face and snuggled close, nestling his head in the crook of her neck and sighing in contentment. She hugged him tight. "You don't even have a name, do you?" she whispered.

The dog whimpered softly.

"I know what that's like. At the clinic they just called me Jane. I think I knew right from the start it wasn't my real name." She scratched the dog's head, and he seemed to like that. "But I guess I have a name now, don't I?" She closed her eyes, recalling the pain in his voice when he'd said it. "Penny," she whispered. "He called me Penny."

The dog licked her face.

"It feels so…strange…but good, you know?" She rubbed the dog's head. "You should have a name, too. Would you like that?"

"Mmmmuff."

She was still shaking all over, and shivering despite the heat. But holding the dog...it seemed to comfort her somehow. She'd focus on that for the moment, until her mind stilled and she could think about the frightening encounter—decide what to do next.

"Let's see, you're a Texas dog. So you need a Texas name. What about...Billy Bob?"

The dog seemed to scowl.

"Okay, what about Jimmy Jack?"

"Grrrrrr…"

"Okay, okay. Something more suitable to your personality, then. Let's see, you're living on the streets, stealing for a living. I know. I'll call you Oliver. How's that?" The dog tilted his head to one side.

Frowning, Penny took a closer look at the dog and noticed the "he" was a "she." "Oh. I guess you'll have to be Olive. Ollie for short?" she added.

"Woof," Ollie said, and she stuck her bottom teeth out.

Penny could have sworn it was the dog's version of a smile. But then Ollie turned away, staring out into the street, ears pricking forward. Penny leaned close and listened. And soon she heard it. A deep, plaintive voice calling, "Penny?" Then silence for a short interval, and then he would say it again, with a lilt at the end that made it a question—a hopeful one. "Penny?"

She peered out and saw him. That blond-haired Brand, searching faces and calling that name that must belong to her. Looking as desperate and alone as she felt.

"I should go out there," she whispered. "I should...I can't. I'm afraid."

Penny. The more times she heard him say it, the more odd it felt. Not unfamiliar, but so eerily strange. Like that deja vu feeling you get when you walk into a place you know you've never been before and feel strongly as if you have. When she looked toward the man again, he was heading for a phone booth. Maybe he'd given up.

She sighed in relief. Okay, he was gone. She was safe now. She had to think.

He knew her. She couldn't doubt that any longer. But what did that prove? It had been pretty obvious by the look on his face that he hadn't expected to see her here. And maybe that was because he knew she was supposed to be stuck in that clinic in England. Maybe he was involved in whatever Dr. Barlow had been up to back there.

And now he was calling someone. The police? She had to admit, with her talent for eluding them so far, she was beginning to wonder if she'd been a criminal in the life she couldn't remember. What if she had been? What if he was calling the cops now to tell them he'd spotted her?

Or maybe he was calling Dr. Barlow to tell him where she was. Maybe that was it. Would Barlow come after her? Would he take her back to that small white room where there was little to do all day besides watch TV mysteries and read Agatha Christie books?

She wasn't sure she wanted to know who that cowboy was calling. But she was just as sure she'd be better off if she did. It was a matter of self-preservation. So she crept closer, crossing the street when his back was toward her and clinging to nearby buildings for cover until she was close enough to hear his end of the conversation.

"I know it sounds crazy, Garrett, but I saw her."

Garrett. He was talking to someone named Garrett. And he sounded tortured. She couldn't see his face, but his voice said he was in some kind of agony.

"No. No, I've made up my mind. Penny is here, running around El Paso someplace, and I'm damned well going to get to the bottom of it. No, you can't change my mind. Get the wheels in motion right now, today, Garrett." He drew a breath, lifted his chin. "I want her body exhumed."

Exhumed! My God, she was supposed to be dead? Suddenly trembling all over, she could hear the tin-can-on-a-string sound of the raised voice on the other end. Then the blond man said, "You finished? Good. While we're at it, I want you to contact the El Paso police, show them her photo and... What? I don't know, take the one I keep on my dresser. Fax it to them and see if they'll keep an eye out for her."

A photo. Of her? On his dresser?

She felt dizzy, and her stomach pitched. The headache worsened.

"And if you can, Garrett, do it without telling them you think I'm completely insane, would you?" There was a pause. "No, I don't know when I'll be home. I can't..." The big man had to clear his throat then. "I can't bring myself to leave El Paso, knowing she's here somewhere, Garrett." Another pause. "I'm not indulging in wishful thinking, dammit, it was her. It was Penny, and I'm not giving up until I find her again." He slammed the receiver down, then leaned forward, head lowered and pressed to the glass side of the booth. She thought she saw a tear glimmering on his lashes. Then he turned and hurried off again—in search of some woman who didn't even exist anymore. A woman she might have been once—Penny.

A woman who was supposed to be dead and buried.

She felt cold inside and out.

~

Ben had his little sister take care of canceling his afternoon classes for him, and spent the day searching El Paso. Not that he had any luck. It wasn't long before Garrett and Adam showed up, as well, but he could tell their hearts weren't in it.

Garrett's big pickup pulled up beside Ben, and his two

brothers got out. They searched his face, probably for signs of insanity.

"You didn't have to come."

"The hell we didn't," Garrett said. "You've got me scared, Ben."

Ben sighed in exasperation. "I saw her. If you came to help me look, fine. If not, you may as well go on back to the ranch."

"We came to help," Adam said. "Don't get all defensive, Ben. You can't blame us for worrying. Hell, you'd worry, too, if one of us was acting the way you've been lately."

Ben sighed, lowering his head. Adam had a point. "I've been everywhere."

"No luck?" Garrett asked.

"No. Did you bring the picture, Garrett?"

Garrett nodded, yanking open the pickup door and snatching a framed photo off the seat. "I brought it."

Ben took it, but when he looked down at his wife's beautiful face and twinkling, mischievous brown eyes, his vision blurred. He blinked and averted his face, handing it back to Garrett. "Let's go talk to the police, then."

"Ben, you're going to ask them to look for a dead woman. They aren't gonna take this very seriously."

"So I shouldn't bother?"

"Of course you should." Adam clasped Ben's shoulder and squeezed. "Garrett just wants you to be prepared, is all."

"Hell, I don't think anyone could be prepared for something like this," Ben muttered. He got into the pickup and slid over to make room for Adam.

Garrett just shook his head and walked to the driver's side. It was a short ride to the Texas Rangers' El Paso office, and they didn't have to wait when they got there. Garrett knew most of these guys, worked with them on occasion, and walked right up to the desk of one of them, a tall slender fellow with dark hair going silver at the edges.

The Ranger got to his feet the second he saw Garrett and extended a hand. "Garrett, good to see you!"

"Matt," Garrett said. "These are my brothers, Adam and Ben."

Matt nodded to each of them in turn. "You guys look about as cheerful as pallbearers. I take it this isn't a social call?"

"Afraid not," Garrett said, and he handed the photo to the man. "We're looking for—"

"Where did you get this?" Matt asked, looking up from the picture with surprise in his eyes. "Do you know this woman?"

Garrett opened his mouth, but Ben spoke first. "Why, Matt? Do you?"

Matt looked from Ben to Garrett. Garrett sighed. "Trust me on this, will you? If you've seen her...just give us what you know. I'll fill you in later, once we figure out what's going on."

"If you know who she is, Garrett—"

"It's personal, Matt."

Matt met Garrett's eyes, then slid his gaze to Ben's again. "Okay. Yeah, you might say I've seen her. Look, why don't you guys sit down, pull up some chairs. You want coffee?"

Ben closed his eyes and sought patience. "Please, just tell us." His voice came out strained and hoarse.

Matt cleared his throat. "Had a call yesterday from a hotel not far from here. Some woman had checked in using a stolen credit card. While we were there, checking it out, she showed up." He pointed to the picture. "But she ran to her car before we could grab her. Turns out the car was stolen, too."

Garrett's eyes were as wide as saucers. "You're sure it was her? This woman in the photo?"

"Couldn't have been her," Ben said. "She'd sooner dig ditches than take something that wasn't hers." He felt disappointment clear to his toes. But he knew Penny. Knew this couldn't be her.

"I looked right at her through the car window, closer than you and I are right now, and tried to get her to unlock the danged door and get out."

Garrett frowned. "If you were that close, how'd she get away?"

He smiled a little and shook his head. "Damned spitfire didn't give me much choice, Garrett. She took off, and…well, hell, I wasn't gonna shoot at her. I…I don't know, I kinda liked her. She had spunk."

Ben felt a knife slide into his heart, but managed to speak again, through the pain. "Did she say anything? Give you any clue where she might be going or…or…." He shook his head, his voice trailing off.

"She said she'd done us a favor by stealing the junk car before the dealer could sell it to somebody for twice what it was worth. Said she intended to return it and pay for using it when she could. And then she cracked the window a little and handed me that hot credit card, and said she'd pay that back, as well." Matt shook his head. "It was the damnedest thing," he said. "I asked her name, and she said she didn't know. And I'll tell you something, boys. I believed her."

Adam and Garrett exchanged alarmed glances. Ben stood there feeling as if he'd been hit in the belly with a two-by-four. He turned and wandered to the nearest window, staring out. Wondering where she was, what had happened, how she could be alive at all. Maybe she wasn't. Didn't they say everyone had a twin somewhere? Maybe this was just a look-alike.

He heard Garrett talking. "Chances are pretty slim your suspect is the woman we know," he said.

"Yeah, well, people change."

Ben closed his eyes. People change. Maybe, but from dead to alive?

"I can tell you this much, if it is her, she's no criminal, Matt. I don't know what's going on, but the woman we're thinkin' of is as honest as the day is long. And maybe not in the best of health right now."

"A bit of an understatement, don't you think?" Adam muttered.

"I'll make sure the boys know," Matt said. "If we find her, Garrett, we'll treat her with kid gloves, you've got my word on that."

"I'm obliged to you, Matt."

They talked some more, but Adam sidled away and came to stand beside Ben.

"She's out there somewhere," Ben said slowly. "It's gonna be dark soon. Dammit, she's got no money, or she damned well wouldn't be stealing. Could be cold. Hungry—"

"We'll find her, Ben. And listen...I mean, I don't want to be the hard-ass here, but you have to remember, this might not be Penny at all. Maybe it's just someone with a striking resemblance, even a relative of hers."

Ben shook his head. "I know. I keep telling myself that. But dammit, Adam, I looked into her eyes."

"Ben, she was dying. No, I know you don't want to hear this, but you have to. Even if it hadn't been for the accident, Penny would have been gone by now. You know that."

Ben shook his head, staring out at the streets again. People passing, everyone looking like Penny to his longing eyes until they got close enough so he could see that they weren't. "She looked so scared, Adam." His heart was breaking all over again. And he wasn't ashamed when a teardrop squeezed loose and rolled down his face.

Rangers came and went, and phones were ringing. Everything seemed to be going on just as if the whole world hadn't suddenly turned upside down.

Garrett came up behind him and slapped his shoulder. "Let's go. I'm gonna put in a call to Judge Reynolds. With this new information, he'll put that exhumation order right through. Then we'd best head home, prepare the family, just in case."

Ben shook his head. "I can't leave. I can't."

Garrett sighed. Adam said, "Ben, you saw her in Quinn. And last night, right out at the ranch. She obviously knows where to find us. And if it is Penny, Ben, she'll come home. You know she will."

"Do I?" he asked. "It's been over two years, boys. Don't you think if my wife wanted to come home she'd have done it by now?"

Adam looked at Garrett. Garrett just sighed. "You'll need to sign papers, Ben, in order for the body to be exhumed. You might as well get that done, get some rest. You can always come back."

Adam nodded hard in agreement. "You'll feel better once you know for sure who's buried in that grave, Ben. You know you will."

Ben swallowed hard, but knew they were right. Besides, he'd already searched El Paso all day long. And he knew Penny well enough to know that if she didn't want to be found, she wouldn't be. She'd read enough detective novels to know how to hide. But he also knew she'd come back to him. Sooner or later. Especially if she was in trouble. Because she always had. Best he be where she'd expect to find him, in case she did.

∽

Getting back to Quinn, Texas, proved to be a whole lot easier than she'd expected. That big ol' pickup truck those fellows had arrived in had a tarp in the back. And Penny—she was starting to get used to thinking of herself by that name—gathered her stubby little dog in her arms and made a dash for it as soon as the three men had gone into the police station. She curled up underneath the tarp and waited. Ollie seemed content with this new situation. She turned around a few times and snuggled down beside her. A few minutes later the runt was snoring so loudly that Penny was half-afraid they'd hear her when they came out.

A short while after that, she heard the door slamming closed and the engine starting up. Then the truck pulled into motion, and Penny's heart pounded harder than the tires over the potholes. They'd be heading back to that beautiful, sprawling ranch, she figured.

What the hell was going to happen to her when she got there?

CHAPTER THREE

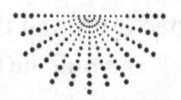

The truck stopped only minutes after it started, and Penny carefully lifted one corner of the tarp to see what was going on. The blond cowboy—the one she was starting to think of as *her* Brand—got out, and walked within inches of her. She froze as he passed, knowing if she moved, even to duck, he'd spot her there. So she just went still, and watched him.

He was tall. Taller than she'd realized when she'd watched him from a distance. There was well over six feet of man under the crown of that hat he wore. And he was big—but he moved easily, his step light, like a much smaller person might move. She'd noticed that grace about him before, and it still impressed her. Such a contradiction.

He looked weary. Tiny lines seemed permanently etched at the corners of his eyes, and his wide shoulders could have been wider if they hadn't been bowed slightly, as if they bore a heavy load.

As he passed, she caught his scent. Leather and spice. Familiar...

A piercing pain knifed through her head, and she almost

cried out at the suddenness and severity of it. Gritting her teeth, closing her eyes tight, she managed to keep quiet. He finally passed, and the scent faded along with the sound of his footsteps. The pain ebbed a little, at least enough so she could open her eyes again.

He was getting into another pickup. Of course, she should have known. He'd been here alone earlier, so he'd have driven his own vehicle. He started it up, and the headlights flashed on, and this time she did duck and pull the tarp down to cover her.

The vehicle she was in began moving again, and the one behind followed closely. Oh, hell, if she moved or the tarp blew up, he'd see her for sure!

She had to lie very still. She told Olive this was necessary, but the didn't seem to have a problem with it. As long as Penny lay beside her, she seemed perfectly content to stay snooze. The trip back to the ranch was far shorter in the newish pickup truck than it had been in that smoke-belching car she'd used. Almost pleasant, even, in spite of the fact that the bed was hard and she was aching from lying so still. The area beneath the tarp smelled faintly of fresh hay and molasses. And the aromas were soothing, somehow. Sooner than she could believe, she felt the rumble beneath the tires that told her they'd turned off the paved roads and onto the dirt one that led to the ranch. She relaxed just a little, though she should have been more nervous than ever.

She must not have been as uncomfortable as she'd thought, curled on the bed of that truck, because she never felt it come to a stop. She fell asleep waiting to arrive, and wondering what she should do when they did.

When she woke again, it was morning. Sunlight slanted beneath folds in the tarp and bathed her face, and she heard people moving around outside. Walking back and forth past the pickup where she hid. She peered out and saw the Brands— God, but there were a lot of them!— walking into the stables nearby, riding out again on horseback and heading into the fields. The blond one wasn't among them. It was several long moments before she heard his voice, and the creak of a screen door.

"I have to be there, Chelsea," he was saying. "You can understand that, can't you?"

"Of course I can," a woman answered. "I just can't believe they're doing it so soon."

"Your husband can pull strings with the best of them," he replied. "Judge Reynolds owed Garrett a favor."

"Everybody owes Garrett a favor," she said. Then, her voice softer, she went on, "You go ahead, Ben. I'll get a sitter for little Ethan, and we'll all come to the cemetery as soon as chores are done."

There was a pause. Then the blond Brand said, "I think I want to be alone for this."

The woman sighed. "I doubt wild horses can keep your brothers away, Ben. But I'll do my best."

"Thanks," he told her. Then there were heavy steps on the porch. "Tell Garrett I appreciate the pickup. I'll take a look at mine this afternoon. Probably just a loose belt."

"You sure you can't eat a little something before you go?"

"Not even if I wanted to," he said. And then the pickup moved with his weight, and Penny was off for another ride.

One she was certain she didn't want to take. Because she was pretty sure she was headed to her own grave, and that was something she was afraid she couldn't bear to see. She held her dog closer and prayed she was wrong.

∼

Ben stood in the familiar spot, looking down at the rose granite headstone he'd had made for his wife and the flowers he replaced every week. He tried hard not to bawl like a newborn calf when he heard the backhoe rumbling near. But it was damned hard.

They likely wouldn't start digging until Garrett arrived. He figured as sheriff, Garrett would have to be present at the exhumation, whether Ben wanted him here or not. He crouched down to gently gather up the flowers. Then he straightened, clutching them in his hands.

"Narcissus," he muttered. "You always loved the smell." Then he brought the perfect white petals to his nose and inhaled, and as he did he could picture her doing the same.

For the first time he thought he could feel Penny's presence here. All this time he'd come here looking for that feeling, and never found it. Ironic that today of all days, he sensed her close to him. Felt it so strongly that he almost regretted making this decision. She was here. It was no stranger lying in this grave; it was his wife. Maybe he'd only imagined seeing her. Maybe it was therapy he needed, not an exhumation.

Who was he kidding? No therapy was going to fix what was wrong with him. Nothing ever would. But maybe if he could just know for sure….

"Don't let them dig it up," a trembling voice whispered from right behind him.

Ben went stiff, lifting his head away from the flowers with their red-rimmed centers and heady fragrance. And he felt his fist clench reflexively around the tender stems.

A breeze riffled his hair and the lush green grass at his feet.

"Please," she said, "I don't want to see this."

Very slowly Ben turned around.

Penny stood not two feet from him. She wasn't looking at him, but past him at that pink-hued granite marker with wide, frightened eyes that brimmed with tears. His wife stood in front of him, staring at her own grave.

Ben's hands moved slowly, reaching out, touching her shoulders, very nearly jerking away again when he found warm, solid flesh instead of some ghostly mist. She was real. And he closed his hands on her instead. "Penny?" And finally her eyes met his. "God, Penny, is it really you?"

Her lower lip trembled, but she quickly blinked away the tears that tried to pool in her eyes. "You aren't going to believe this, but...I don't know," she told him in a soft voice. "Is it?"

Ben let his eyes feast on her face, probe hers, and there was no question. This was not a look-alike, and not some distant relative who bore a marked resemblance. This was Penny. And he couldn't talk because his heart had jumped up into his throat and its beat was trying to choke him. His eyes blurred with moisture, and his chest heaved spasmodically. And it was like a reflex action when Ben wrapped her up tight in his arms and held her, and he knew. This was Penny. This was his wife. He didn't know how or why, but he knew the way she felt in his arms. Like heaven. He crushed her tight to him, kissed her hair, her face, her neck.

"Cut it out," she muttered.

"It's okay, Penny. I've got you now, and everything's gonna be okay." He buried his fingers in her soft, dark hair, holding her head to his chest. He was shaking all over, and his knees were weak. God, how had this happened? Why? It didn't matter. Nothing mattered except that she was here, back in his arms where she belonged, and he was never going to let her go again. Not ever.

"Let go of me!"

His hand in her hair stilled, and he realized she was struggling in his arms, not hugging him back. It was like the bubbling cauldron in his belly just got flash frozen. He felt the chill, the sudden foreboding. She wasn't acting like the Penny he knew.

Slowly he eased his grip, changed it. But he didn't let her go, half-afraid she'd run away again. Half-afraid that if he stopped touching her, she'd vanish, and he'd realize she'd been no more than an illusion. Stepping back slightly, he searched her face.

Wide eyes, as frightened as a trapped animal's but hiding that fear beneath a furious glare, stared back at him. The branches overhead swayed in the stiffening wind, and the morning sun cast lively shadows over her face.

"Penny? Honey, what is it? What's wrong?"

She shook her head slowly, pulling against his hands, but he only held on more tightly. And when it seemed she understood that he wouldn't release her, she stopped fighting and stood there, breathless, staring up at him.

"Talk to me," he whispered. "Jeeze Penny, say something."

Closing her eyes slowly, she lowered her head. "I don't know what you want me to say." Her voice was soft, ragged. "I don't know you."

"Don't be ridiculous. Of course you know me, Penny. What are you—?"

"I don't know you!" Her head came up fast, her eyes meeting his and holding them. "And I don't know me. I don't know anything." Her lips trembled, and she caught them in perfect white teeth as her gaze slid past him to fix itself to the headstone again. "Is this...is this grave...is it supposed to be mine?"

He was too shocked to do more than stand there and nod. His hands seemed to lose their strength and they fell to his sides. Penny moved past him to stand before the headstone, and as he turned to watch, her knees seemed to melt, and she sank into the thick green grass.

"Penny Lane," she whispered, her fingers tracing the letters chiseled into the granite. "That's almost funny."

"Your parents thought it was beautiful," he told her. "So did I."

Her hands moved, fingers pausing on the last name he'd given her, the one they shared. "Brand?" she asked, not looking at him.

He didn't answer, not sure what to say. What was wrong with her? How could she claim not to know him? He moved closer, so close his legs brushed her back as she knelt there, and he watched her tracing the letters, heard her reading aloud in a soft monotone that held no emotion. "Beloved Wife." She turned and stared up at him. "Whose beloved wife was I?"

Was? What the hell did she mean, was? "Mine," he told her, and he knew there was a wealth of power behind the word. "And you still are, Penny. I don't know what the hell is going on, how any of this could have happened or why you're pretending not to know me, but you're my wife."

She nodded, taking his words in without flinching, looking as dispassionate as if she were listening to a news report. "And what about the 'beloved' part?"

He winced. "How can you ask me that?"

Gripping the headstone, she got to her feet. Ben vaguely heard the backhoe rumble to a stop nearby, but chose to ignore it as Penny turned to face him squarely. The wind blew from behind her, so her hair danced over her face. "It's not such a strange question," she told him. "I woke from a coma in a clinic in a foreign country to be told I had no one. That my family had washed their hands of me. That they hadn't once called or visited or even shown an interest in knowing whether I was still alive, and I want to know why." She lowered her head, shaking it. "I guess you're right. It was a stupid question." Head still down, she started to walk past him.

He panicked! She couldn't just leave, not now! Ben gripped her arms, twisting her toward him once more. "We thought you were dead," he nearly shouted. "Dammit, Penny, we buried you. We didn't know—*I* didn't know!"

Blinking slowly, she stared at him, and her eyes were wary. "Is that the truth?"

And gradually the blankness in her eyes finally got through to him. It was as if the love that used to glow from behind them had been extinguished, and Ben searched her face with his heart in his throat. "If you remembered what we had, you wouldn't be asking me that. My God, Penny, you don't, do you? You don't remember...."

"No." She drew a breath, lifted her chin. "Until I heard you say it, I didn't even know my name."

"But...but you came here. You found me again...." He didn't want to believe her.

"I found an address on a piece of a crumpled envelope that had fallen into the lining of my jacket. That's all. I thought...if I came here...I might find some clue who I had been." Averting her eyes, she added, "A husband was the last thing I expected...let alone a grave with my name on a cold granite headstone."

Ben looked down sharply, then glanced sideways at the backhoe operator, who was watching, looking confused and unsure what to do next.

"Who's buried here?" Penny asked. "If it's not me, then who?"

"I don't know," Ben whispered. "Someone who died in your car."

Her eyes narrowed. So many times he'd seen her look at other people the way she was looking at him now. The old Penny, not the weak, dependent one she'd become once the illness took hold. She'd doubted everything anyone told her back then, until she had proof it was true. And more than once, he'd seen this very look trained on some person she believed to be lying to her.

But he had never once seen that look trained on him. He'd never expected to.

"Penny...honey, the car burned. The body...." He shook his head and didn't go on, seeing the horror appear in her eyes, though she hid it quickly. "Whoever it was, they were wearing... this." As he spoke he pulled the chain from beneath his shirt. Penny's wedding band dangled from the end. He'd worn it since the day he'd lost her.

She touched it. Fingered the onyx and diamond chips.

Frowned and tilted her head. Then let it go and squeezed her eyes hard as if her head hurt.

"Penny?"

She massaged her temples, scowling. "It'll be gone in a second," she said.

"You should see a doctor. I can call—"

"No!" Her eyes flew wide, and she took a step away from him. "No doctors. I won't. You try to make me, and I'll be out of here so fast you'll—"

"Okay, okay. Take it easy." He spoke softly, frightened by the panic in her eyes, eager calm her, take care of her the way he used to. "Listen, no one's going to make you do anything you don't want to do, I promise you that. All right?"

She eyed him, wary and ready, it seemed, to take flight at any moment.

"I want you to come home with me," he said very softly. "To the ranch."

"No." She looked panicky again.

Ben pushed a hand through his hair and told himself to slow down or he'd scare her off. There were so many questions, so much he didn't know. But apparently there was a lot she didn't know, either. He had to be careful, go slow with her. He had to remember how fragile she was. How delicate.

"That didn't come out just right," he told her. "It wouldn't be just you and me there. Half my family still lives there, and the other half are in and out constantly. Penny, it's where we lived before...before you went away." She was still shaking her head, backing away from him. God, she couldn't be afraid—not of him— could she? "Honey, if you're around familiar things, maybe you'll remember...something. Please, just think about it. It's your home, Penny. It's where you belong. I can take care of you there...."

Her hips backed into the headstone, and she stopped, looking ready to run, maybe feeling a little trapped. "I...I...can't just pretend to be...to be her. I'm not...I'm not your wife anymore. God, I don't even know your name."

It was as if she'd slapped him. He stopped and stood stock-still, aching and bleeding. He lowered his head, keeping his voice carefully level, hiding the pain and frustration and anger at whatever forces had taken her from him, robbed her of her memory. "Ben," he said softly. "My name is Ben. And I know that you can't just come home and pick up where you left off." Where they'd left off, despite their love for each other, hadn't been such a good place anyway. She'd been so sick. She didn't look sick now, but he knew all too well that she had good days, as well as bad.

"Just come home, Penny. You want to know about us—and I want to know what happened to you. And...and take care of you."

"I can take care of myself."

He flinched when she said it. But he knew better. She needed him.

"We have plenty of rooms," he told her. "You'd have your own. You'd be a guest, Penny. Free to...come and go as you please." He chanced a peek at her face. She was studying his. He wanted to wrap her in his arms and kiss her. He wanted to shake her until she remembered him. He couldn't believe she could forget how it had been between them. God, she looked half-afraid of him now. And one hundred percent distrustful of everything he said.

If she left him again, he would die. He'd lie down right on this spot with his heart torn out and never get up again. But if he told her that, she'd run screaming. He didn't want to push, to scare her off. So he'd use logic. Penny had always responded to logic.

"Penny, what options do you have right now? You need me... you need us." He reached for her, then stopped when he heard a low growl from behind him, and looked down to see the funny-looking, filthy dog baring its teeth at him.

"She's telling you that we don't need anyone," Penny said. "We've been getting by just fine on our own. All I want from you are some answers."

The dog glanced up at Penny, then seemed to shrug her wide shoulders and returned to chewing the branch that looked as if a beaver on steroids had attacked it.

Shaking his head, Ben focused on Penny once more. "Listen to me," he said. "You haven't been getting by fine on your own, Penny. You've had to steal. The Penny I know never would have done that unless she was desperate."

"Maybe I'm not the Penny you knew." But she averted her eyes, and he knew she felt guilty for what she'd done to survive. He also knew she'd had no choice.

"Of course you are," he told her gently. "Penny, I don't care about what you've done. Just listen to me, what I'm telling you makes sense. The police are looking for you. You know that, right?"

She didn't admit it, but she didn't deny it, either. Just stared at him with huge brown mistrusting eyes.

"If you go off on your own, they're going to catch up with you sooner or later. You'll be safe at the ranch. I promise, Penny, it will be okay. Give me some time, and I can take care of all of this. Just try it for a day or two. If you're not comfortable there, if you want to leave—"

"One day."

He blinked at the way she dropped the words.

"I can only think about one day at a time right now. So one day. And you don't need to take care of anything for me. I just need to get my bearings, and then I'll find a job and—"

"You'll do what?" He gaped at her. What the hell was she talking about finding a job for? She was sick— shouldn't even be alive right now. But the look in her eyes when he questioned her that way made him think twice. Just get her home. Deal with the rest later. "All right," he said finally, carefully. "Whatever you want, Penny. One day. Okay?"

She nodded. "And the dog comes with me."

Ben glanced down at the misshapen animal and the pile of sawdust at its feet that used to be a twig. "Dog, huh? I was wondering."

"She's all I have in the world," she whispered.

Ben felt a blade twist inside his heart. You have me, he thought. You always have…and always will.

And damn, he'd never thought he'd see Penny with a dog.

Aloud he said, "The dog's welcome. Blue could use a little companion." He crouched down and reached for the animal. "You wanna go for a ride, Stubby?"

The dog crouched, too, and growled at him again.

"Her name is Olive," Penny said. Then she bent and picked the mutt up, and the dog licked her face.

Ben felt a rush of irrational jealousy, but quelled it. Stupid to be jealous of a dog. "You can go ahead to the truck," he told Penny. "I'll just tell Joe over here to take the backhoe home until further notice."

She nodded, and turned to walk toward the pickup. Watching her go, Ben felt a moment of panic, and called after her. She turned, looking over her shoulder at him.

"You won't run off again, will you?" Dammit, he sounded desperate. He hadn't meant to sound that way. Would she change her mind now about coming home with him? Would she bolt?

She tilted her head to one side, probing him with her eyes. The little dog looked at Ben, too, then up at the woman who held her, whimpering softly. "I'll wait in the truck," Penny said slowly.

Ben nodded. "I'll only be a minute."

~

How could a man believe his wife had died if she hadn't? Penny wondered. How could a woman be cooped up in a clinic far away for over two years and her own husband never have a clue about it? Someone had to arrange it. Someone had to pay the bills. Maybe there was some reason for getting rid of her. For letting the world think she was dead and shipping her off to Dr. Barlow. Maybe there was some motive here for what he'd done.

If there was, Ben Brand certainly wasn't showing it.

She had never been more terrified in her life. Not of him. Not really. She was afraid of herself and of the strange emotions being near him evoked in her. It was not natural to sit beside a perfect stranger and try to imagine what it would feel like if he should kiss her. To keep remembering the feel of his strong arms around her, and the sound of his heart hammering in his chest. It was too intimate, too personal. He'd been her husband. He knew things about her that she didn't even know about herself.

And maybe he couldn't be trusted.

Damn. It would be awfully easy to swallow every word he said, hook, line and sinker. To believe whatever he told her, because she'd never seen a more honest-looking pair of blue eyes. But she couldn't let herself do that. There were too many unanswered questions. When she got the answers, she wanted to be sure they were the correct ones.

He was big, powerful, and there was a pit of emotions boiling inside that man, emotions he was keeping well contained. But despite all that, she didn't think he would hurt her. Not physically. In fact, he seemed to act as if he thought she'd break in a strong wind. He helped her into the truck, buckled the seat belt around her as if she was a child, kept asking if she was too cold or too warm. But there was a need burning in his eyes that frightened her in its intensity. She felt as if everything she said or did suddenly had enormous power. As if he was the fragile one here. As if the big blond man's very life hung from a thin thread—a thread she held between her fingers.

Or so he wanted her to believe.

Facing his family was frightening, too. A houseful of strangers who must know her nearly as well as he did. It might almost have been better if she could have been alone with him.

She glanced across the pickup at him, recalling the power and passion in his embrace when he'd crushed her against him before. No. It was better to face the family. Being alone with him would certainly be far more dangerous.

As he drove, Ben pointed out landmarks as they passed, looking at her expectantly each time as if he thought she was going to remember. The diner where he'd bought her dinner on their first date. The school where he'd carried her books. The scraggly pasture full of cows that had been the drive-in they'd frequented fifteen years ago. They passed another truck, and she recognized the driver and passenger as the two men who were with Ben in El Paso. The dark, smaller one gaped, wide-eyed as they passed, and the driver stared so long he wound up on the shoulder throwing up dust. Ben motioned at them to follow, and soon the big truck was pulling a U-turn and coming up behind them.

More people to face. How could she do it? All these strangers who knew so much about her, while she knew absolutely nothing about any of them. She felt naked, and blindfolded, and surrounded by a crowd of people she couldn't trust. Damn.

"It'll be okay," Ben said softly. "They love you. They all love you, Penny. They're your family, too."

"Loved," she said. "Past tense. And not me, but the woman I was. They don't even know me." She lowered her head. "How can they, when I don't know myself?"

He looked at her strangely. He couldn't understand. How could she expect him to? Ollie crawled onto her lap, sat facing her and lowered her head to Penny's shoulder. Ollie understood. She hugged the dog close and lowered her head to let the dirty fur absorb her tears and at the same time hide them from the stranger beside her.

CHAPTER FOUR

𝓑en pulled into the driveway of the ranch, beneath the arch, and stopped in front. There were already several vehicles parked there, and the other truck pulled in behind them. She looked up only briefly before hiding her face in Ollie's fur again. So many people.

"You're scared," Ben said.

She shook her head against warm fur. She could already hear the screen door banging, and knew people were piling out of the house onto that wide front porch, gaping at her. That pickup truck's doors slammed, too, and she felt the eyes of its passengers searing her. She wanted to curl into a dark corner and hug her dog until they all went away. "I'm not scared," she lied.

"We can turn around and leave if you want," Ben said. "Or I can make them all leave. It's up to you. Just tell me what you want. Penny?"

She lifted her head and stared down into Ollie's brown eyes. "You wouldn't run, would you, Olive?" she asked. "No, you'd dive in headfirst and come up with a juicy bone in the process." She sniffed and thought there was no better way to learn about her past— find out what had happened to her and who was involved—than to begin meeting the suspects. "Let's just get this over with," she said.

Ollie barked as if in approval. Ben was watching her, looking a bit hurt, maybe because she spoke to the dog and all but ignored him. Maybe he wanted to help her through all this. But he couldn't. He didn't even know her.

She grasped the door handle, shoved it open and got out. Ollie leaped to the ground and waited for her, then stayed at her side as she made her way around the vehicle and faced the crowd of people who stood on the porch. Ben came close to her other side, and though he was a stranger to her, it did bolster her somehow when his big warm hand closed around her small one. His grip was strong but gentle at the same time.

"Penny?" a female voice whispered. "Oh, my Gawd, Penny!" A tall, slender young woman with short-cropped auburn hair bounded down the porch steps, and in the blink of an eye Penny found herself wrapped tight in her arms. The girl was crying, hugging her hard, kissing her face. She stood back a little, her hands smoothing Penny's hair back, her big eyes wide and wet and happy. "I can't believe it. Penny, you're home! Oh, you're home." Her watery smile trembled.

Penny could only lower her head and whisper, "I'm sorry." She couldn't live up to the joy in the girl's pretty eyes. Couldn't share her elation. She'd only disappoint her—all of them.

Others were crowding closer now, exclaiming and asking questions all at once, but Ben held up a hand. "Listen up. There's a whole lot going on here that you don't know about." He touched the girl's shoulder, easing her away from Penny a bit. "Give her some room, Jessi."

Jessi shook her head, searching Penny's face in confusion. "But…."

"She doesn't remember," Ben said. And all the chatter died. Stunned silence spread over them like a blanket as every pair of eyes stared at Penny. "She doesn't know what happened. Only that she woke up in a clinic someplace, alone and scared. She doesn't remember anything before that." He slid his arm around her shoulders in a gesture that was almost protective. Almost as if he was shielding her from all these strangers...from the world.

She thought she should object to that. After all, she didn't need protecting from anything. But...but something about it felt right.

"But...but how?" Jessi asked. Her wide gaze returned to Penny's face. Then softened. "It's true, isn't it? You don't remember us? Oh, Penny...." She looked as if she was going to cry again. And as Penny scanned the faces of the others, she thought they all looked like they were attending a funeral, as well. Gazes lowered, heads shaking sadly, sympathetic glances toward Ben.

"Then we'll just start fresh," another woman said in a voice that bordered on cheerful. She was petite, no bigger than Penny, and had tresses of red-gold hair curling over her shoulders as she came forward. "You wouldn't have known me anyway," she said. "I came into the family while you were...away. I'm Chelsea Brand." The woman extended a slender hand.

Hesitantly Penny took it, almost relieved to be meeting someone who didn't expect to be remembered.

"My husband is Garrett, the big guy with the badge," Chelsea said, smiling and nodding at her husband. "He's Ben's older brother and the town sheriff. And that little guy playing with your dog there, is ours. His name is Ethan, but the boys insist on calling him Bubba."

Penny hadn't even noticed that Olive had left her side, but she followed the woman's gaze, and frowned as she saw Ollie licking the toddler's face. An irrational stab of jealousy flashed through her, but she shrugged it off and focused on Garrett, with his badge. He could mean trouble for her if he wanted to.

"Now, you'll never keep us all straight at first, Penny," Chelsea went on, tugging Penny's hand and leading her forward. "So don't worry about it right away."

Penny glanced back at Ben, but he nodded encouragingly, so she went along with Chelsea. He kept pace, staying close to her side.

Chelsea stopped in front of a couple who looked very much Native American, both of them dark haired and ebony eyed and beautiful. "This is Ben's brother Wes, and his wife, Taylor. They raise Appaloosas on a ranch nearby, and Taylor teaches at the university."

Each of them took Penny's hand in turn. Wes unsmiling, grim faced, unsure of her, she thought. Taylor's grip was warm, her eyes friendly. "You wouldn't remember me, either," Taylor said. "But I'm glad to know you now."

"Th-thank you." Okay, so if Chelsea and this dark beauty—Taylor—had both come into the family while she'd been away, that ruled them both out as suspects. Wes, on the other hand, didn't look overjoyed to see her.

Chelsea moved on to a whipcord young man with reddish-gold hair. "This is Elliot, Ben's youngest brother. He lives here with us, helps run the ranch and causes general mayhem on occasion."

Elliot hugged her gently. "Me and Jessi used to tag along after you and Ben all the time," he said. "Even on dates. Ben was always trying to get rid of us, but you never did. Welcome home, Penny."

A dull, thudding pain began behind her temples, and Penny closed her eyes against it. Elliot. She filed his name away in her mind. He and Jessi both seemed genuinely happy to see her, and their smiles were warm, and even misty. But then again, if they'd been involved in what had happened to her, they would try to hide it, wouldn't they? And giving her a warm welcome home would certainly be a good way to do that.

Just the way Ben had done.

"Are you okay?" Ben was leaning close, searching her face. Could such intense concern as that in his eyes right now really be false? If it was, he was an incredible actor.

She nodded. "Fine."

"I'm Adam," a deep voice said, and yet another hand clasped hers. "Another of Ben's brothers. And I'm going to help you both through this, you can count on it."

"Adam is staying with us for now," Chelsea explained. "But he lives on the East Coast most of the time."

"Might be hanging around longer than I intended to," he said softly.

Penny narrowed her eyes on him. Just what did he mean by that?

Chelsea squeezed Penny's hand. "Almost done now. Hang in there." And she led her to a handsome brown-eyed man who held a baby girl in his arms.

"Lash Monroe," the man said. "I'm Jessi's husband."

Jessi, standing now at the man's side, said, "And this is our little angel, Maria-Michele."

The baby cooed and smiled, but Penny couldn't manage to smile back. This man wore a badge like the other one— Garrett. And she was all too aware that they both probably knew she wasn't in very good standing with the law. Ben must have felt her stiffen, because his arm around her tightened. Why didn't she shrug away from him?

Why did she want to lean closer?

"Lash is Garrett's deputy," Chelsea explained. "Jessi's the town vet. They live in Quinn, right near her clinic."

She nodded mutely. "I'm a little overwhelmed."

"And a little scared," Ben said, gazing down at her with a gentle smile. "Don't be, Penny. Garrett, we can take care of her scrapes with the Rangers in El Paso, can't we?"

"I'll get on it right now," Garrett said. "But you both know, there are a hell of a lot of unanswered questions here, and we're going to have to get busy answering them. First and foremost being, who did we bury and how did they end up in that car, wearing Penny's wedding band?"

He looked at Penny as if she could tell him what he wanted to know, when he knew perfectly well she couldn't. It irked her and made her instantly defensive. "If I had the answers, I'd give them to you, Sheriff Brand, but—"

He moved closer, and his hand on her cheek was gentle. "It's 'Garrett,' hon. I'm as much your brother as Ben's, and don't you forget it. We're gonna see you through this, Penny. We'll get to the bottom of it."

She frowned in confusion. Did they all think she was really falling for this?

"Yeah," Adam said. "And I have a pretty good idea where to start." All eyes turned toward him, and he shook his head, looking angry. "With Kirsten."

Jessi rolled her eyes. "I shoulda known you'd find a way to blame all this on her, Adam. You know, just because she stood you up at your own wedding doesn't make her responsible for every bad thing that happens in the universe!"

"No, Adam's right," Ben said softly. He looked at Penny. "Kirsten was your best friend," he explained. "If anyone might have a clue what happened that day your car went off the road, it would be her."

"I'll call her," Adam said, his voice grim.

"I think maybe someone else should do that," Jessi put in, with a meaningful glance at her brother.

"Meanwhile," Chelsea said, breaking into the planning session with her soft voice, "are you okay, Penny? Is all this too much for you?"

Penny couldn't help but like the woman. The way she took charge and tried to ease things for her. And she didn't even know her. Maybe that was why she liked Chelsea. She was too new to the family to have been involved in the plot to get rid of her. She had no expectations of her. She wasn't looking at her now and mentally comparing her to the woman she'd been two years ago. The way she felt Ben doing every time his blue eyes probed so deeply into hers. The way they were doing right now.

"I'm okay. Just tired...and my head's aching some."

Chelsea's eyes met Ben's, and something passed between them. It was Ben who turned to Penny. "I know it's a lot to deal with all at once," he told her. "Especially when you're still so sick. I don't even know how you've managed this long on your own in your condition. Come on, why don't you come inside, lie down for a while."

Penny crinkled her brows, studying him. "I'm not sick," she said. "Aside from losing my memory...and these damned headaches...the coma didn't cause any side effects at all."

He just stared at her. Unblinking. Wide-eyed.

"Penny..." He gave his head a shake. "Penny...do you know what caused you to go into that coma in the first place?"

She blinked at him. "You said something about a car accident."

A long breath escaped him, and he closed his eyes slowly. When he opened them again they were wet, and something closed off in Penny's throat.

"Wasn't that what it was? I mean, I thought that must have been how I was hurt, and why you sent me—why I had to go to the clinic..."

"Honey, nobody sent you anywhere. I'd have killed anyone who tried." He reached for her, pulled her into his arms, kissed her hair. "But it doesn't matter," he told her. "You're home now and you look better than you ever did, and that's all that matters right now."

He stopped speaking when she didn't return his embrace, and very slowly he released her. "I'm sorry."

He looked so hurt, so torn, and happy and sad all at the same time. It touched her a little, though she tried not to let it. "No, it does matter. Why would you say I was sick? Why shouldn't I look as well as I do?" She searched his face, then scanned the eyes of the others. "Is there something you aren't telling me?"

Ben eased a palm over her face, parted his lips, but then closed them again and glanced at his brother Adam. "I can't…"

"Penny," Adam said, stepping closer to her. "It looks as if you were never in that car when the accident happened. But you were sick before that."

She frowned. "How sick?"

Adam lowered his head. "Pretty sick."

Tilting her head to one side, she realized slowly that she'd been lied to again. Dr. Barlow never told her she'd been ill, but didn't correct her when she assumed she'd been injured in some way and that was what led to the coma. But she shook her head, brushing it off. She'd get all the answers she sought, eventually. "I see. I don't remember being sick. But I suppose it makes no difference. I'm not sick now."

When she said that, Ben averted his eyes fast—as if she'd given him a sudden pain he didn't want her to see. What was going on with these people? "Really," she said, glancing around at their surprised faces. "Aside from these headaches, I feel great."

"You certainly look great," Chelsea said. "C'mon, I think you could use a little rest all the same. You've been through the mill, and besides, I want you to know where you are."

"I know where I am," Penny said as Chelsea took her arm. "In Quinn, Texas."

"No," Chelsea said. "You're home, darlin'. You're home."

For some reason she couldn't name, Chelsea's words made her eyes burn a little. She started for the porch, then glanced back in sudden panic when she realized Olive wasn't beside her. But then she spotted the dog, still rolling on the ground with the little boy.

"I'll bring her along in a minute or two," Jessi offered.

"All right." Penny thought it was ridiculous to be afraid to let the dog out of her sight, much less to have become so damned attached to her in such a short time. But it didn't help calm her stomach. Olive had become like a living security blanket somehow.

She walked up the front steps, glanced at the porch swing and went still, staring at it. For just a second she saw herself sitting there...and Ben beside her, his big arm slung around her shoulders, her head resting upon his as the swing moved gently back and forth. Her head pounded harder, and the vision faded. Then she went through the screen door with Chelsea at her side, and heard it bang closed behind them.

~

Ben held on just fine until she was out of sight. But once the screen door shut behind her, he lost it. He felt his body slump, shoulders sagging, head hanging low, as he battled the damned tears that burned his eyes and fought to catch his breath. And then Adam was there, and Garrett and Wes. Even Elliot. He could hear Jessi gathering up that damned dog, and little Bubba. She and Taylor and Lash wandered off to give him space. Let him be. But not his brothers. Elliot was gripping his arms, Adam squeezing his shoulder and Garrett asking if he was okay. Wes stood nearby, silent, brooding. But close enough to touch him should the need arise. They closed in on him like locusts the second Penny was out of sight, and he thought if they hadn't he'd probably be on his knees by now. The big pains in the backside.

"This must be killing you," Adam said. "God, Ben, I don't know what to say."

Ben nodded once, meeting Adam's eyes, hoping the anguish didn't show too much in his own. "Not much to say. My wife is back from the dead. Somehow...some way. And I ought to be glad, you know? I ought to be on my knees thanking God almighty for this miracle, this chance to spend a little more time with her. But all I can think about is that I'm going to lose her again. And...dammit, she doesn't even know she's sick."

Adam closed his eyes, lowered his head. "You're going to have to tell her. You know that."

"How can I? How can I break that news to her all over again, Adam? Did you see her? How she is right now?"

Adam nodded, meeting Ben's eyes, his own grim. "Yeah. She's like she was before...before she got sick in the first place."

"Exactly." Ben glanced toward the house. Wide and old, if it could talk, it would have some stories to tell. He remembered the nights he and Penny had rocked on that very porch swing, arm in arm, lips on lips. His throat went tight. "It destroyed her the last time she got news like this. God help me, I don't think I have the strength to tell her. To say those words and watch that light in her eyes go out like it did before."

Garrett shook his head, sighed heavily. "It'll be hard, Ben, but you have to do it. You have to tell her. For God's sake, you can't just let her go on not knowing—"

"Now, hold up a minute," Elliot cut in. He turned to pace a few steps away. Then he turned to face them all again, swiping the hat from his head in the process. "I think you all are over-lookin' the obvious, here."

Wes straightened from where he leaned against the pickup's shiny fender. "And what's that, little brother?"

Elliot lifted his brows and hands at the same time. "Did she look sick to you? Because I'm telling you, boys, she sure didn't look sick to me. Not even a little bit."

There was silence as Ben glanced at each face, each set of eyes, and saw hope flashing only in one of them. Elliot's. "Doc was sure about the diagnosis," he told his optimistic younger brother softly. "And the symptoms were getting worse all the time. There was no doubt it was HWS."

"That's just my point!" Elliot shook his hair with his hands and then replaced his hat. "Hillman-Waite Syndrome is progressive. Gets steadily worse. There's no remission, no sudden recovery. Doc made all that pretty clear to you back when he first diagnosed Penny with the disease. So, as sick as she was just before the accident, how the heck is it that she's walking around looking just like peaches and cream now?"

Ben dragged his gaze away from the youthful hope and zeal in Elliot's eyes and met Garrett's instead. Garrett shrugged. "You gotta admit, it's a good question."

"You should get Doc over here, have him take a look at her," Adam told him. "Maybe there's more going on here than we know. I mean, she said she was in Europe, right? They're always coming up with new treatments and—"

"Don't say it, Adam." Ben held his hand up to stop his brother. Then he turned slowly, putting his back to all of them. He braced his arms straight out against the pickup and let his head hang between them. It ached. His whole body ached, but most particularly in the area where his heart was being systematically shredded. "Don't even think it."

"But if there's hope—" Adam began.

"Hope can be a cruel thing, Adam," Wes said slowly. "It can lift you higher than you've ever been, and then just let you go— no net, no parachute and no anesthesia. I think Ben would prefer to keep his feet on the ground for now."

Ben said nothing, but felt his brothers' eyes on him. Felt their concern touching him even when they kept their hands at their sides.

"That's probably the best thing to do," Garrett said, reverting to the parental tone he used whenever he felt his full-grown siblings needed to hear it. "Be realistic, and don't go falling for that old wishful-thinking trap. This is hard enough without false hopes. But it's okay to wish it was different, Ben. It's okay to wish she wasn't sick, and it's sure as hell okay to hate that she can't remember you."

The red-orange sun blazing down from the huge Texas sky made the fender warm on his hands, and yet Ben still felt chilled to the bone. "Penny's the one who feels like hell, not me. Imagine how it would be to wake up one day and realize you've lost your whole life. Your past. Everything." He lifted his head, turned around slowly, knew his eyes were probably red rimmed. "And on top of that, imagine being told you probably won't live long enough to make any new memories to replace the ones you've lost."

Elliot shook his head hard. "She'll get her memory back, Ben. She has to!"

"I don't know about that."

"But she has to remember you. She loves you!"

Ben faced his youngest brother, seeing the hope in his eyes, despite Garrett's warnings against it. God, to be that young again, to be able to see everything with optimism, to believe in happy endings. "Loved me, Elliot. Now…now she doesn't even know me." Ben's voice broke, and he had to avert his eyes.

Wes clasped Ben's shoulder, his own voice slightly choked, raspy. "Whatever we can do…."

"We're here for you," Garrett said. "You know that. We're family, Ben."

"Yeah." Ben looked at each of his brothers in turn. When one Brand stubbed his toe, another one cussed. They were that close. He prayed they always would be. "I know," he said.

"You okay for the moment? Up to talking? Because in the meantime, Ben, we have a hell of a hornet's nest to deal with here. And the sooner we get moving, the better."

Ben drew a deep breath, squared his shoulders and nodded. "Let's get to it, then."

Elliot lowered the tailgate on the pickup and used it as a seat. Wes pulled up a bale of hay and settled there.

"Tell me what we need to do, Garrett," Ben said softly.

"First we go ahead with the exhumation. We have to find out who's in that grave. They might have family, too, somewhere. I'll see to that myself. Then there's the matter of Penny's little crime spree."

"I'll pay the dealer for the use of the car. Hell, I'll buy it if he wants. Give him more than he's asking," Ben said.

"He'll probably go along with that. And I imagine the hotel in El Paso will drop the charges if we explain things and settle up with them. The stolen credit card, though...." Garrett shook his head. "See, there's more to that. The owner of that card has come up missing."

Ben's head came up fast.

"She was a nurse," Garrett said. "From England. The good news is, the police know Penny was here in the States before the woman vanished. Bad news is, they still think she might know something about it."

"They'll want to question her, then," Ben said softly. He shook his head. "You know I'm not gonna allow it, Garrett. She's sick. I have to take protect her."

Garrett nodded. "I'll put them off as long as I can, Ben."

"Good Lord, what in the world has that wife of yours been up to?" Wes asked.

Ben shook his head, realizing this was the first Wes had heard of Penny's crimes. "Long story, and I don't know half of it."

"Kirsten will know," Adam said. He'd been leaning against the pickup, but he straightened now and that old grimness was back in his eyes—always was when Kirsten's name came up. "It's high time she get over here and answer a few questions."

Garrett put a hand on Adam's shoulder. "I'll call her. You're still too angry. But not today. We have enough on our plate without adding another course just yet. Meanwhile, Ben, don't you think we oughtta have Doc come by and take a look at Penny? After all she's been through, and given her condition and all?"

Ben shook his head. "She's dead against it. Threatened to take off if I tried to push the issue. Which makes me all the more curious about that clinic in England. What the hell happened to her there that left her like this? I'm telling you, Garrett, when I suggested she see a doctor, she went white. She was scared. Hiding it, like she always did, but scared."

Garrett nodded. "Take it slow with her, Ben. If you can get her to tell you any more about the place, maybe I can have it checked out." His eyes were sympathetic and worried. "We'll get to the bottom of this. I promise you that."

Wes nodded. "In a few days, when she's more comfortable, maybe she'll reconsider about letting Doc take a look at her. Hell, he delivered her."

Ben nodded. "And he was with her parents when they died." He lowered his head. "Tough to believe she doesn't even remember them. Or me." Drawing a deep breath, he went on. "I'll convince her to see Doc, though. Don't see that I have much choice about that."

"And you'll tell her about her condition...." Garrett prompted.

Ben met his brother's eyes, set his jaw. "Not until Doc sees her and confirms it." Garrett frowned, but Ben held his gaze. "I can't do it to her, dammit. Not yet. Let's give her a few days of peace before we tear her world apart all over again."

Garrett held up a hand in surrender. "All right, okay, we'll keep quiet until you decide to tell her. But don't wait too long, Ben. She has a right to know."

"Damn, this is hard." Ben shook his head slowly. "I want to hold her, touch her...but I have to keep reminding myself that as far as she's concerned, I'm a stranger."

His brothers nodded. And he knew that Garrett and Wes, at least, could understand. They had wives they adored. The thought of losing them, then getting them back only to realize they really were still beyond their reach—that was one they could sympathize with. "I have her back for a little while," he said softly. "But I don't. Not really."

"One step at a time, Ben. Just hold on, okay? Hold on to us," Adam told him.

Ben nodded. If there was one thing he could count on, it was his family. They'd be holding him up right to the end. No matter what.

"I'm going to head into the office," Garrett said. "Get started on straightening out her legal problems. Gotta get them moving again on that exhumation, too. I'll let you know what I find out."

"Thanks, Garrett," Ben told him.

"Elliot and I can handle your classes for today, if you want," Adam offered. "Not that we know spit about martial arts, but—"

Ben pressed a palm to his forehead. "I forgot all about the kids." He glanced at his watch. "I have three groups today. I already cancelled the older kids who come in from ten to noon, but there's still the middle schoolers after lunch from one to three, and the toddler class from three to five."

"We can handle it," Elliot said. "We'll just tell them to do whatever it was they did last time." He looked at his watch as well. "Heck, Adam, we just about have time to get there."

Adam nodded, squeezed Ben's shoulder and turned toward his shiny black sports car that looked as out of place on the ranch as an Armani suit in the stables. Everyone had his own personal theory as to why Adam had driven the car down instead of flying in from New York. And every one of them involved Kirsten and the rich man she'd married.

"Taylor and I can handle the chores around the ranch today," Wes said. "Take your time in town, Garrett. Do what needs doing and don't worry about things here."

Garrett nodded. "You okay, Ben?"

"No," Ben said. "But I'll manage." He looked toward the house, half eager to go inside, half afraid to.

Wes nodded. "I know," he said. "But I remember a time not too long ago when you told me you'd give your right arm for another chance with Penny. Now you have it, Ben, even if it is only for a little while. Not many men get that kind of miracle."

Ben nodded. His brother was right. He had to make this work, make her remember, make everything the way it was before and make the most of every minute he had left with her. He had to.

CHAPTER FIVE

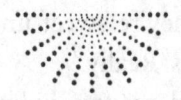

Chelsea led her through a sprawling house, where every room seemed like a big, inviting haven. She glimpsed a large kitchen and a formal dining room, but the living room was her favorite. Open and wide, with broad windows that were uncovered to reveal the lush, rolling fields beyond. A huge fireplace took up a third of one wall, and the furniture was overstuffed and comfortable. A braided oval rug covered most of the floor, and a hound dog who looked like his coat needed ironing lifted one eyebrow as she passed.

"He...won't hurt Olive, will he?" Penny asked.

Chelsea grinned. "He can barely work up the energy to hurt his food at mealtime. I think your bulldog is safe. Ol' Blue never hurt a flea."

She led Penny to an old-fashioned, steep staircase and started up it. "There's more to see downstairs," she said. "There's a den, and an office down there, plus the bath. But I thought you'd rather get upstairs where you can be alone and try to digest all of this."

"I appreciate that," Penny said.

Chelsea led her to a bedroom at the end of the hall and

opened the door with a flourish. Penny saw pink. Pink patterns in the wallpaper, and pink lacy curtains to match the pink bedspread.

"This was Jessi's room before she married Lash and moved into town. She hated all the pink, but she never had the heart to tell her brothers."

"They decorated it for her?"

Chelsea nodded. "They're sweet underneath all that macho they wear with their hats. Really."

Penny thought she'd reserve judgment on that. But they certainly seemed sweet so far. She sighed and walked to the row of windows that overlooked the barn and stable, and closer, the cluster of Brand men gathered in the driveway around a pickup truck that seemed to be their focal point. Ben glanced up as she looked down, and their eyes met. Something shivered down her spine, right to her toes, and she quickly turned away.

"It's better than white," she said, picking up the thread of the conversation. "In the clinic everything was white."

Chelsea gently touched her arm. "It must have been awful for you."

Shrugging, Penny scanned the kind woman's face. "I wasn't awake long enough for it to be awful," she said. And she reminded herself that Chelsea was not a suspect here. She couldn't have been involved in whatever scheme had resulted in the mess she now had for a life. "Chelsea...do they talk about me much?"

Chelsea frowned a little, but sat down on the edge of the bed and patted a spot beside her. She waited until Penny joined her there to begin speaking. "You were loved here," she said. "That's pretty obvious to me. Every time anyone brings your name up, it's usually with a teary smile. With everyone except Ben, that is."

Penny lifted her gaze. "Ben doesn't talk about me?"

"Ben doesn't smile. He's probably the saddest man I've ever known, Penny. He never got over losing you."

A little lead ball formed in Penny's stomach. She tried to ignore it, but it only got bigger.

Chelsea clasped her hand. "But you're back now."

And Penny shook her head. "Not really. I mean, I'm back... but I'm not the woman he's been mourning all this time." She closed her eyes and wondered why she felt so much regret when she said that. As if she might want to be that woman...the woman Ben Brand loved. Imagine that. And it was a stupid way to feel, since for all she knew he might have been involved in her disappearance.

She sighed heavily and shook her head. "I think I'd like to be alone for a little while."

"Sure," Chelsea said, and squeezed her hand. "If you feel like talking later, you just say the word. For now, it's understandable you needing some time to yourself. I'll make everyone leave you alone."

Penny nodded her thanks.

"I'll bring you up some tea in a few minutes. You just call me if you need anything else, okay?"

"You don't need to wait on me, Chelsea."

"Indulge me," she said with a wink.

Chelsea left then, and Penny returned to the windows, parting the lace curtains to stare once more down at the men gathered below. The Brand brothers sat or leaned or stood around Ben. Talking about her, no doubt. Ben seemed tortured. And she couldn't believe the stunning impact of seeing him in so much pain. Maybe because it was such a contradiction. Such a big, powerful man—his denim shirt straining across the expanse of his shoulders—looking so wounded. She felt badly for him. If he'd really loved her once, it must be hard for him now. Seeing how different she was. It was obvious she was not the woman he remembered.

And if she'd really loved him….

Had she? Had she ever looked up into his eyes the way she'd seen Chelsea look into Garrett's today? Had she slept curled up snug in Ben's arms? Made love to him?

A lonely pain writhed in her stomach, and her headache worsened. What must that have been like? To hold such a man inside her? To be that close to him?

He was a beautiful man. Hair like old corn silk, long and untamed. Blue eyes as deep and sad as the ocean.

She had to turn away, because staring down at him caused an unidentifiable pain in her belly, in her heart. How could she forget being with a man like Ben Brand? How?

Sighing, she spun around and collapsed on the bed. And she lay there for several minutes, waiting for her pounding headache to ease.

There was a gentle knock on her door, and she turned, expecting to see Chelsea with her tea. Instead she saw Olive, cleaner than she'd ever seen her. Her fur was actually white now, and she had a brown spot on her backside that Penny had never noticed before. As Penny got up, Olive looked across the room at her, then raced forward, stubby legs flying, and launched herself. Penny crouched down and gathered the little dog close, nearly toppling backward from the impact, but hugging her all the same, wet fur and all. It was only as Olive kissed her face that she heard the deep laughter from the doorway and looked up to see Ben standing there. Though he was amused, he came forward quickly to ease the dog from her arms.

"You shouldn't be carrying her. She's too heavy for you, Penny."

"Don't be silly." Penny took the dog back and hugged her tight. "Ooh, you look like a million bucks!" she said.

Olive kissed her face again.

"Hope you don't mind. Jessi thought a bath was in order.

And Bubba wanted to help. By the time I found those two, they were wetter than Stubby here."

Penny watched Ben's face. Saw the way he was still eyeing her uneasily and barely restraining himself from reaching out to help each time the dog made a sudden move. "I don't mind. I was going to give her a bath myself."

"Um, Jessi found more than dirt." Ben came farther inside, reached back to close the door behind him, but then seemed to think better of it.

"What do you mean?"

"Put her down, Penny. Please, you're making me crazy."

Frowning, Penny lowered Olive to the floor. Olive didn't mind. She immediately put her nose to the carpet and snuffled along like a living vacuum. "Okay. She's down." She didn't like his insistence on treating her like a weakling. "What did Jessi find?"

"Your dog is expecting."

Penny blinked. "Olive is pregnant?"

"My kid sister's a vet, remember? She's pregnant, all right. All fifty-plus pounds of her, and I'll hazard a guess she'll be even heftier in the next few weeks."

Penny shook her head and crouched down on the floor to bring herself to Olive's eye level. "I never would have guessed! I mean, look at her. She doesn't exactly look like the glowing mother-to-be, does she?" Ollie tilted her head to one side as if listening, looking for all the world like a fighter who'd been hit in the face too often. "Puppies, Olive! You're going to be a mommy."

Ben cleared his throat. She couldn't quite believe he was competing with her dog for her attention, but that was the feeling she got. She stood up again, brushing her hands together. "She's quite a dog."

"Jessi seems to think so. Pure English bulldog, she says. Where did you get her?"

Ollie barked as if to say it was about time someone recognized her greatness. Penny smiled at her companion. "I found her outside a diner in El Paso. The owner tried to kick her, I threatened to kick him and we've sort of been together ever since."

Ben stared at her as if he wasn't certain who she was. Join the club, she thought.

"You threatened to kick a grown man?"

"Oh, it was more than a threat. I'd have done it in a minute. He said she'd been there for weeks, though, and since she has no tags and no collar, I figured she was as alone in the world as I was."

She saw him wince, and wished she hadn't blurted that.

"I'm sorry you were alone, Penny," he told her. His blue eyes bore into hers intently, yet managed to convey gentleness at the same time. "You have to believe that if I knew you were alive, no power in heaven or earth could have kept me from coming for you."

Her breath rushed out of her lungs all at once. He said that with such passion. Could it be true?

She didn't know what to say, how to respond to that.

He seemed a little surprised by his own words, as well, as if he'd blurted them without intending to. And he averted his gaze. "I…I thought you came up here to lie down."

"I did. My headache's better now."

"Still…."

"I think I'll take a shower and then…then I'd like to look around the ranch, if that's okay."

He frowned as if it was the last thing he expected to hear from her. "I don't know if that's such a good idea…."

"Why not? It's a beautiful day and I want to see this place I'm supposed to know so well. I'm curious."

"But you should rest—"

"I can rest when I'm dead," she quipped, then stilled when

Ben's face went so chalk white she thought he might pass out cold. It must have been instinct that made her rush close to him, gripping his firm shoulder in one hand and cupping the base of his neck with the other. "Hell, I'm sorry. That was a stupid thing to say. Are you okay?"

"Sure, fine." His voice was little more than a rasp. Then he looked down into her eyes, and she was still touching him, and she knew he wanted a lot more. To hold her. To kiss her. She could practically read each thought that crossed his mind. "If, um, if you're sure you feel up to it, I'll take you around the ranch this afternoon."

"I'm not so sure *you* feel up to it," she said.

Ben stared down at her face. "You would tell me…if you were…under the weather or…or anything."

"I can't think of any reason why I wouldn't."

Studying her face, he nodded. "Okay," he said. "Okay."

"Guess I'll take that shower now."

He glanced toward the bathroom. "I'll run you a bath—"

"For heaven's sake, Ben, was I a complete invalid before, or what?"

He blinked at her as if searching for words. "I just…" He gave his head a shake. "Sorry. I'll get out of your hair." He turned to go, then turned back. "Jessi says pregnancy can be tricky for bulldogs…not that there's anything to worry about. Just, when you feel up to it, we ought to bring her by the clinic for a checkup."

"When I feel up to it?" Penny repeated.

Ben shrugged. "Right."

"Okay. I'll do that."

He nodded and then left her alone. Penny lay back on the bed, head throbbing all over again, eyes wet, longing with everything in her to remember the past she'd lost. Wondering why her husband seemed to think she wouldn't have the energy to go into town for something as simple as taking her dog to the vet. Why he'd seemed shocked she'd felt like exploring the ranch.

She was going to have to sit him down and make him tell her the truth. And part of her wondered why she hadn't done that already.

She knew why. The look in his eyes scared the hell out of her. And part of her thought maybe the truth was something she really didn't want to know.

Ollie stood with paws on the edge of the bed and barked until Penny pulled her up. Then the little dog curled close beside her. In seconds she was snoring.

"You sure don't snore like a female," Penny whispered, stroking the still damp fur.

Ollie groaned contently and snuggled closer, while Penny found herself a notepad and a pencil, and began to list her newfound relatives and, beside each name, the reasons why it was so hard to believe any one of them had been involved in trying to get rid of her.

∽

The Texas Ranger kept looking at him, and Dr. Barlow didn't like the suspicion in the man's eyes. "And you say your name is…?"

"Jenkins," Dr. Barlow lied. "Now, I know my wife has been here. Please, sir, if you know where she is, just tell me. She's seriously ill, and—"

"She didn't look ill to me, sir."

Barlow went still, eyes narrowing. "Then you have seen her?"

The Ranger nodded, but the doctor noticed the way he pressed his lips together. As if mentally telling them not to say any more. "I saw the woman in this photo, yes. But I have no idea who she is or where she is."

"Where was she when you saw her?"

"In a car."

"Heading in what direction?"

"Sittin' still." The Ranger picked up a pen and tapped it on his desk. "You want to file a missing-persons report on her?" he asked, and he reached for a form. "Just need to see some ID, then you can give me her full name and—"

"No, no, I don't think that will be necessary." Barlow couldn't show him identification, much less give him Penny's real name. In case she hadn't figured it out on her own yet, then the fewer people who knew, the better. But he still had a bad feeling in the pit of his stomach...a feeling that he knew where to look next.

"Tell you what," the Ranger said with a helpful smile. "You tell me where you're stayin' while you're in town, and I'll give you a call if she turns up."

"Thank you kindly," Barlow said in a drawling imitation of the officer's semi-charming accent. "But I believe I'll call you instead. Simpler, you know. What with me being on the road, as I am at present."

"Fine by me." The Ranger glanced at the phone on his desk for the third time.

Dr. Barlow had an inkling the man was in a hurry for him to leave so he could place a call. And he had no doubt the call would be about him, and his interest in finding Penny Brand. He was glad he'd used a false name, then, though it wouldn't do much good. She'd have advance warning. Time to run away and hide from him again.

The problem was, there wasn't a thing he could do to stop the man from placing that phone call. So he guessed he'd just have to track her down before she had the chance to run away again.

Ben went outside to help with morning chores, which had been delayed already by all the excitement. He came back a couple of hours later, walked into the house, glanced around and didn't see Penny. He did see the morning paper and a handful of coffee mugs scattered across the kitchen table, though. He hastily cleared up the mess, shaking his head and muttering under his breath. Penny had always hated clutter. She'd been a neat freak of the highest order.

Chelsea came into the kitchen when she heard the cups rattling. "How you doing, Ben?"

He gave a distracted shake of his head. "Where's Penny?"

"Still up in Jessi's room."

He instantly got worried. "I knew it. She wasn't feeling as good as she tried to make us all think. If she's been in bed all this time, she must be...." He didn't finish. Just swallowed hard, closed the dishwasher and started for the doorway.

"Ben, I don't think she's been in bed. And, um, she could probably use some time alone."

He flinched as if she'd slapped him. "She's had two years to be alone for crying—" Biting his lip, he closed his eyes slowly. "Sorry, Chelsea. I had no call to snap at you that way."

"You're frustrated," she said. "It's understandable."

He shook his head. "I've been thinking about it, Chelsea. And I think—hell, I just have to be patient. She'll remember me once she's been home awhile. I know she will."

She studied him as if studying a puzzle piece that didn't quite fit. "What if she doesn't, Ben?"

"She will."

Drawing a slow breath, Chelsea took a mug from the tree on the counter and filled it with coffee. She added fresh cream from the fridge, gave the brew a stir and then set the mug on the table. "Sit down, Ben. Give her a few more minutes. I want to talk to you."

He didn't want to sit down. He didn't like the look in

Chelsea's eyes. Like she was about to pop the big bright balloon he'd so carefully created for himself, the one filled with the hopes he'd told himself not to let in. Too late. It had been too late the second he'd looked into Penny's brown eyes. He had to hope, dammit. He had nothing but hope right now.

He sat down, only because he wasn't sure what he was going to say to Penny when he went to her. Maybe he'd think of something in the next few minutes. He didn't want to tell her about her condition. Not yet. He wanted to pretend it didn't exist.

And it would be easy. God, she looked so healthy.

Not that hope. Not that one, come on, Ben, don't dig yourself in too deep here.

"You're not a headshrinker just yet," he reminded Chelsea when she sipped her own coffee and eyed him over the top of the cup.

"No, but I'm the closest thing to one you've got at the moment." She took another sip. They were alone in the house. Through the kitchen window Ben could see Wes outside, holding little Bubba in front of him in the saddle as he headed out to check the fence lines. Taylor rode beside him, dark hair flying. The others had all gone.

"You know I only want the best for you, Ben," Chelsea said. "And I really hope Penny's memory comes back on its own. But I think you need to consider the possibility that it might not happen that way."

He lowered his gaze, staring at the caramel-colored coffee. Chelsea knew him well enough to make it just the right shade. So she ought to know him well enough to realize he wouldn't accept what she was saying if he didn't want to. And he didn't want to, dammit.

"We don't have any idea what caused the amnesia," she went on. "Until she sees a doctor or we get a look at her medical records, we won't know, Ben. And even when we do, we may not be able to guess whether her memory will come back. We might very well have to just wait and see."

"She'll remember," Ben said.

"Okay, maybe she will." Chelsea slid her hands over Ben's, where he clutched the handle of his cup. "But in case she doesn't, Ben, maybe you ought to try the idea on, see if it's something you can deal with. She might come back someday, or maybe she never will. You have to start over, Ben, right now. Get to know who she is, and don't expect her to be who she was."

He set his cup down and pushed away from the table. "Who she is" he said softly, "is a woman who doesn't know me and probably wouldn't like me much if she did. Who she was, is a woman who loved me. Now, if you were in my shoes, Chelsea, which one do you think you'd be looking to find behind those brown eyes?"

"Who you'd rather find doesn't make any difference. She can't be a person she doesn't remember, no matter how badly you might want her to be."

"She'll remember," he said. And he got to his feet.

Chelsea sighed and got up, as well. "I hope so." But she didn't look real hopeful about it. "Meanwhile she looks to be about my size. I've sorted out a pile of clothes for her. They're in the basket in my room."

Ben felt badly for being short with Chelsea. The woman was sweet as honey, and her heart was spilling over with enough love for every Brand on this place and any strays who wandered in, besides. "That was thoughtful of you, Chelsea. Thanks."

She shrugged. "There are still some of Jessi's clothes in her room, but I figured they'd all be a good six inches too long. We petites have to stick together." She sent him a wink.

Ben headed through the living room and up the stairs. He stopped off in Chelsea and Garrett's room, the master bedroom that used to belong to his parents. The basket sat just inside the door heaped with jeans and blouses and other things, all neatly folded. He scooped it up, and moved on down the hall all the way to the end. The room next to his had been his baby sister's. Now it was his wife's, and he could hear music coming from beyond it. The radio, he guessed. Something to fill the silence. He knew that need to have noise around to drown out the scream of loneliness. Feeling like a school kid and hating it, he raised his big hand and tapped gently.

"Come in," she called.

Ben opened the door and stepped inside. And then he just stood there, feeling like a hapless traveler who'd stumbled into the twilight zone. The music was loud, the beat driving, the lyrics sexy as hell, or at least they were if he was understanding them right, and he was only getting about every other word. The bathroom door stood ajar, and he could see wet towels and puddles on the floor in there. Out here, in the bedroom, the clothes Penny had been wearing were flung haphazardly over the back of a chair. An empty teacup lay on its side on the bedside stand. The bedcovers looked like a wrestling match had just taken place on the bed.

Penny wore Jessi's old bathrobe. She was down on all fours, holding an alarm clock in both hands and pulling for all she was worth. The cord stretched out straight from the clock, and Ben had to step farther inside to see what was on the other end, though he could have guessed.

That stubby bulldog held the cord in her teeth, pulling hard and snarling like a pit bull with a toothache.

It threw him. All of it.

He set the basket on the bed, and then reached over to flick the radio off. "You need some help there?" he asked. "Your dog sounds like she's going to take your hand off any minute."

"Olive would never hurt me. She just won't give back the clock, and I'm afraid she'll ruin it." She tugged. Olive growled louder and tugged back.

Everything in him wanted to scoop Penny off that floor before she hurt herself, but he'd already figured out that kind of thing would irritate her—now. Didn't use to.

When she was sick, she'd come to depend on his taking care of her.

But he resisted the urge. "Try setting the clock down," he suggested instead.

Penny stopped tugging, and turned to frown up at him. It hit him like a kick to the breadbasket, because her soft brown hair was hanging in her eyes, and she wrinkled up her nose when she scowled up at him like that. He wanted to kiss her. Instead, he cleared his throat and tried to swallow.

Then she nodded. "Okay, it's worth a try. Here you go, Ollie. I surrender." She put the clock on the floor.

Olive immediately dropped the cord and sat very politely, tilting her head at Penny as if to ask why she'd given up so easily.

Penny picked up the clock, and the dog snatched the cord and began tugging and growling again.

"It's a game," Ben said. "She's playing with you."

Shaking her head, Penny put the clock on the floor again, and Olive dropped the cord, looking disappointed. "She's the craziest dog I've ever had."

"Probably the only dog you've ever had," Ben said. Penny turned, looking at him with lifted brows. "You were always a cat person," he told her. "You put up with old Blue, but you always said it was only because he'd been living here longer than you. Said you'd rather have cats."

Penny tilted her head. "That's funny."

"Why?"

She blinked and pushed the hair out of her eyes. "When I found her...I don't know, I got the feeling I'd always wanted a dog."

She was right. She had wanted one, but she'd refused when

he'd wanted to bring her a puppy. Because she'd known she was dying. And she didn't want a pet who would become too attached to her or dependent on her. So she'd stuck with arrogant barn cats who tended to hang around for a month or two and then move on to greener pastures.

"Anyway," she went on, "now I'd rather have dogs."

"I can see that." And he thought that once she knew...once he told her, she might change her mind about keeping Ollie. And then she looked at the dog, and there was something so genuine in her eyes that it made his own burn.

She got to her feet and turned to glance at her reflection in the vanity mirror. "I'm different now, aren't I?" she asked him.

He glanced at the towels and puddles on the bathroom floor. She used to be so tidy. But she obviously wasn't anymore. And she used to like country music, soft and low. But that seemed to have changed, as well.

She used to love me, he thought vaguely. And then he closed the door on those thoughts. They'd do him no good now. "I haven't been around you enough to tell for sure," he said. "You might be a little different."

"I'm a lot different." She turned to face him, leaning her hips and hands back against the vanity. "Must be a real letdown to you."

"You're alive, Penny. How could that possibly be a letdown?"

"If it's not, then why do you look like that? What's wrong, Ben?" She studied him with sharp, probing eyes.

What, besides the fact that I'm standing here talking to my wife as if she's a total stranger?

"Nothing," he said. "I, uh, brought you some things." He nodded toward the basket on the bed. "Chelsea sorted through her closets for you." He stuffed his hands into his pockets, mainly to keep himself from touching her.

"That was really kind of her." Penny walked to the bed and pawed some of the clothes in the basket. "I'm glad," she said.

"Jessi said I could use her stuff, but this robe is way too big for me."

"Jessi's a bit more than a size six, petite."

Penny looked at him quickly, a flash of surprise in her eyes for just a moment before she blinked slowly and banked it. "It seems strange that you know so much about me."

"That's funny," he told her. "It seems strange to me how little I know about you now."

She turned, sat down on the edge of the bed. "This has to be pretty hard for you."

He stood closer, reached down to take hold of her hand, and as he held it, his thumb glided lazily up and down the back of it. "I've done hard before, Penny. I can handle it. And I'm well aware it's twice as hard for you."

"I don't know about that." She cleared her throat, and he thought she'd pull her hand away. But she didn't. Instead she studied it, enfolded within his. "I had no expectations when I came here. And your family has been more welcoming than I could have hoped for. But I've just been…just been a huge disappointment to all of you." She lowered her head, shook it. "Maybe it would have been better if I'd stayed away."

Ben moved forward impulsively, cupping her chin in his hand and tilting her head up, and then forcibly resisting the urge to kiss her lips just once. He'd missed her taste so much, dreamed of kissing her again. But he knew he couldn't do that. Not now. Or…not yet.

"Don't say that, Penny. You belong here. This is your home, and everyone here is family."

"Maybe they were once," she said, looking around her. "Now, I don't know." She met his gaze again. "Ben…your family…did they always like me as much as they seem to now?"

He frowned. "I'm not sure I know what you mean."

She averted her eyes, and he got the feeling she was hiding something. Or maybe just not saying everything she was thinking. "I mean I couldn't have been perfect. No one is. They're all being really sweet, but I can't help but wonder...if I had any... unresolved issues with any of them."

His frown grew deeper. If he didn't know better, he'd think she was on one of her fishing expeditions, probing a witness for clues the way she used to when she was sixteen and seeing a conspiracy around every corner.

He touched her cheek, just with his forefinger, and turned her face toward his so he could look for the telltale mischief in her eyes. But she kept lowering her lids so he couldn't be sure if it was there.

"Penny, you never had a quarrel with anyone in this family, unless it was with Wes for leaving the seat up in the bathroom or Jessi for getting into your favorite lipstick. They love you just as much as I–" Ben bit his lip, averted his eyes. "They love you, Penny."

"Loved me," she said softly, and when he glanced her way she was looking into his eyes and there was something there in hers. Longing, he thought, and it made his stomach convulse. And then she looked away.

"Give it some time," he told her. "You'll feel better once your memory starts coming back...and I'm convinced it will come back, Penny."

"Maybe...I just hope it doesn't turn me back into the woman who needed waiting on hand and foot."

"What makes you think you were like that?" he asked quickly. Had someone let something slip?

She shrugged. "The way everyone seems to want to wait on me hand and foot now," she said. "Especially you. Why is that, Ben?"

"I always...liked taking care of you." He searched her face. "You never minded it before."

She frowned at that. And he wondered if he'd said the wrong thing.

"So when do I get my tour?"

He thought she asked just to change the subject "After lunch, if you—"

"If I feel up to it, I know."

He had to stop saying that. She seemed almost offended by it. "If you don't mind waiting until after we eat," he said instead.

"Depends. When do we eat?"

"Just as soon as you can get yourself dressed and downstairs."

She glanced down at the floor where Olive sat patiently beside the chewed-up clock cord, watching the two of them and waiting for someone to take up her challenge again. "Can Ollie come with us?"

"Does she chase cattle?" Ben glanced up from the dog to Penny.

Penny shrugged. "I honestly don't know."

Damn, but she didn't like the idea of being away from the funny-looking dog for a minute. He could tell by the look in her eyes. How did she get so attached to the animal?

Maybe, he thought, because she hadn't had anyone else.

"I guess we can rig up a leash for her and take her along."

Penny nodded, looking relieved. "Okay."

He stood there a second longer. It was so hard to leave. So hard, when all he wanted to do was hold her, kiss her, tell her how glad he was she'd come back to him. Make the most of whatever time he could have with her.

And beyond that, he had so many questions...unanswered questions. His mind was hopping with them, but it would do no good to ask her. She couldn't know the answers.

Her gaze lowered, dancing across his lips for the briefest moment, making him wonder if she was feeling some of the same things...and he felt his blood heat. Then he made himself get to his feet, turn toward the door.

A muffled bark made him turn back to see Olive sitting at

his feet, behind him. She had the alarm clock in her mouth, and when he looked down she shook it as if she was trying to scramble its insides. He reached for the clock, and the fat little dog immediately crouched and began growling, daring him to try to take it from her.

Ben shook his head and smiled grudgingly. "She's cuter than any old cat anyway," he said.

"I'm glad you think so, seeing as how she's about to multiply."

Ben looked at Penny with his brows raised. Then he sighed slowly and eyed the dog once more. "I guess we'd better buy some more alarm clocks."

CHAPTER SIX

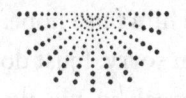

*B*en led Penny all around the house first, then took her outside to show her the barn and the stable, and the pasture where the horses grazed. Aside from a dull headache, she felt no reaction to the place other than admiration. It was beautiful.

He led her back to the house, sat her down on the porch swing and took a seat beside her. "Surely you remember this?" he asked her.

It was probably the tenth time he'd uttered the phrase, and it was getting to her. "No," she said as she'd said each time he'd asked it, and she knew he'd next tell her exactly why she should remember it. The man was developing a pattern. Not that she could blame him for hoping.

"We used to sit out here after dates. For hours we'd swing and talk...make plans for the future. Neck a bit, until Garrett would see us and flick the porch light. That was always our cue to knock it off."

He looked at her expectantly, waiting for her to snap her fingers and yell, Oh, yeah, I remember all that. It was like facing a kid on Christmas morning and telling him Santa had forgotten to stop by, and she was beginning to feel like a real grinch for having to do it to him over and over again. He seemed so vulnerable right now.

But she had felt something when she'd first spotted this swing on the broad front porch. Hadn't she? Had it been a memory…or just a fantasy? She didn't know. How could she know? She looked at Ben's expectant eyes and realized how cruel it would be to give him false hope.

Sighing, she said, "I'm sorry. I just don't remember."

And with his heartbreak in his eyes, he said, "That's okay. You will sooner or later." Just as he'd said every time they'd repeated this little dance.

She was really beginning to doubt he could have deliberately plotted to rid himself of her. He seemed to want her back very much.

Olive sat on the porch beside the swing, her leash still in Penny's pocket. Ben got to his feet. "I'll get the horses saddled up. You can wait here."

"Okay." But as she watched him go, she wasn't sure she was ready for another verse of the "remember this?" song. Still, maybe he needed this as a sort of confirmation that she didn't remember, that she maybe wasn't going to. She pulled Olive up into the swing beside her, stroked the dog's head and swung very slowly.

Pretty soon Ben came out of the stables with two nearly identical horses saddled and ready. He stopped near the porch and held out a hand to her.

"I'm not real sure about this," Penny said, getting to her feet. "I don't know the first thing about riding one of these things."

Ben looked blank for a second. Then, his voice unbearably sad, his eyes averted, he said, "You're the best rider I know, Penny." He sighed deeply, hid his heartache and faced her again, stroking the brown mare's nose. "This is Agatha. You claimed her the day she was born, named her even."

Blinking in surprise, Penny came down from the porch to stand in front of the mare. She searched the huge brown eyes, and ran her fingers through the thick, nearly black mane. "After Agatha Christie?" she asked, not looking at Ben.

His breath escaped him in a rush. "You remember?"

"No," she said quickly, turning toward him. "I guessed." He lowered his gaze, and she impulsively touched his face, pressing her palm to his cheek. "I'm sorry...I didn't mean to make you think...."

"Don't be sorry." His hand covered hers where it rested on his face, and then he turned and pressed his lips softly to her palm.

She caught her breath at the touch of his lips. But then he released her hand. And she felt, oddly, as if she hadn't wanted him to. She bit her lip. She should leave here before she broke this big man's heart beyond repair. But instead she walked around to the horse's side. She gripped the pommel and let Ben help her into the saddle. She settled her feet in the stirrups and gathered the reins into her hands. She didn't remember. But it didn't feel unfamiliar to be sitting here this way. Her headache thudded harder.

"They're twins, you know," he told her, looking again at the horses. "This one's Brutus."

"Their names are almost as bad as Olive's," she said in an effort to lighten things. "Oh, I almost forgot Olive!" She reached for the leash.

Ben took it from her, but glanced worriedly at the little dog. Olive didn't notice. She was standing at the top of the porch steps looking down at the horses, ears perked, head tilting from one side to the other.

"I'm not sure that's a good idea, bringing her along for the ride," Ben said. "With those stubby legs of hers she'll be winded in ten minutes, and she looks like heart-attack material to me."

Penny frowned down at the fat little dog. "You're right.

Besides, she shouldn't be straining herself if she's going to be a mother."

"I agree, and I think Jessi would, too. I'll just put her inside." He looped his reins around the rail that stood in front of the porch, and started up the steps. But as soon as he reached for her, Olive seemed to read his mind, and she darted under his hands, between his legs and down the steps, quicker than lightning.

Penny's mount danced when the dog raced around its feet, and the horse's dancing seemed to excite Olive all the more. She barked, crouching low and looking up at the horse with a "let's play" kind of gleam in her eyes.

The horse reared, no doubt with an "I don't think so" kind of look in her own eyes.

"No!" Penny shouted, jerking the reins and turning the mare in midair. "Don't trample my dog!"

The hooves landed hard, barely missing Olive, who thought the whole thing was a riot and wanted to do it again. Olive barked and lunged, the horse bolted and Penny held on for dear life.

Penny's horse was off like her tail was on fire, and the dog's legs were throwing up dust as she raced after the spooked mare. Ben snatched up the dog just as Chelsea came running out the front door, onto the porch. He shoved the mutt into Chelsea's arms, leaped into the saddle, whirled his mount around and dug in his heels. Damn! Ahead of him Penny bounced up off her saddle every time her horse's flying hooves touched the ground. She wobbled from one side to the other as if she'd never been on a horse before in her life. And the way her legs were slamming against Agatha's sides with every impact would only urge the mare to run faster.

Ben leaned over his own horse, pushing for more speed. He was gaining on her, but too slowly. Damn! Two years ago she'd have been able to sit a runaway mount without even thinking about it. Now....

She was coming up on a fence. And dammit, the horse was still charging full speed—too fast to stop in time. And if Agatha tried to turn, Penny would be thrown for sure. She'd probably break her neck. Ben's heart jumped up to block his throat, so that when he shouted her name no sound came out. He had the horrible feeling that he was about to lose her all over again.

And then something happened. She settled into the saddle. Her legs stopped flopping like wet rags and suddenly clamped tight to the horse's sides. The horse charged right at the fence, and Penny leaned over the pommel, weight in the stirrups, backside lifting slightly from the saddle as the mare launched herself. Like a pair of well-matched dancers, Penny and the horse sailed over the fence, landing easily—and safely, thank goodness—on the other side.

Ben followed, unsure what to think. Penny's horse was still running, but its pace slowed now, and he could see her easing back on the reins, stroking the sleek, sweat-damp neck, leaning close to speak softly. He caught up in a few seconds, but by then she had slowed the animal to a trot, and then a brisk walk, and finally drew her to a stop there in the middle of the south pasture.

Ben drew his horse to a stop, as well, sliding quickly to the ground and hurrying over to Penny. She leaned forward in the saddle, her head in her hands, pale and trembling. Without even thinking about it first, he reached for her and lifted her down. But he didn't set her on her feet. Rather he cradled her like a child in his arms and searched her face.

Her brows were bunched up tight, eyes closed. But she didn't argue about being held this way. Instead she let her head rest against his shoulder.

"You're hurt?"

"No." She pressed both hands to her forehead again. "Damn, it's my head. God, it's throbbing."

"All right. All right, Penny." He held her closer, massaging the base of her neck with one hand, kneading her scalp with his fingers. Gently, rhythmically. "You're okay."

She released what sounded like a pent-up breath. "That feels good."

"Then I'll keep on doin' it."

He carried her closer to the stream, a crystal blue strand that ran through this pasture and kept on going all the way to Wes's place, bisecting his land, as well. Choosing a grassy spot close to the water's edge, Ben sat down. He arranged Penny so she was reclining against his chest, and began massaging her head with both hands now. Fingertips rubbing gentle circles at her temples while his thumbs curved around to press at the base of her skull. Slow and steady he worked, half-amazed that she didn't object. Her headache must be pretty bad for her to let him touch her like this. He hated that she was hurting—but loved that he could hold her.

"Is it any better?"

"A little."

He peeked down to study her face. "Close your eyes," he told her. "Relax. You're scrunching up your face so much you're starting to look like that dog of yours."

"Hey!"

"That's better. At least you stopped scowling. You always did have a killer scowl."

"Did I?"

She flinched a little. As if the pain was suddenly worse again.

"Forget it. I want you to try something for me, Penny."

"I've been trying," she told him, tensing up all over again. "I've tried and tried, but I can't remember, Ben."

He sighed softly and shook his head. "You just did, sweetheart. Whether you know it or not, you remembered how to ride. If you hadn't, you'd have never made that jump without a few broken bones at the very least."

A long, slow breath escaped her. "I didn't remember. Not really. I just...I just did what seemed best."

He nodded. He knew better, of course, and suddenly he had more hope than ever. Horsemanship was lurking somewhere inside Penny's mind, and the knowledge had come to the surface when she'd needed it. Who was to say that all the rest of her past wasn't still there some-where, as well? Who was to say it wouldn't emerge just as subtly as this bit of memory had? He might have her back—all of her—even if it would be for a brief time. Too brief.

"Doesn't matter right now anyway," he told her. "I wasn't going to ask you to try to remember. I had something else in mind."

She turned her head, glancing up at him with a hint of alarm in her eyes.

"Relax," he told her. "And listen." He gently turned her head around to its former position, and resumed massaging her headache away. "You hear the stream?"

She frowned a little, but then the frown eased away. "Yes. It's like...laughter."

He wanted to kiss her so much it was like a pain inside him. But he didn't. It was too soon. She'd remembered how to ride that horse, how to jump the fence, how to control the animal and calm it. He had to believe the rest would come, too. He just had to give her time.

And he refused to listen to the voice inside, reminding him that time was something she did not have.

"Just listen to the water," he said softly. "Let everything else go."

He kept massaging her head, his touch light, fingers moving slowly through her dark, silken hair. Her breathing slowed and deepened. Gradually he felt her body relaxing against his. They sat that way for a long while. Ben sorely wished he could calm his mind the way he was helping her to calm hers. But it was impossible for him to reach that relaxed state when she was lying in his arms. He wanted her so much he could barely contain it. But he would, for Penny's sake.

Eventually she blinked her eyes open and whispered, "I can't believe it."

"What?"

"The headache's gone." She sat up then, turning to face him, surprise etched in her pretty eyes.

He didn't want her to sit up. He'd so enjoyed holding her, touching her. "I'm glad."

"They usually last so much longer."

Ben nodded. But he was worried. Headaches had never been part of the myriad symptoms she'd suffered. "When did these headaches start, Penny?"

Lowering her gaze in thought, she frowned just a little.

"Just before I left the clinic," she said. "But they got a lot worse once I came here. I think the first time one hit me this hard was the night I drove past this ranch for the first time." Meeting his eyes again, she went on. "Stress, I imagine. Wanting so badly to remember and not being able to. It's enough to give anyone a headache."

"That could be it." He drew a slow breath and dearly hoped he wasn't about to bring her headache screaming back again. "But it might not be. Penny, you were so sick…and you said yourself you spent two years in a coma. Don't you think it would be best to make sure these headaches aren't something a lot more serious?"

She bit her lip, averted her gaze.

He reached out to cup her face. "I'm not going to push you, okay? Whatever you decide is fine by me. But I'm worried about you, Penny."

She nodded. "I know that." She sighed heavily, tipping her

head back and staring up at the big blue sky. "I woke up a month ago, in a hospital bed. The nurse—her name was Michele—she looked like she was going to faint from shock when I opened my eyes and spoke to her. It didn't hit me right away. I mean, I was so overwhelmed and frightened, not knowing who I was or what I was doing there. It was a couple of weeks before I started to feel like something...something wasn't right."

"Physically, you mean?"

She shook her head. "No. I felt fine, getting stronger every day. It was the way they acted. Dr. Barlow, and the nurses." She studied his face as she spoke. "Don't get me wrong, they treated me like a princess there. But they kept saying I had no family, no friends, no reason to be in a hurry to leave. And it just felt wrong to me, like they were keeping something from me, you know? I got...I got really suspicious."

Ben smiled. For a second he'd spotted a familiar gleam in Penny's eyes. "Nancy Drew," he muttered.

"What?"

He shook his head. "Nothing. Go on, please. I want to know everything."

Taking a breath, she leaned back on her hands in the grass. "I realized that I'd never seen another patient in the clinic. Dr. Barlow told me I'd been in an accident, and had spent two years in a coma. And he told me this clinic was solely for the treatment of patients like me, with the same type of injury. But when I asked to see other patients, talk to them, he got...weird. Put me off, you know?"

Ben nodded, imagining how the old Penny would have reacted to the doctor's vague answers. And he was also wondering about this doctor, and filing that name away in his mind. Barlow.

"So what did you do?"

"They gave me a sedative to help me sleep every night," she said. "So one night I just didn't swallow it. When the nurse left, I got out of bed, flushed the pill and waited until the place was very quiet. Then I slipped out of my room and had a look around the clinic." She sat up, looking troubled, meeting his eyes. "There were other patients there, all right. In every room I checked. But they were all unresponsive, and hooked up to IV's and monitors." She bit her lip. "This is going to sound really farfetched, Ben."

He almost grinned at her. To have her here, telling him something farfetched, was almost too good to be true. He couldn't count how many times she'd started a sentence that way in the past. "Tell me anyway," he said.

She nodded. "I think I was the only one in that place who ever came out of their coma."

Ben sat up a little straighter. "Are you sure?"

She shook her head. "No. I mean, I couldn't search the whole place. But the letterhead at the nurse's desk read Barlow Hospice." Licking her lips, closing her eyes, she went on. "A hospice is where people go to die, Ben. Not to get well. And I got to thinking about how surprised they all seemed when I woke up. And how they'd been calling me Jane and saying they had no information about my background, and that I'd told them I had no one when I'd arrived there, before slipping into a coma. And suddenly I just didn't believe any of it."

"You think they were lying to you?"

Penny nodded slowly, and her eyes narrowed. "There was something going on in that place. I'm sure of that."

There was a remembered fear in her eyes that made Ben shiver. "Did you confront them?"

"Would you? If I was right, and I let them know I was onto them, they'd have never let me out of that place."

"So you ran away?"

"Not for a while. First I got them to take me walking every day, so I could get strong again. Eventually, I knew the clinic backward and forward. They even let me go outside into the yard a few times. That was when they finally had to give me the clothes I'd arrived with. When I found the torn, crumpled bit of an envelope in the lining of the jacket pocket, I knew I had to come here. It was my only hope of finding the truth."

He stroked her hair. She didn't object, so he did it again. "It couldn't have been easy, coming all that way...not knowing what you'd find."

She shrugged. "I got into the nurse's lounge and stole Michele's credit card along with her goofy hat and sun-glasses. She caught me in the act."

Ben stiffened. "Holy...."

Penny's eyes gleamed and Ben fell silent, recognizing that look. He hadn't seen it in a very long time. Since long before the accident and her supposed death. Since they were teenagers.

"I had to tie her up and leave her in a closet. Mean, I know, but I had no choice."

He shook his head in wonder. "Maybe the old Penny isn't completely gone after all," he said softly.

"Why do you say that?"

"Because that's just the kind of thing she would have done."

"Really?"

Ben nodded, searching her face, wanting to ask her if this new Penny had any sort of feelings about him. Wondering if things like desire or attraction had survived in her memory along with the ability to ride and the tendency to see mysteries around every corner. He wanted to ask her. But he didn't. Maybe because he was so afraid to hear her answer.

Instead he said, "So you think you were more or less a prisoner there?"

"I don't know. Maybe. I didn't wait around to find out."

"And that's why you're so wary of doctors."

She nodded. "They stick together, you know. If I saw someone, they might just ship me right back to the clinic."

Ben shook his head. "You think I'd let that happen?"

She stared at him, but said nothing.

"They'd have to go through me to take you away again, Penny," he said softly. "And if they managed that, they'd have the rest of the family to contend with. You're safe with us, Penny. No one can hurt you now that you're home." She blinked, bit her lip, and he knew she was close to giving in. "Would it help if I told you the doctor I have in mind is the same one who tended your mother when you were born? And tended her again when she and your dad passed on later?"

Penny's eyes closed suddenly. "My parents are dead," she stated in a flat tone.

Ben groaned. "I didn't mean to drop it on you like that, Penny. I'm sorry. I wasn't thinking—"

"Was it…while I was…gone?" she whispered.

Ben clasped her small hand in his large one. "You were by their sides, honey. Your daddy had a year long battle with cancer. He died when you were still in college, and your mama had a heart attack a couple of weeks later. Almost like she couldn't live without him."

She blinked away a few tears that crept into her eyes. "Maybe she couldn't."

Ben nodded. "I know just what she was feeling."

Her gaze dropped, touching very briefly on Ben's lips, and he forgot about the time that had passed and leaned closer and brushed her mouth with his. Softly, too briefly. She tasted so sweet.

Her eyes widened a little, but a second later they fell closed, and her lips touched his again. Ben gathered her close to him, and kissed her. Gently, tenderly, he caressed her mouth with his. Until she drew away shuddering, lowering her head again, rubbing her temples.

"Penny?"

"We should get back," she said, getting to her feet.

He shouldn't have done that. Dammit, he was moving too fast. "I'm sorry," he said. "I didn't mean—"

"No." Her timid whisper stopped him in mid-sentence, and he searched her face. "It...it's okay."

She looked up, met his eyes, and he could see her headache had returned. But he could also see the flush of pleasure in her cheeks that hadn't been there before.

"I'll see this doctor of yours if you think I should, Ben. But only if..." She lowered her head, bit her lip.

"Only if what?"

Averting her gaze, she said, "Only if you'll be there with me."

Didn't she know he'd be with her twenty-four hours a day, seven days a week if he had his way? "I'll be there," he promised. He took her hand, and led her slowly back to where the horses grazed.

～

What was happening to her? It was frightening, and shook her right to the core, whatever it was. She'd been terrified when the horse had taken off with her like that, scared senseless when she'd seen the fence looming before her. But then something had come over her. Something unfamiliar and strange. Almost like someone else had taken over her body and her mind. She'd felt possessed by some foreign soul.

But when it happened, somehow she'd known exactly what to do. Her body had acted without her consent, and she'd found herself suddenly at ease in the saddle, anticipating the horse's every move, even urging her forward, instinctively aware she had no choice but to jump the fence. And when the horse sailed easily over it, it felt like the most natural thing in the world. And every part of her seemed to remember having done this before. Every physical part. She'd felt all of this before. The wind rushing across her face, carrying the heated scent of the mare. The percussion of thundering hooves on the ground beneath her, the elation of flight and then the impact of the landing. Her body knew those things, recognized them. Her mind didn't. She couldn't remember them. But the knowledge was there. The sensory memories remained.

And they had been there again when Ben's soft lips had brushed hers. Her body had come alive. It knew the feel of those lips even if her mind didn't. She'd tingled all over, and something…something was teasing at the edges of her mind—something she couldn't quite grasp. Just as it had with the horse.

And just as it had then, her head began pounding like a jackhammer, feeling as if it would split at any moment.

Was she starting to remember? Would this continue? Did she want it to, when each hint of memory seemed to bring on such intense pain?

Yes. It would be worth anything to get her identity back. She knew that. Besides, it wasn't as if she had much choice in the matter. But she didn't tell Ben any of this. She could just imagine the way his eyes would light up with hope if he knew. And how disappointed he'd be if nothing more came of it. She had more than sufficient reason to believe nothing would.

She'd asked Dr. Barlow if her memory would return. He hadn't said maybe. He hadn't said time would tell. His reply had been a sad but simple "No." And though she suspected the man might have lied to her about other things, she couldn't think of a single reason he might lie to her about that.

But could he have been wrong?

Ben helped her back into the saddle. He looked at her for a moment, then nodded. "It's like riding a bike," he said. "Once you learn, you never forget."

She shook her head as he mounted his own horse. "I've read about people with amnesia who have to learn to walk and talk all over again. I imagine they forgot how to ride a bike."

"But you didn't," he said, gathering the reins and looking at her, and even though she hadn't told him the truth, she saw that gleam of hope in his eyes all the same. "It's gonna come back to you, Penny. All of it. I know it is."

"What if it doesn't?"

He'd nudged his horse into a gentle walk, and Penny rode along beside him. Though it was early autumn, the sun beat down, warming her. It felt good. All of it. The breeze that cooled the sun's hot kiss, the saddle creaking beneath her and smelling of leather.

"What do you mean?" Ben asked.

She lowered her head. "I'm different now," she said.

"Not in any way that matters."

"How have I changed?" It wasn't what she really wanted to know. What she wanted to ask him was whether he thought he could learn to like her again, get to know her as the woman she was now, rather than the woman he remembered. Because this new Penny might be all she could ever be. The one he longed for so much might be just as dead as if she really was in that grave she'd seen.

But maybe not. Because being with him here in this place felt so right.

He thought about his answer. "You never used to throw your towels on the floor after a bath," he said.

She felt her cheeks heat and bristled a little defensively. "I did pick them up when I got around to it."

"Before, you'd have wiped the tub dry, and the floor, and folded the damned things before you put them in the hamper."

So he thought she'd turned into a slob. She glanced at his face and found him grinning.

"Used to drive you crazy when I'd toss mine aside after a shower. And your neatness obsession used to drive me just as nuts."

She blinked in surprise. "Then it doesn't bother you if I'm sloppier than I used to be?"

"Bother me?" He looked at her sharply. "You saying you'd be upset if it did?"

Penny quickly averted her gaze, not knowing how to answer that. It would upset her, she realized, but she wasn't certain she understood why.

He saved her from having to reply, though. "You could trash the whole place, and I wouldn't mind, Penny."

She tried not to smile, but smiled anyway. His voice was deep and soft. It made her feel warm inside. "How else am I different?"

He shrugged. "You never had a dog before. I told you that, though. Then there's the music."

"Music?"

He nodded. "You were listening to some rock station when I came into your room this morning."

"And I didn't used to?"

"Never. You were strictly country. Knew all the words to every song Reba ever did."

She frowned. "Reba who?" Then she wished she hadn't said it, because he looked at her again, and his eyes were so sad it cut like a knife. But he covered it quickly.

"You, uh, you cut your hair."

"You let yours grow," she said.

Ben's eyes widened and, drawing his horse to a sudden halt, he stared at her, gaping. "Did you hear what you just said?"

Penny blinked, searching her mind. "It just came out," she said. "I don't know where it came from, Ben, it just sort of spilled out of me without warning." Her head ached a little harder. She closed her eyes.

"No," he said gently, and his hand came to rest on the side of her head, right where it ached. Easing, comforting her. His touch was magic to her. And each time he stopped touching her, she found herself wishing he'd touch her again. "Don't try to force it. Just let it go, pretend it didn't happen. Seems to me more comes back to you when you aren't trying than when you are."

She shook her head, opened her eyes. "Please don't get your hopes up, Ben. It wasn't a memory. I don't know what it was—it was just there."

He nodded slowly, clicking his tongue at the horse, and both animals began walking again. The steady plodding of their hooves over the lush, grassy ground was soothing somehow. The house was in sight now. And Penny felt an odd twinge of regret that their ride together was coming to an end.

"So, about the hair," Ben said, sending her a sideways glance. "Do you think I should cut it again?"

She smiled at him, but her throat went dry as she studied his dark gold hair, pulled back with a band, and thought about how it would feel to run her fingers through it. "I…kind of like it the way it is."

He turned his head so she couldn't see his reaction to that. "I like yours, too."

"Better than before?"

He faced her, and his smile was gone. His eyes, deep and solemn as his gaze moved over her. "I liked it long. I like it short. I'd like it even if it all fell out."

Her stomach tied itself into a painful knot.

"It isn't the hair, Penny. It's the woman underneath who gets under my skin. Always was."

She closed her eyes. "The woman underneath," she whispered, wondering why his words hurt so much. And then she knew. Because there was no woman underneath—not the one he knew, at least. Not anymore. And there might never be again.

CHAPTER SEVEN

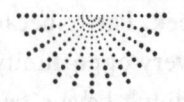

They sipped iced tea on the porch swing, and Ben studied her face, searching for signs of fatigue. But he saw none.

"What are we going to do now?" she asked eagerly.

"Haven't we done enough?" She'd insisted on brushing down Agatha herself. She should be exhausted by now, but wasn't.

"Not by a long shot." Then she frowned, searching his face. "You must have things you should be doing, though. The dojo...."

"Elliot and Adam are handling things there for me," he said softly.

She tilted her head. "They're into martial arts, too?"

Ben smiled at her. "They're clueless. But they'll be fine. Fact is, there's only one class left today." He glanced at his watch. "The preschoolers should be arriving in a half hour for their lesson, and then the boys are done for the day."

She sat up straighter. "Let's let them off the hook."

Ben frowned, not sure what she meant. "You want me to go in and teach that class?"

Smiling softly, she nodded. "If I can come, too. I mean...if you don't mind...."

"Are you sure you're not too tired?" He couldn't get over how much energy she had. He'd expected her flat on her back in bed by now.

"I'm not tired at all. And I want to see that place...from the inside, I mean."

Ben stroked her cheek. Partly because he couldn't seem to resist touching her at every opportunity, but mostly because he wanted to be sure she didn't have a fever. She didn't. Her skin was warm and soft, and her eyes sparkled. "Okay," he said. "If you insist, we'll go teach the class. Together." In truth he'd always dreamed of showing his wife what he'd built from what had once been a grain warehouse. He was proud of the dojo. But not being able to share it with her had always detracted from his joy in it.

They arrived twenty minutes later, and he saw Penny admiring the dragon painted on the red door as he opened it for her. They entered the huge main room, stepped over the mats scattered on the floor and stopped in the center.

On the far end, Elliot executed a clumsy spinning back kick, while Adam shook his head and said, "No way. I've seen Ben do it, and that's all wrong."

"Is not," Elliot countered. "I know I'm doing it right."

"You are if you're supposed to look like you just stepped on a banana peel."

Ben laughed. "You two ought to sign up for lessons if you really want to learn."

His brothers both turned to face him, Elliot looking surprised, while Adam sent a worried look toward Penny. "What are you two doing here?"

"Relieving you both of command. Penny and I will take the final class. You can go home."

Penny and Ben moved forward, and Adam said, "Are you sure you're up to this, Penny?"

Penny tilted her head. "Why is everyone always asking me that?"

Adam shrugged. "We get overprotective of our sisters. You don't believe me, just ask Jessi." There was affection in his eyes as he studied her face, looking, Ben knew, for signs of fatigue just as he'd been doing himself all afternoon.

"To hell with asking Jessi," Elliot said. "Ask Lash."

Ben lowered his head when Penny sent him a searching look. "We weren't exactly...gentle with him."

"Poor Lash," Penny said.

"He came out okay." Ben glanced toward the door as it opened and a few three and four-year-olds came inside. "I'd better go change. Be right back." He headed toward the locker rooms, but inclined his head at Elliot as he went. When they were out of earshot he said, "On your way home, stop at Garrett's office and tell him the clinic was called the Barlow Hospice, and the name of the doctor in charge was Barlow, as well. Maybe he can check it out."

Elliot nodded. "Hope he can find something," he said.

Ben did, too, but he saw Penny looking at them, and knew she'd be curious as to what they were discussing. He didn't want her worrying about it. So he slapped Elliot on the shoulder, and muttered, "Stay with her until I get back out here, okay?"

"Sure, Ben."

Ben headed into the locker rooms, leaving Penny in the care of his brothers.

Elliot greeted the children, while Adam drew Penny aside. "You sure you feel okay?"

"Fine. Shouldn't I?" She should grill him, she really should. But she didn't think he'd tell her a thing. She'd have to get her information from Ben. And she would. Soon.

Adam nodded. "Did you get any answers today, Penny? Are

you any closer to knowing what really happened to you two years ago?"

Sighing, she shook her head. "I don't know much more than I did when I got here." She studied his face, wondering at his interest. But saw only caring and concern in his eyes.

"You will," he told her. "You just relax and try not to worry. I'm gonna take care of this for you. Okay?"

"Adam, do you know something you're not telling me?"

He lowered his head. "I know someone who might." Then he met her eyes again. "But like I said, I'll see to it." He searched her face and smiled. "Damn, it's good to have you back home where you belong. I don't know if I've told you that." Then he hugged her, and she thought it was impulsive and unplanned, and she hugged him back.

If Adam was keeping something from her, she realized it wasn't that he'd plotted to get rid of her. He couldn't. His caring was genuine, she felt it right to her bones. "Thank you, Adam," she said as he stepped back.

"Hey, what's this?" Ben called. "I turn my back for a minute and find my wife in my brother's arms?" But there was humor in his voice.

"That's what you get for leaving her alone with such a handsome devil," Adam told him with a wink. "C'mon, Elliot, let's get out of here before he decides to demonstrate that spinning back kick on my face."

When they left, Penny found a vacant mat in the corner, and sat down there to watch Ben work. He'd emerged from the locker room dressed in the same white uniform the children all wore, but his was decorated with a black belt. The children lined up in front of him, pressed their palms together in front of them and bowed, and Ben did likewise. She saw his eyes gleam as he talked them through several simple movements, saw the way the kids responded to him. He suppressed laughter when they messed up, and patiently helped them get it right. They called him "Sensei" and looked at him with adoration in their young eyes.

He loved these kids, and they him, she thought. And then she thought it was no wonder. Ben Brand would be an easy man to love.

When the session ended and the mothers arrived to collect their kids, Ben waited until the last one had gone. Then he shut off the lights, locked the place up and walked Penny back to the pickup truck.

She got in, turned to face him and said, "So where do I sign up?"

He glanced toward her, startled. "Sign up?"

"For lessons," she told him. "It's so beautiful, what you do. I want to learn."

His smile was gentle, but unbearably sad, as he reached out to stroke her hair. She expected him to ask her if she was sure she was up to taking lessons from him. But he didn't. And it made her wonder....

"Is this something I knew before? Something else I've forgotten?"

"No. I took up martial arts after you...went away. I thought it might help me find some kind of...peace."

That made her throat tighten up. "And did you?" she asked him.

"Not until you came back to me, Penny."

She lowered her head, feeling guilty because there was so much feeling for her in his eyes. "I figured my coming back had only made things harder for you."

"Nothing could be harder for me than being without you."

Why did she feel on the verge of tears? She moved closer to him on the seat of the pickup. And Ben slipped his arm around her as he put the vehicle into gear.

"Penny...it's hard for me to remember that all of this is

brand-new to you. If I...if you feel like I'm pushing...if I overstep...just tell me, okay?"

He was so gentle, so careful with her. "I will," she whispered, and then she let her head rest lightly upon his shoulder, and she heard his sigh of contentment.

He stopped once on the way home. Home. God, was she really beginning to think of the Texas Brand that way? As her home?

He ran into a small shop while she waited in the truck, and when he came out, he was carrying a tiny brown bag. He got in and handed it to her.

Frowning, Penny reached inside. She pulled out a bag of dog treats, a brand-new leash and lastly a white rubber bone with a red ribbon around it. She squeezed the thing, and it squeaked loudly. She thought her heart was overflowing as she smiled up at him. "Ben, you didn't have to...."

"Sure, I did. Ollie's part of the family now, too. Besides, if she has a bone to chew, maybe she'll leave the clocks alone."

It wasn't that he was worried about the clocks. She knew that. It was because he cared so much about her, and he knew how much she loved the dog. Was he trying to win her affection, then, by buying things for Olive?

If he was, she realized, he needn't have bothered. He'd already won it.

∽

Penny had gone up to her room to lie down right after dinner, and while Ben missed her company already, Old Blue seemed relieved to be rid of Penny's bulldog side-kick. The stubby dog had been running circles around the old hound all evening, trying to get him to play. Blue's most ambitious response had been to crook his eyebrows on occasion, yawn and settle more comfortably onto the braided oval rug. But he had an indulgent, mildly amused look in his big hound-dog eyes as he watched the bull-dog's shenanigans. Unlike the look in Penny's eyes when Ben had begun referring to her precious pal as Stubby. But that was okay. Her velvety brown eyes lit up again when he gave her the rubber bone he'd bought for the dog. You'd have thought he'd given her a diamond ring the way she smiled.

Man, she did love that short, fat, smush-nosed mutt. But Ben was rapidly discovering it was hard not to love a dog with as much personality as Olive had.

He was sitting now in front of the dead fireplace, wondering what the hell to do next, how he woudl sleep later, knowing she was in the room next door. How to keep himself from going to her room tonight, even if it was just to look at her as she slept.

Then he heard voices on the porch.

A female one he didn't recognize at first, said, "Why won't you tell me what this is all about?"

Adam's deeper voice replied, "You'll find out soon enough."

The screen door banged, and the two stepped inside. Adam, and the woman who'd jilted him and broken his heart five years back. Kirsten Armstrong. She was just as pretty as ever, with masses of light brown hair like doe hide, spilling over her shoulders. But she'd changed. She wore clothes that might as well have had their expensive price tags still dangling instead of the jeans she used to live in. Her shoes had deadly looking heels, and their color matched the little purse she carried. She wore makeup and big long fingernails painted the same shade of red as her lips. It was like the old Kirsten had been the rough draft, and now she was polished to perfection. But Ben thought he'd liked the rough version better. She'd been more real back then.

Adam was trying hard to look angry, but Ben could see the pain in his eyes.

"Dammit, Adam, why the hell has your brother been calling the estate all day, and why did you drag me all the way out here?"

Adam rolled his eyes. "The estate, is it? Haven't we just moved up in the world? But I hear marrying money will do that for a girl."

"Don't go there, Adam." She glared at him, but Ben thought he glimpsed a hint of pain in her eyes, as well.

"So has your old geezer got one foot in the grave yet? He didn't make you sign a prenup, did he? Be a crying shame if all you've been giving him went to waste, wouldn't it?"

"Shut up!" she spun toward the door, but Adam gripped her arm, and for a moment they stood there staring at each other, sparks practically leaping between them.

Ben cleared his throat, and they both looked toward him. "Let go of her, Adam. This isn't about you two. You can save it, okay?"

Adam drew a breath and released her. "Wait here." He stalked past Ben and headed up the stairs, and Ben knew he was going to get Penny. Penny, who still didn't know about the condition that was supposed to have killed her by now. His heart beat a little faster.

Kirsten sighed heavily, but came farther into the room, slapping her handbag down on the coffee table and staring up the stairs after Adam disappeared. She turned toward Ben, and her frown eased a bit.

"Hello, Kirsten," he said. "Been a long time."

She nodded but didn't meet his eyes. "I'd have stopped by. I just thought it would be…awkward."

"You thought right."

"Your brother would just as soon shoot me as look at me."

"Can you blame him?"

She looked away. "I can't change the past. Why can't he just let it go?"

"Like you have?" Ben asked.

She sighed, still not looking him in the eye. "I've done a lot of things I regret, Ben."

"Was not showing up for your wedding one of them?"

She looked up quickly. "I didn't say that." She paced to the bottom of the stairway, looked upward, then turned and paced back again. "Do you know what this is all about, Ben?"

"Yes." He said nothing more. She was nervous; that much was obvious. But he supposed having her former fiancé haul her to his home without explanation was partly to blame for that.

"Are you going to tell me?"

"You wouldn't believe me. I think you'd best just wait a second and see for yourself. But first I have to warn you to watch what you say, Kirsten."

Her eyes narrowed, and she blew an impatient sigh. "This is ridiculous. I'm leaving."

"Wait. Just give me a minute, Kirsten—"

"Tell Adam, when he wants to act like an adult—if that day ever comes—he can call me." She snatched up her bag and stalked toward the door. "Until then—"

"Just a minute, Kirsten," Adam called, and then his footsteps came slowly down the stairs. "You might walk out on your husband-to-be, but you wouldn't do it to your best friend, now, would you?"

Adam and Penny descended the stairs and stood side by side at the bottom. Adam looked smug and Penny confused.

Kirsten kept her back to him, reached for the door, and Penny said, "Adam, what's going on? Who is she?"

Kirsten froze where she was. Her designer handbag fell to the floor, but she didn't seem to notice. Very slowly she turned, and when her eyes fell on Penny standing there, she went chalk white. Her lips moved, but no sound came out. And when she stumbled, Ben lunged from the chair. Adam beat him to Kirsten's side, though it was unnecessary. She didn't faint. She caught hold of the back of a chair and stood there blinking at Penny as if she was seeing a ghost. Hell, she probably thought she was.

"P-Penny?"

Ben dragged his gaze from Kirsten's stricken face and saw Penny nod. And then Kirsten moved slowly across the room, shaking her head in disbelief. When she reached Penny, she touched her hands as if she couldn't believe she was real. And then she wrapped her arms around Ben's wife much the way he had when he'd first seen her. And she cried, clutching Penny close, rocking her in her arms, all her polish suddenly as transparent as glass.

"How? Penny, how is this possible? They said you'd slipped into a coma, that you wouldn't survive another month....I don't...." Then she stepped back, bit her lip, lowered her head.

Ben stood there, digesting what he'd just heard. But it was Adam who spoke. "You knew, didn't you, Kirsten? You knew Penny didn't die in that car accident. Didn't you?"

Kirsten's shoulders were shaking now, but she didn't answer.

"Speak up, dammit!"

"That's enough, Adam." Ben put a heavy hand on his brother's shoulder, silencing him. "Kirsten, you have some heavy-duty explaining to do." He lowered his eyes, the pain of a friend's betrayal stinging like acid. First things first, however. "Penny, this is Kirsten Armstrong. She was your best friend from the time you both started kindergarten together. We thought she might know—"

"What are you saying?" Kirsten interrupted. "Why are you telling her who I am when she...." She searched Penny's face. "You know me, Penny. You know me...don't you?"

Penny lowered her head. "I'm sorry. I don't."

"Kirsten," Ben said softly, "she doesn't remember anything before waking up in a clinic in Europe. Apparently you're the only one who can tell us how she ended up there."

"Oh, my God," Kirsten muttered. She pressed her palms to Penny's cheeks. "But look at you. You look...you look...healthy."

"Kirsten," Ben said, a warning tone in his voice. He wanted

an explanation—not the revelation Kirsten seemed about to drop on Penny.

"Everyone keeps saying that," Penny told her, and she shot Ben a questioning glance. "Was I that sick before...before the accident?"

Kirsten frowned at Ben. "She doesn't know?"

"Kirsten," he said again.

"Doesn't know what?" Penny turned to Ben, wide brown eyes searching his face. "Ben, what is it you haven't told me?"

"Nothing that won't keep, Penny."

"I don't want it to keep. I want to know now."

"Oh, God," Kirsten muttered. "I'm sorry...." She glanced at Adam. "You should have told me."

Adam shook his head, looking as if he'd finally realized how badly he'd screwed up. "I wasn't thinking." He glanced apologetically toward Ben.

"You rarely do where Kirsten is concerned." And as a result, they'd gotten way off the subject

"Will someone please tell me what's going on here?" Penny demanded.

Ben lowered his head. Damn, but he didn't want to do this to her. He didn't want to see the life ebb out of her again the way he'd watched it do before.

Kirsten reached out a hand to gently touch Penny's face, and she smiled through a flood of tears. "What happened, happened because of love, Penny. Mine for you, and yours for Ben." She sniffled. "I wished for you so many times. God, Penny, if only you knew...but you don't even remember me."

Penny shook her head, then reached up to take Kirsten's hand in hers, moving it slowly away from her cheek. "It's obvious we were...close," she said.

"Closer than sisters. Oh, Penny, I've missed you so much."

"Then help me. If you know what's been kept from me, please, Kirsten, please tell me. I need to know."

Lowering her head, Kirsten sighed deeply, brokenly. She backed away from Penny and sank into a chair, and Ben could see clear through her polish now. She was shaken. Trapped. Scared. Suddenly she was the same awkward, insecure girl she'd been when they were all kids.

"God, just how sick was I?" Penny asked.

"I'll tell you," Ben said softly. "Penny…God help me, I wanted to wait. I wanted you to see Doc first, because…you just look so damned healthy and I can't help but wish—"

"Ben, it's impossible. You know that. Don't do it to yourself." Adam came to stand beside his brother, one hand on his shoulder.

Ben met Adam's eyes. "Leave us alone, will you?"

Adam nodded, turning to Kirsten. "This doesn't let you off the hook. I still want answers, Kirsten."

"You aren't getting any." She held Penny's confused, frightened eyes, never even glancing at Adam. "When you're ready, Penny, I'll tell you all of it. But only you. No one else."

"Then you do know what really happened," Adam accused her.

She looked at him, then lowered her head and moved away, grabbing up her bag and fishing something from it. A small card, which she laid on the table. "My number," she told Penny. "Call me when you want to talk."

Penny nodded mutely, and then Kirsten turned to walk out the door. Adam cussed under his breath, then followed, muttering that he had to drive her back to the estate. He said the words as if they left a bad taste in his mouth.

Ben's heart felt as if it had turned sour when Penny looked up at him, all her questions in her eyes.

"Kirsten knew I didn't die in that accident," she said softly.

Ben nodded. "It looks that way. I can't believe she kept it from us. She was like family, back then." He closed his eyes. "I could choke her for this."

"Maybe she had a good reason," Penny said, "but she was still surprised to see me alive."

Ben drew a deep breath, and it felt as if there was a sharp blade piercing his chest. "Yeah."

"Why?"

He moved closer to her, reached up to run one hand through her silken hair. "You were real sick, Penny. For a long time. We knew about your condition before we were married."

She stepped back a little so she could search his face. "What kind of…condition?"

He gripped her shoulders in gentle hands. "It's called Hillman-Waite Syndrome. It's a degenerative disease."

"Degenerative." She repeated the word, and he could see her mind working through it before she met his eyes again. "But treatable?"

Ben felt his throat tighten. "No. The symptoms worsen slowly, leaving you more and more helpless, until at the end you just slip into a coma and never wake up."

She paled, right before his eyes, and he could feel the shudder that worked through her. "Are you saying…Ben, are you telling me I was dying?" She pulled free of him, pushing her hands through her hair, shaking her head. "Then…if there's no treatment, no cure for this thing– My God. My God."

He reached for her, wanting to pull her into his arms and hold her, make it better for her somehow, even though he knew nothing could. But she was stiff, standing where she was, refusing to come closer. "I survived the coma…I made my way back here…only to find out…." She closed her eyes, pressing a hand to her forehead. "No. This isn't true, this can't be true."

"I wish it was me instead of you Penny. I'd do anything to take this away."

She stared up at him, horror in her eyes. And then she just sank to the floor, shaking violently as tears flooded her face. She lowered her head into her hands, shoulders bowing forward, sobs racking her.

Ben was beside her in a heartbeat, scooping her up into his arms and cradling her there. And she didn't fight him this time. She curled against him like a frightened child. Her face pressed to the crook of his neck, her tears wetting his skin. "Dammit, Penny, I'm sorry." He carried her across the living room, up the stairs and into her bedroom. But he didn't put her down. Instead he sat on the bed, still holding her, and he lowered his head to kiss her hair.

She sniffled, and tipped her head up, red-rimmed eyes searching his. And then she lifted her hand, and she touched his cheek. "You're crying," she whispered.

He pressed his lips together and swallowed hard.

"You really did love me, didn't you?" she asked him, blinking away tears that were quickly replaced by fresh ones.

"I still do."

"I want to remember." Sobs made her draw gasping, unsteady breaths that broke her words into fragments. But she parted her lips slightly, and leaned up to press them to his.

Trembling as much as she was, Ben kissed her deeply, but tenderly. And her taste was so familiar that his heart swelled. He felt it would burst with the bittersweet emotions—overwhelming joy at having her in his arms again, and crippling grief so intense he could barely breathe.

And when he lifted his mouth away from hers to stare into her eyes, she whispered, "Hold me, Ben. Make it like it was."

He hadn't thought he could hurt any more. He'd never been more wrong.

CHAPTER EIGHT

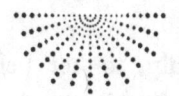

It was heaven and hell at once when Penny wrapped her arms around him, held him as if she would never let go, kissed him in a way he hadn't been kissed since the day he'd lost her. The way he'd dreamed of so often these past two lonely years.

But he couldn't deny her. He knew the crippling pain she was feeling right then, because he felt it, too. And like Penny, he wanted to remember. He wanted to make love to her and make the rest of this nightmare disappear. He wanted to hold her again, like before.

He turned to lay her down, gently on the bed, and with his eyes he asked if she was sure, and without a word she told him she was. She reached up with trembling hands to unbutton his shirt. And when she pushed it open, her palms slid across his chest, and he closed his eyes in agonizing pleasure.

The shirt slid from his shoulders, and he bent over her to reciprocate. He peeled her blouse away, and tossed it to the floor, and freed her of the bra she wore, throwing that aside, as well. And then he looked at her, lying there in nothing more than a pair of Chelsea's jeans. And her breasts were as small and round and perfect as he remembered. He closed his hands over their warmth, and Penny closed her wet eyes.

His mouth watered for her. He lay down on the bed beside her, and kissed her mouth again, and then he slid lower to kiss her body. Her breasts were warm and salty against his lips, and their peaks stiffened on his tongue. She arched her back as he suckled her, and her fingers tangled in his hair as she held him close to her.

He flattened one palm to her belly, and slid his fingers beneath the waistband of her jeans. She reached between them to caress the swollen hardness beneath his. Ben stopped breathing. "I want you," he whispered. "I've dreamed of this…."

"I have, too…only…I could never remember when I woke. But I wanted to remember, Ben."

He freed the button and zipper of her jeans so he could slide his hand deeper. And when he found the soft moistness between her legs, he touched her there, the way she liked. Her hips arched, pressing her against his hand, and she sighed deep and raggedly.

He kissed her, pulled her body tight to his and worked her jeans lower. And somehow she managed to undress him, as well. And then he was lowering himself over her, slipping inside her. Feeling as if he'd come home after a long, long journey, he moved deeper into her body. She wrapped her legs around his and held him there, lying still, opening her eyes and staring up into his. And for just a moment he thought he saw the old Penny there. The look of love, shining from her eyes just the way it had done before.

Then she closed her eyes, and the look was gone. But the feeling remained. He moved inside her, and she moved with him, and it was as if they'd never been apart. He knew every sound she made, every breath that shuddered out of her. He knew when she climaxed, because she held him tighter, pressed him more deeply into her, and because she whispered his name in that same broken way she always had. And he lost himself to sensation when he joined her in ecstasy.

And then he cradled her close, and kissed her face, and whispered that everything was going to be okay. He only wished it wasn't a lie.

～

She didn't know why she'd reacted the way she had. Fear was certainly a part of it. Coupled perhaps with a desire to cling to her life, whatever it had been, for as long as she could. Because it might end, all too soon.

Whatever, she knew one thing. She didn't regret it. Ben had made her feel more alive than she had since waking from that coma, and there was no way she could regret that. Her feelings were all mixed up. Intense sorrow and devastation warred inside her with a stubborn urge toward denial. All of it wrapped up in a soft, newborn glow as fragile as a firefly's tail. Newborn, yes. But old, too. Like a soul beginning its next incarnation, her feelings for Ben were born again inside her. Fresh and new, but drawing somehow from the old ones she couldn't recall.

And there was something else. Some sense that turning to Ben Brand when disaster hit her in the face was something as natural to her as breathing.

So much was going on in her mind. She couldn't believe she'd suspected him of trying to rid himself of her by faking her death and shipping her off. He wouldn't have done that. First because he'd have had no reason to, knowing she was dying anyway. And second because he'd obviously loved her—adored her—once, a long time ago.

He said he still did.

She closed her eyes and nestled closer to him in the little bed, and his arms tightened around her. He said he still did, but of course he couldn't possibly, could he? He didn't even know her now.

And maybe he never would. Maybe there wouldn't be time.

"It's so odd," she said. "I feel so good, except for the headaches. I just don't understand how I can be..." She didn't say the last word. Dying. She didn't even want to think it. So instead she sat up slightly, staring down at him. He'd long since dried away her tears with his kisses. She vowed she wouldn't shed any more. She had far too little time to waste it on crying.

"What kind of shape was I in before that accident? Physically, I mean?"

Ben closed his eyes. "Bad," he told her, and she thought from the lines of tension at the corners of his eyes that he must be remembering. "You couldn't walk through the house without becoming breathless and dizzy. You'd stopped riding. Stopped going out, even. You had to lie down a lot, take naps during the day." He opened his eyes, studied her face, and the tension eased. "Nothing like you are now."

"Was I in pain?"

He winced visibly. "It was pretty bad. Doc medicated you as much as he could, and that just made you even more tired all the time."

She nodded, searching her mind for the memory of all of this, but not finding it. "I don't feel tired at all now. And there's no pain." She tilted her head. "But you said it was a degenerative condition."

"Yeah. The coma...the coma was supposed to be the final stage of the illness."

A tiny tongue of fire leaped to life in her breast. "Is there...is there any chance it was?"

He studied her, and she could see him trying not to let himself hope too much. "Doc said there was no cure for HWS, Penny."

She drew a breath, then let it out all at once. Closing her eyes, she lay back down. "Then...this disease is still inside me."

"We'd be fools to think otherwise," he said softly. "But we can't bet on anything until you see Doc." Ben rolled up onto his side, cupping her face in his hands. "Whatever time we have, Penny, we'll be together. We'll make the most of it. I want to give you everything you've ever wanted, take you anywhere you want to go—"

"I don't want to go anywhere," she told him. "I want to be here. I want to remember."

"I know," he whispered. "I know." He leaned closer, brushing her lips with his.

The knock at the door made her go stiff, but Ben didn't even flinch. He just called, "Wait a minute," and got out of bed, pulling on his clothes. Then he glanced down at her, and gently tucked the covers around her.

She felt like crawling underneath them to hide from this cruel new reality she was being forced to face. She wanted Ben here with her. He could make her forget.

Ben opened the door then, and she heard Garrett's voice, though he spoke so softly she had to strain to catch his words. "Need to talk to you, Ben," he said, and he sounded grim. "Alone."

Frowning, Penny changed her mind about crawling under the covers. What was this? More secrets? Lord, this family seemed to have more than its share of them!

Ben glanced back toward Penny, then stepped into the hallway, pulling the door closed behind him.

Penny scrambled out of the bed, yanking on the robe that hung over the back of the chair. She tiptoed to the door and listened by pressing her ear to the wood, but only muffled tones made their way through. Damned old-fashioned builders and their love of hardwoods and high quality! She glanced around, spied a water glass on the bedside stand, chugged its contents so fast her belly ached. Then she put the glass to the door and her ear to the glass.

Ah, better.

"Why the cloak-and-dagger routine, Garrett?" Ben was asking.

She wondered why it relieved her to hear something that seemed to indicate this round of "I've got a secret" wasn't Ben's idea.

"Adam told me what happened," Garrett said. "I figure Penny has more than enough to deal with right now. How is she taking it?"

"How do you think?"

There was a deep sigh. Then Garrett asked, "How 'bout you, Ben?"

"I feel like I've been gut-shot and left in the desert. But she's with me, so I don't want to leave. Does that make any sense at all?"

Penny's eyes welled up when he said that. She blinked her tears away and tried to focus on the conversation instead of on her state of health and on her emotions. She could picture Garrett's worried gaze moving over his brother's face, picture him shaking his head in sorrow.

"I figured there was no sense scaring her when she was going through so much."

Penny's heart tripped and stuttered. Scaring her?

"Scaring her?" Ben asked.

"Ben, I think we got trouble. I had a call today from Matt Bauer, over at the El Paso Rangers' Station. He said there was some fella there lookin' for Penny."

Penny's throat went dry. Ask for a description, she thought desperately.

"What sort of fella?" Ben asked.

"Midforties, balding, lean. Spoke with a British accent."

Dr. Barlow! Penny's heart raced faster.

"Ben, this guy had a photo of Penny. Claimed she was his wife."

"That's bullshit," Ben snapped. But then he was quiet for a long moment.

"That's what Matt thought, too. He said the guy refused to say where he was staying, or even fill out a missing-persons report on her. Took off as soon as Matt started asking questions. Thing is, Ben, I tried to check on this Barlow Hospice in London, where Penny said she'd been, and on the doctor she mentioned by the same name. Both seem to have vanished from the face of the earth."

"How's that?" Ben asked.

"The building is empty. Barlow sold it to a real-estate agency for half what it was worth and disappeared, along with whatever patients might have been in his care. No one can find any records…there's just nothing."

Penny drew a sharp breath. Gone? The clinic and the doctor? Just gone?

"What about former employees?" Ben asked.

"The ones they can locate don't know a thing. They showed up for work one day, and the place was locked up and empty. None of them have a clue of anything shady going on there, Ben, but I gotta tell you, it sounds fishy to me. I mean, I know Penny is suspicious of little girls selling cookies, but I think this time she just might be onto something."

She heard movement. Pacing. She thought it was Ben. Then it stopped. "You said the employees they can locate…."

"Yeah," Garrett said. "There are a handful who've vanished along with the doc. And then there's one they did find, but she isn't talking. The nurse, Michele Kudrow—the one Penny stole the credit card from—she was found in her apartment."

"Found?" Ben asked. Then, more softly, he asked, "Dead?"

"Yeah."

"Murder?"

"Suicide."

There was a long pause.

Suicide, my eye, Penny thought. Michele knew too much! Then she blinked slowly. Come to think of it, she might know too much, too. She just didn't remember. But what if she did? Or what if Dr. Barlow thought she might?

God, what was that man hiding?

"We're gonna have to find this Barlow, Garrett. I don't care what it takes. Whoever is responsible for costing me two years with my wife is going to pay. I should have been with her, coma or no coma. I should have been there. Someone robbed me of that. And I can hardly stand to speculate on the reasons why, what the hell his motives for keeping Penny there in secret might have been. I want that bastard to look me right in the eyes and tell me, Garrett. And then I want to see him pay for what he's done."

Penny closed her eyes, awed again by the force of the emotions the man still held for her. It was overwhelming to know he cared that much. She wanted to know those answers just as much as he did. And there were two people who might be able to provide them, Kirsten and Dr. Barlow.

A little chill raced up her spine as she realized that in all likelihood, they were both in town. But only one of them could be approached. Kirsten. She might be an enemy but Penny could handle her. The other must be avoided at all costs. Or she was sorely afraid she'd end up just like Michele Kudrow.

∼

Dr. Gregory Barlow hadn't wasted any time once he'd discovered that his Jane—Penny Brand—had indeed managed to locate her family. He didn't know how she'd done it. His files hadn't been touched. And no one, not even his most trusted employee, had known her real name. Or anything at all about her, or any of the others.

So there was only one answer. She must remember. And if she remembered, she might well remember things that could destroy him. Comatose patients often heard much of what went on around them. He'd known that. But it hadn't mattered, or he'd thought it hadn't mattered. Because he hadn't expected her to ever recover from that coma. And even if she did, he hadn't intended for her to ever leave his clinic. And even if she managed that, she should never have regained her memory enough to find her way back to her family.

Somehow, though, the mite of a woman had done all of those things. And soon she and her family would manage to put it all together. She was a danger to him. A threat to everything he'd worked for, everything he'd accomplished. God, he was so close, closer than he'd ever been!

Well, he simply couldn't let her ruin it all. He couldn't.

Already he'd had to phone that unscrupulous attorney and make hasty arrangements. Sell the clinic, move the patients, set up again under a new name and begin seeking out new employees. Take care of anyone who knew too much.

Michele. He'd been half in love with her. But she was soft. She'd have given it all up if pressed. He knew that.

Now all that remained was his one-of-a-kind patient. The one who represented his greatest work so far.

She was going to have to surrender to his care, come back with him. Or she was going to have to die.

~

Ben stepped back into Penny's bedroom, feeling worried as hell and trying not to show it. He expected to find her in the bed where he'd left her, but instead she was up and dressed. Bright eyes, though puffy from crying. Pink cheeks. Gleaming hair. She looked healthier than he did. What alarmed him was that she seemed to be packing. Methodically removing the clothes Chelsea had given her from the dresser, and stacking them on the bed. Maybe she was just sorting through them again.

"Honey, you ought to rest," he told her.

"Resting is the last thing I want to do." She averted her gaze when she said it, but quickly hid her distress, and opened another drawer.

Ben was thoroughly confused. "But…"

"But nothing." She faced him, hands on her hips. "Look, I don't know how this kind of news hit me the last time, Ben. I can only tell you how I feel now."

He stepped close to her, pushed her hair out of her eyes, loving the silkiness of it against his palm. "And how's that?"

"Like I have a whole lot to do, and maybe not a lot of time to do it."

He closed his eyes. God, to hear her say it so matter-of-factly….

"Besides, if I'm going to be as sick as you say I was before… well, I might as well try to do what I want to while I'm still able."

He sighed, nodded. She was right. He'd tried to bring her around to thinking this way the last time. But she'd been so different, then. Sicker. In pain. Devastated. Beaten. She'd just given up.

It was good to see her this way. The fighter she'd been before she got sick in the first place. But God, did she have to leave him? She'd told him she wanted to stay here. To find her old life while there was still time.

"So…where are you going?" he asked her.

She turned slowly, looking up into his eyes, almost startled. Then her eyes darkened with understanding. "I'm sorry, Ben. Did you think…?" She glanced at the clothes on the bed, then back at him. And then she smiled very gently, but sadly, and reached up to stroke his cheek. "Not far," she told him. "Just one door down."

"One door..?" He blinked and searched her face, afraid to believe....

"I thought...but maybe I should have asked first. I thought, Ben, if you still want me...I'd like to try being your wife again. I was going to move my stuff into your room...our room."

He smiled slowly, and felt a huge weight lift from his shoulders. Oh, plenty was still there, bearing down on him, but a little bit of it floated away. He pulled her into his arms and kissed her. And then he released her.

"In that case, I have something to give you."

She tilted her head, studying him curiously as he slowly took the chain from around his neck. The one he'd been wearing since he'd lost her. Undoing the clasp, he slipped her wedding ring from the silver chain as she watched, and he saw her eyes grow moist. He brought the ring to his lips, then took her hand and gently slipped it onto her finger. Penny caught her breath when he lifted her hand and kissed the place where the ring encircled her finger.

~

Penny knew she'd made this decision impulsively and under tremendous emotional strain. And yet she couldn't quite bring herself to regret it. She spent that night in the arms of her husband. And the fact that he was a stranger to her, a man she barely knew, didn't detract from the comfort he gave to her. It didn't matter that she didn't love him. She had once. She was sure of that. And right now he was the only thing she had besides an empty life, barren memory and the anticipation of an early death. He was here, offering to fill her brief time up with his love, and it was an offer she couldn't refuse.

And though she didn't love the man...sometimes, when he

held her, or looked into her eyes...it felt as if she could almost remember what loving him felt like. Almost as if it was still there in her heart, but faint and distant. A tiny voice, a whisper straining to be heard.

The ring on her finger felt right. Warm and secure, and she knew it had been placed there with love.

She woke up beside him, his strong arms holding her close, her head pillowed by his broad chest, his scent all around her. And for just an instant—that minuscule space between one heartbeat and the next, between sleeping and waking—it was as if she'd never been away. As if this was the way she woke up every morning. As if...as if she remembered it all perfectly.

And then it was gone again, and she was left with a morning headache.

"Good morning," he said very softly when he felt her stirring.

She managed to smile past the pain when she looked up at him. "Morning."

"How do you feel?"

She thought about that for a minute. "Lucky, I guess. Sounds pretty strange, knowing I'm carrying this disease around in my body." She looked into his eyes. "But I'm not alone anymore."

Ben smiled, his blue eyes twin wells of emotion as he stroked her hair. "You couldn't be less alone if you tried." And he sent a meaningful glance toward the foot of the bed.

She followed his gaze to spot the white lump lying there, sound asleep. "At least she's not snoring," Penny said.

He laughed. God, he was a saint He'd even put up with Olive in his bed, if that was what it took. She wondered if she'd ever been worthy of this kind of love. She wondered if any woman ever had.

This room—it felt so familiar and yet somehow new to her at the same time. The curtains and bedspread were both a soft, piney green, and the photos on the walls were mostly of family members. But there was one shot with people she didn't recognize.

"Who are they?" she asked Ben, pointing at the framed photo on the wall. "Someone else I've forgotten, I imagine."

Ben's eyes were clouded when he answered. "The man is John Brand. My father's brother. That's his wife, Sally, and their two kids, Marcus and Sara."

"Did I know them?"

Ben nodded. "They used to come out to the ranch for a week or two every summer. Best time those kids had. But, um, they're gone now."

Penny blinked at him in shock. "Gone? You mean—"

"Yeah." Ben gazed past her at the photo, and she saw the tightness in his jaw. "John got involved with organized-crime figures, did money laundering for them and got greedy. I don't really know the details, just that someone found out he'd been skimming. Some thugs went to their house…and…."

"My God," Penny gasped, looking at the photo again. The dark young boy, and the girl, little more than a toddler. "Even the children?"

Ben nodded. "Wiped out the whole family. They never even found all their bodies."

"That's horrible." Penny looked at the photo until she couldn't bear to look at it any longer.

Ben pulled her into his arms and held her gently. "Too horrible to think about right now. We have enough to worry about, Penny. We shouldn't be dwelling on old nightmares."

"You're right." She snuggled closer and let his warmth, his nearness, chase the horror away.

"So, what do you want to do today?"

Penny lowered her gaze. She'd been lying here awake thinking about just that, and though the task before her was not a pleasant one, she had to get past it. Get it out of the way so she could move on.

Drawing a deep breath, she met Ben's eyes. "I know you're anxious to find out what really happened that day when I was supposedly in a car accident, Ben. I am, too. I want to know who took me away from the only family I had, just when I needed them most. And it seems like this…Kirsten…has some information that can help us. Maybe she had something to do with it, herself."

"Kirsten?" He searched her face. "She adored you, Penny."

Penny bit her lip. She thought the pretty Kirsten might just have adored Ben rather than his wife. She'd seen the glances the two had exchanged. Secretive and full of feeling. It bothered her, but she wasn't about to tell him that.

"Doesn't matter," Penny said. "What I'm trying to say is that I'm as eager to talk to Kirsten—find out what she knows—as you are. But there's something else I have to do first, Ben. Because I just can't focus on anything until I know." She sat up in bed as she spoke.

Ben sat up, as well, slipping an arm around her shoulders, nodding. "You want to see Doc," he said.

She turned to face him, surprised. "Know me pretty well, don't you?"

He nodded. "To tell you the truth, I'm not going to be able to think about anything else, either—not until we get this done. I want to know how you are. Inside, you know. How…." He lowered his gaze.

"How much time I have," she finished for him. "Me, too." Her eyes tried to moisten, but she blinked rapidly. "However much that is, though, I'm not going to waste it crying over things that can't be changed."

He looked at her, his eyes sad and admiring. "You're stronger than you ever were before, Penny. You know that?"

She cocked her head to one side. "Am I?"

He nodded. "I'll call Doc. I have no doubt he'll come right over."

He was wrong about that, as it turned out Doc had back-to-back appointments at his office in town, but when Ben told him on the phone that Penny was not dead, that she was in fact at home with him right now, Penny could hear Doc's surprised shouting all the way across the bedroom.

She'd showered first, and was sitting on a chair that felt made for her, in front of a dressing table she felt belonged to her, brushing her hair with a silver brush that felt so familiar in her palm she could scarcely believe it. When she heard Doc's shouts from the phone, she glanced up to meet Ben's eyes in the mirror. He looked mildly amused, but there was a gut-deep fear underneath it. She knew. Because she felt it, too. Fear of what they would find out today. Fear of dying.

"Okay, okay," Ben said. "We'll come over there, then. All right, fine, an hour."

Even as he hung up, Penny's heart rate accelerated.

"Doc can't come to us," Ben said. "So we'll go to him." He came over to stand behind her, took the brush from her hand and resumed brushing her hair for her. But she couldn't relax beneath his soothing touch.

As if sensing her turmoil, Ollie opened her eyes to peer at Penny from the bed. Then she stretched and jumped down to come sit beside her chair.

"I'm not sure going out is such a good idea, Ben."

"Why not?"

She didn't answer right away, and Ben stopped brushing and frowned at her in the mirror. "Honey, you're as white as a sheet. Look, I know it's scary." He set the brush down, squeezed her shoulders with his hands. "But we'll get through this. Together."

"I know," she told him. "It's not that, it's...." She bit her lip, lowered her gaze.

"Okay, come on. Spill it." Ben turned her chair around so she faced him. Then he braced his arms on either side of her and looked her in the eye. "What's got you so shaken, Penny? Other than the obvious."

She drew a breath and swallowed hard. "I...I sort of overheard what you and Garrett were talking about outside my room last night."

Ben blinked. Then he frowned. "Not without bugging one of us, you didn't. We were practically whispering. How...?"

"Water glass to the door." She peered up at him, shrugged slightly. "You'd be surprised how well it works."

Ben's frown eased, his eyes sparkled and he cupped her face in both hands. "I should have figured. Hell, Penny, you always were into playing detective."

She lifted her brows. "I was?"

"Yeah. Even took a course once. But then you got sick and...."

"And what?" she asked him.

"You let it go." He shook his head. "But we're off the subject, Penny. How much did you hear?"

"Enough to know that Michele Kudrow is dead and Dr. Barlow has vanished. And I can tell you right now, Ben, that nurse did not kill herself."

Ben tilted his head. "How can you be sure?"

"I knew her," Penny told him. She got up from the chair and began pacing the room. Ollie paced along beside her. "Ben, she was Barlow's right hand. If anyone might have known what he was up to at that clinic, it would have been her. And now she's dead? Just like that? At the same time he vanishes?" She shook her head rapidly. "No, this was no suicide."

Ben stood still, leaning back against her dressing table, head turning to keep track of her while she paced back and forth. "You think Barlow killed her?"

"Or had her killed."

"But why, Penny?"

She stopped pacing and turned to face Ben. Ollie sat down,

slightly breathless. "To keep her quiet about whatever was going on at that clinic. And, Ben, I'm afraid that's the same reason he didn't want me to leave that place. The reason he lied to me, told me I had no family, tried to make me stay there even when I knew I was well enough to leave." She resumed pacing. This time the dog only sat still, head tilted to one side, ears cocked, looking quite puzzled by Penny's antics. "I think I might know something about all this," Penny went on. "Something I found out before the coma, and forgot when I came out of it. It's the only reason I can think of for him to want to keep me there." She reached the end of her circuit, turned and stood still. "And if that's true, then Barlow can't risk my remembering and telling anyone what he's trying so hard to keep secret."

Ben blinked, then he came forward and gripped her shoulders. "You think he might come after you?"

She met his gaze, held it. "He already has, Ben. The man your brother described, the one who was in El Paso asking about me at the Rangers' Station...it was Barlow."

Ben searched her eyes, maybe saw the fear there. Then he pulled her into his arms and held her close. "We're gonna get that bastard, Penny. I promise you that. And he's not gonna hurt you. I swear to God, I'll never let anyone hurt you."

Suddenly dizzy, and assailed by the sensation of her mind spinning endlessly, Penny looked up at him. "Say that again...."

"I'll say it as often as you need to hear it, honey. I'll never let anyone hurt you," he told her.

Penny lowered her head to his chest, closed her eyes...

~

She was thirteen, and she had a flashlight in one hand, a shovel in the other. She was certain she would find Mrs. Murphy's body buried in her own backyard if she dug long enough. Everyone knew she and her husband fought like crazy, and now she'd been missing for a solid week. Mr. Murphy's tale that she'd gone out of town to visit her sick mother just didn't hold water. Penny had seen the old coot out here earlier this week. Pretending to plant roses. He'd been planting roses, all right! He'd planted Rose Murphy, his wife—that's what he'd planted.

She couldn't just go digging. First she had to determine the man's whereabouts, make sure she wouldn't be caught. So she slipped around the side of the house, and peered through the window, and clicked on her flashlight.

That's when she heard Mr. Murphy roar like a bear. She saw him lunge out of his bed and head for the front door, and even before she turned to run, that door was slamming and the suspect was on the front porch. Penny's heart hammered in her chest as she realized she couldn't escape without running right past him. But she did it anyway. Poured on every bit of steam she had, and she swore her Keds were flinging soil in her wake as she pounded out of there. Mr. Murphy was shouting after her all the while, and scaring the heck out of her. She could feel the cold sweat on her skin, and the tingle in her nape as if he was right behind her.

She ran straight to Ben, knowing him well enough that she knew she'd find him at the makeshift basketball court in town with his brothers and his tomboy sister, Jessi. And just like always, he was right there when she needed him.

She could still hear Murphy yelling, and the thought occurred to her that he might have grabbed his shotgun on the way through the house. She flung herself into Ben's arms without even thinking about it.

He was so tall for his age. Tallest boy in the seventh grade. But skinny as a scarecrow. His straw-colored hair, always too long, and the way his clothes all fit too loosely only added to that image. But his big blue eyes were just as warm as the Texas sky, and Penny had been in love with him since the first time she'd looked into those eyes and felt them looking right back.

And it didn't matter one ounce that she was only thirteen, either.

He put his long arms around her. "You went and spied on Mr. Murphy after I told you it was a bad idea, didn't you?" he asked her, his voice almost teasing.

She nodded.

"He see you?"

"I don't know. I think so."

And his arms tightened around her a little bit more. "It's okay, Penny. I'm not gonna let him hurt you, you know that. I'd never let anyone hurt you. He comes around here, I'll swear you've been with us the whole time. And my brothers'll back me up, won't you, guys?"

His brothers nodded. Those Brand boys sure stuck together. And little Jessi yelled, "Me, too! I will protect you, Penny!"

Ben tousled his sister's hair, but his eyes were staring real deep into Penny's. "Don't you worry," he told her. "I'll make it okay."

She knew it was true. And she felt an odd little melting sensation in her heart, one she'd never felt before.

~

Penny blinked slowly as the memory faded. But when it left her, it wasn't gone. Not entirely. It remained in her mind, where she could pull it up and look it over at will. And something else remained, too. That melting sensation in the vicinity of her heart. That feeling she'd had for Ben in the memory... she could feel it again, exactly as it had been. He had never let anyone hurt her. He'd been her protector, always, even when she'd insisted she didn't need one. And suddenly she knew that running to him when trouble loomed was something she'd always done. No wonder her instincts had guided her to run to him when she'd come out of that coma. No wonder she'd been so driven to come back here, to find this place. To find him.

She was still in Ben's arms. He was holding her tight, rocking her slowly from side to side, and she knew with everything in her body and soul that he'd been telling the truth. He'd protect her. She'd always known that, never doubted it.

She swallowed hard, battling tears that had nothing to do with the fact that she was dying. Maybe they had more to do with the knowledge of what her dying would do to a man who'd vowed he would always keep her from harm. She meant so much to him. He must feel so helpless.

He was stroking her hair now, speaking softly. "I understand why you're afraid to go out, Penny," he said. "But I'll be with you. That bastard isn't gonna get within a mile of you with me there, I swear it." He stepped back slightly, brushed the tears from her cheeks with his thumbs. "Hey, you can wear the huge hat and sunglasses if you want. Consider yourself undercover." And he winked at her.

She managed to smile through her tears. And her heart twisted in her chest. What had she ever done to make this man love her so much?

"All right," she told him. "We'll go. I guess seeing Doc is too important to let some lunatic frighten me out of it."

"That's my girl," Ben said. And the words made her want to laugh and cry all at once.

CHAPTER NINE

Adam was rattling around in the kitchen when Ben and Penny came down the stairs. Ben carried Olive, since they'd discovered that she was physically incapable of walking down a steep set of stairs. Being a bulldog, her front legs were shorter than her back legs, and most of her weight was in her chest. She'd attempted it once, and Ben had caught her just before she'd flipped head over heels. So from then on they carried her. And she seemed to like that solution very well. She had her rubber bone in her teeth, waiting for someone to try to take it away from her, and rode in Ben's arms looking as if she thought she was royalty.

Ben set the dog down in the kitchen. Adam grinned at him, his white teeth flashing in his tanned face, as if he knew exactly what had happened between Ben and Penny last night. Then again, Ben figured, it would hardly be a secret. Probably the first one who'd popped into Penny's room to find her and her stuff gone, had alerted the rest of them. They were an efficient bunch of snoops.

Not half as efficient as Penny, though.

With time to kill before Doc would even be in his office, Ben pulled out a chair for his wife and, as she sat down, he took a careful look at her, falling back into the old habit without even realizing it. He remembered all too well the bad mornings they'd gone through together in the past. He used to be able to predict her worst episodes before they happened, just by watching for the signs in her face. Her cheeks would be ashen, her eyes dull, with dark circles underneath. Her neck would look puffy, and her hair always seemed to go limp. Ben had taken to inspecting her for signs of impending disaster each morning. And toward the end, he'd seen them more often than not.

She was glowing this morning. Glowing in a way he hadn't seen her do since high school—at least, not until she'd come back to him. And in the deepest, most secret place inside him, he nurtured a fragile hope that he knew was all but impossible. He was hoping for a miracle, he realized. He'd only end up more devastated in the end. He knew that, and yet the hope remained.

Adam finished washing his hands and waved Ben away when Ben reached for the coffeepot. "Sit your butt down, brother Ben. It's my turn to do breakfast."

Ben capitulated, and tried to pretend he hadn't noticed the gleam in Adam's eye. "Fine. Just don't poison us, okay?"

"You take all the fun out of it." Adam filled three coffee cups, setting two of them on the table, and keeping one on the countertop where he'd been working. "So what'll it be this morning? Eggs Benedict? Belgian waffles? Fresh berries with clotted cream, or maybe some gourmet bagels with sorbet?"

Ben made a face. "Yeah, yeah," he said. "This ain't New York City, Adam. Let's have a Western omelet chock-full of peppers and onions, dripping good ol' sharp cheese and mushrooms, sausage on the side. And toast with real butter and some home fries."

"You eat like that and you'll die young." Adam slammed his mouth closed on the words, but too late. Ben saw him grimacing and cursing himself, saw Penny flinch and go a little pale.

Then Adam went to her, knelt down in front of her chair, taking both her hands in his and squeezing them gently. "I'm sorry. I could kick myself."

Penny seemed startled. She glanced quickly at Ben. Ben shrugged. Adam said, "Ah, hell, he's not gonna get jealous. You're my sister."

"You...keep saying that, and I'll start believing it." She blinked rapidly as Adam got to his feet.

He smoothed one hand over her hair. "You're a Brand, Penny. You may not have had any family left before you married this lughead over here. But afterward you got more than most. It doesn't matter if you've forgotten that. We haven't."

Ben could see how deeply his brother's words affected Penny. She nodded a little too quickly, sniffed once or twice. "Thank you for that, Adam."

"Forgive me for being a thoughtless fool?"

She smiled then. "If you'll make those Belgian waffles for me," she said. Then she glanced down, and when Ben followed her gaze it was to see Olive, lifting a plaintive paw to Penny's knee. "Right," Penny said. "And one for Ollie, too, please."

"You got it," Adam said. And he proceeded to make them a meal fit for royalty.

By the time he finished flexing his culinary muscle, the rest of the family had wandered in, and the oblong kitchen table was filled to capacity. Ben could see Penny just taking it all in, the noisy chatter, dish passing and elbow bumping that epitomized mealtime at the Texas Brand. He knew she was wishing she could remember having been a part of it. He was wishing the same thing.

Bubba sat in his booster seat, studiously eating the cream without touching the waffle. Naked bits of waffle on his plate, white fluff on his lips, he looked at his mama. "Mo cweam?"

"Eat the waffle first."

"I like cweam."

"Eat your waffle, Bubba," Garrett told him, and the little boy pouted but ate.

"Where are the home fries, anyway?" Elliot asked.

Penny and Adam exchanged glances, and Penny said, "Adam and I discussed it and decided they were bad for your health."

"'Course they are," Elliot countered. "That's why they taste so good."

"It's your turn tomorrow," Adam told his brother. "You can make home fries if you want to."

"Good. Who's on grocery detail? I want ham, and some of those big Spanish onions."

"I think that must be me," Ben said. Then he glanced down at his plate. "I'm afraid I've been slacking off, keeping up with my share around here lately."

"Don't worry about it. You have more important things to do," Garrett told him, with a smile at Penny.

"I'll pick up those groceries today, all the same. Penny and I will be heading into town anyway this morning."

Chelsea looked up, curious. "Oh?"

"I'm seeing the doctor," Penny told her. The smiles around the table seemed to falter. "It's time, you know?"

Chelsea nodded. "Then the last thing you're going to feel up to doing is grocery shopping."

"No, I want to." Penny drew a breath and lifted her chin up. "I mean, what else am I going to do, head back up to my room and brood? Ben and I will get those groceries. I want to feel like...a part of things around here."

Garrett sent Penny an admiring smile. Elliot reached past Ben to clasp Penny's hand for a moment. "You don't know it, sis, but you've been a part of things around here for as long as most of us can remember—even while you were gone." He grinned at her as he released her hand. "But I should'a known you'd be back. Don't they say a bad Penny always returns?" Elliot winked and went back to eating.

"No one told me I was bad," she said, her tone lighter.

Ben was grateful for Elliot's constant levity for once. It eased the tension.

"Yeah, well, you aren't asking the right people," Elliot went on. "Now, old Mr. Murphy would probably tell you just how bad you were. And he'd be likely to claim his rose bushes are still recovering from your shenanigans."

Ben shook his head, remembering. "You really did make a mess of them."

"Hey, she had probable cause," Garrett put in. "She was investigating a murder, after all."

"Yeah," Adam said. "Only nobody was actually dead."

"Well," Elliot put in, "nobody except those roses."

Everyone laughed at that, but Ben's eyes were only on Penny, shaking her head in disbelief.

"You mean I actually went back there and dug them up? Even after he scared me so bad when..." Everyone went silent, and turning her gaze inward, Penny said very slowly, "When... he caught me peeking in his windows..." She blinked, lifting her head, facing Ben.

"You remember that?"

Licking her lips, she nodded. "I...I kind of remembered it last night. But I wasn't sure if it was real...." She shook her head slowly. "It's like someone else's memory, playing out in my mind."

Ben clasped her hand in his. "That's incredible. Honey, you remembered. It's going to come back to you, all of it. I know it is."

Lowering her gaze, she whispered, "I hope so. Then maybe I'll know how I ended up leaving this place." Then, looking around the table at each of them in turn, she went on. "Because I can't imagine why anyone would ever want to."

Adam cleared his throat, and Ben thought he was probably feeling a little homesick himself. He'd been living in New York, only home for short visits, and Penny's words might have touched a nerve with him. "I think we'll get the answers to that even before you get your memory back, Penny. I think Kirsten knows exactly what happened."

Penny nodded. "I got that feeling, too. I'm going to talk to her soon."

"Right," Ben said. "But first we see Doc. Speaking of which...." He tapped his wristwatch with a forefinger.

Penny took a deep breath and set her jaw. But he could see the fear in her eyes. She was dreading this. "Time to go, huh?" she asked him. When he nodded, she popped the last bite of waffle into her mouth and pushed away from the table, attempting a brave smile that probably didn't fool anyone in the room.

∽

Having that huge breakfast with the family had made the time pass more quickly. And it was a good thing, Ben thought, because if Penny was anywhere near as nervous as he was, she'd make herself ill. He felt like he'd developed an ulcer himself. He talked to God inside his mind, as they sat in Doc's waiting room. At least don't let him tell us she only has a short while left, he thought. Let her have a few years, please. Just a few years. Is that so much to ask?

He was afraid to even think about what he really wanted to hear. That the disease had miraculously vanished. That Penny was his, now and forever and...

"Penny Brand?" the nurse called.

Ben saw Penny's head come up. Her eyes were damp, her skin pale. Facing this, hearing it from a doctor instead of from him, God, it must be driving her mad.

He closed his hand around hers, held on tight and got to his feet. She managed to do the same, and they walked together into the examining room, probably looking like a pair of convicts walking up to the gallows.

He wanted to scoop her off her feet, turn around and run from this place. He wanted to take her where they'd never have to face anything like this again. Problem was, there was no such place.

The nurse pointed Ben to a chair in the corner, and he sat down, fidgeting, while Penny was weighed and her blood pressure and temperature were taken. "Okay, good," the woman said, not looking at either of them as she scribbled on a chart. She dropped a paper gown on the exam table. "Undress and put that on. The doctor will be in soon." And then she left.

Ben drew a breath, rubbed his arms. It was cold in here. It was always so cold in doctors' offices. "You're going to freeze in that paper gown," he said.

"Yeah." But she started to undress, and Ben quickly got to his feet to help her. He took her clothes from her, folded them up. When she was in the paper gown, he lifted her up and set her on the exam table. "That nurse's bedside manner left something to be desired."

Small talk. They were skating around the reason they were here as if it was a thin spot in the ice.

"Made the nurses at the clinic look downright bubbly—and they were probably criminals."

Ben tried to smile. He paced some, but thought that was probably making Penny more nervous. So he sat down again, and read the posters on the walls. One was about oral hygiene, and another showed a diagram of the inner ear.

The door opened. Doc came in. His face like shoe leather, silver hair gleaming. The women loved him, and Ben always thought it was due to his Ricardo Montalban voice. His black eyes when they fell upon Penny...were stunned.

"Penny," he said softly. And then he stepped inside the rest of the way and hugged her very gently. "Ben told me, but even then I could not quite believe…." Releasing her, backing away, he studied her face. And slowly a frown deepened between his salt-and-pepper brows. "But look at you!"

He pulled her lower eyelid with his thumb, whipping a light from his pocket to stare into her eyes. "No discoloration." Then he dropped the light, and poked underneath her chin. "The glands, they are not swollen." Then he stopped. Just stopped and stood there, staring at her. "Penny, what is going on here?"

She licked her lips. "I don't know. I truly don't."

"She's lost her memory, Doc," Ben said, getting up from his chair to stand beside the table and his wife. And he told Doc all he knew about what had happened to Penny, which wasn't much. And as he did, he realized that in all of his joy at having her back, and the renewed sorrow at knowing he would soon lose her again, he'd really let the whys and wherefores fall by the wayside. He'd put his questions on hold. But it would soon be time to go looking for the answers.

A little ball of foreboding formed in his stomach. It was like he knew already that those answers were not going to be pleasant ones, sensed it somehow. He'd almost rather not know.

Doc was silent for a very long time. Then he pursed his lips, shook his head and opened the door to call for a nurse. While he awaited her, he returned to his poking and probing of Penny.

"Yes, doctor," the nurse said when she arrived.

"I want you to draw some blood. Two vials, yes? Take a drop or two and prepare a slide for me." He looked at Penny, smiled encouragingly. "It won't hurt, I promise. Not much, anyway." Then eased her back until she was lying down on the table, while the nurse pulled a plastic case full of instruments from a cupboard.

The deed was done in no time, and the nurse was on her way

out with the vials while Penny sat with her elbow bent and a wad of cotton trapped there.

Doc pulled up a tall stool and sat down, taking Penny's hand and looking her in the eyes. "Now we talk," he said slowly. "Penny...Penny, I delivered you. Did you know this?"

"Yes. Ben...Ben told me." She glanced his way, and he put his arm around her.

"So you know that you can trust me. I have nothing in common with this Dr. Barlow person you and Ben have been telling me about. I would not lie to you. Do you believe this?"

She drew a breath, nodded. The nurse returned with the slide, slipping it into place beneath a microscope that rested on the counter. Doc patted Penny's hand, and went to it, leaned over it, peering through the lenses for what seemed like a very long time.

When he straightened, he rubbed his eyes. And Ben wondered if it was from looking so hard for so long, or for some other reason.

"It is good that you trust me, Penny. Otherwise you might not believe what I have to tell you. I'm not sure I believe it myself."

Penny blinked, glanced at Ben, then focused on Doc again. "What is it?"

Doc licked his lips. "You have no symptoms of Hillman-Waite Syndrome," Doc said. "None. Now, the blood tests will tell us for certain. And we will have those results tomorrow, I promise you. But *chicacita*, I have seen HWS cells in the blood before, and I do not see any in yours. These blood cells I've just examined, they appear to be perfectly normal."

She just stared at him. Ben felt as if he couldn't breathe.

"Beyond that," he said with a wave of his hand, "if the syndrome were still in your body—quite frankly, Penny, you would be dead by now."

Ben blinked, almost afraid to believe what he was hearing. Penny seemed frozen in place.

Doc looked from one of them to the other, pursing his lips at their silence. "The HWS gets progressively worse, the coma signaling the final stages. You were there. You were at the end, and now you are back." Doc shook his head. "I have never seen anything like this before."

Penny tried to speak, but her voice was like dried straw. "Are you telling me I'm not sick anymore? That I'm not going to die?"

Doc smiled so hard Ben thought his lips would split. "The blood tests will confirm it, Penny. But I think the results will show exactly what I expect. I am not a young man. I have been a doctor for a long time, and so, you see, I am good at this. I see no trace of HWS. No, Penny, you are not going to die."

"Oh, my God," she whispered. She turned slowly to Ben, stunned and blinking and shaking her head.

He closed his eyes tight and wrapped her up in his arms. He couldn't believe this. It was like a dream. Maybe he was dreaming. Maybe he'd wake up, and none of this would be true. Maybe...

"I'm not going to die," Penny said, full volume now, and she leaped off the table, clinging to him. Ben spun her around in a circle, and let his wary heart accept this gift. And the grief seemed to chip away like plaster, until his heart was free and beating again.

He held her, kissed her. "Thank you," he kept saying over and over. "God, thank you."

Finally Doc cleared his throat loudly enough so that Ben was reminded of where he was. Gently he set Penny down on the table again, but he couldn't take his eyes from her face. Tears gleaming on her cheeks. Rosy cheeks. Rosy with the blush of health.

"All right," Doc said. "Now we talk about this amnesia, yes?"

Ben looked at Doc, but he stood close enough so he was touching Penny, one arm around her. Almost afraid to let go.

"This Barlow, you say he told you your memory would not return, is this true?" Doc asked.

"Yes. He said he was certain. There was no chance of me regaining my memory."

Doc nodded. "But you know he was lying, don't you, Penny?"

Penny blinked, said nothing.

"He would have no way of knowing this if your amnesia was due to the coma. Coma patients sometimes recover their memory, sometimes... not so much. But only time tells us which will be the case. So...why would this Barlow tell you such a lie?"

Penny studied Doc's face, and Ben could see her trying to decide how much to tell him about her suspicions of Dr. Barlow. But before she could speak, he went on. "My guess is you have remembered something already, have you not? A tiny flash in the mind? A dream too vivid to be just a dream? A feeling of recognition about something? Any of that?"

"Yes," she said, nodding emphatically. "And the headaches... every time I remember something, my head just throbs."

This made Doc pause. He tilted his head to one side, searching Penny's face. "Tell me, Penny, while at this hospice under this man's care, was he giving you any medication?"

She nodded. "Pills to help me sleep, and a shot every day—"

"And...did you ever wake up with a bitter taste in your mouth?"

She frowned. "How did you...?"

"Would this doctor—if he is a doctor—have had any reason to *hope* your memory would not return?"

Penny glanced at Ben. Ben nodded at her.

"Maybe," she said. "Why?"

Doc shrugged and made a note on the chart. "Could be nothing. But I will have one more test run for you. I think we took enough blood for both."

"Do you think there's a chance she might remember after all?" Ben asked, almost afraid to hear the answer.

"Your Penny, she has beaten a fatal disease, by all appearances," Doc said, smiling. "And that she is already remembering, this is a good sign. I would say where this wife of yours is concerned, anything is possible." He turned to Penny. "Now, you can get dressed. I'm going to write you a prescription, Penny—a very mild drug for these headaches. But you take it only when the head is aching, okay?"

Penny nodded. "Okay."

"Good." Doc grinned as he finished scribbling, tore the illegibly written sheet from his prescription pad and handed it to her. Then he leaned close. "We share an interest, you and I."

"Do we?"

Doc nodded, grinning. "We both like solving puzzles. I'm going to help you solve this one, I promise you that." He squeezed her hand, then turned and left them alone again.

Ben looked at Penny for a long time. "Come here," he said softly, and then he pulled her into his arms and kissed her like he hadn't kissed her in years, without a single hint of sorrow detracting from the passion.

Penny didn't know when Ben had slipped away to call his family with the news, but he'd managed it. Maybe sometime during their stop at the grocery store in town or at Mr. Henry's drugstore while they waited for her prescription to be filled. At any rate she'd been looking forward to sharing her good news with the rest of the Brands.

It was an odd feeling, this knowing that her own happiness meant so much to other people. People who'd been strangers to her only days ago, but who were slowly somehow becoming her family. She had no doubt they'd all be overjoyed for her. And the fact that she'd initially suspected any one of them of being involved in her disappearance seemed ludicrous now.

When she walked through the front door that afternoon, a

sudden chorus of shouts had taken her by surprise. She looked around, blinking. The entire living room was filled with people. Streamers and confetti littered the place, music bawled from unseen speakers, and Ollie barked a greeting as if joining in the happy celebration.

Chelsea grabbed Penny and hugged her hard. "You weren't here for your birthday, Penny. But this is even better, don't you think?"

"My birthday...." Penny blinked and turned to Ben. "God, I don't even know when I was born."

Ben smiled. "Thirty years ago last Sunday, hon. Same day as Nancy Drew." He smiled at her, and she felt warm inside. "We'll call today your rebirth day. The day you got a new lease on life."

"And a chance to start over," she whispered.

Ben nodded, and ushered her into the midst of her rebirthday party. Chelsea walked close to her other side, and urged her toward a table full of gaily wrapped presents. Penny blinked tears from her eyes. "All this...for me?"

"Who else?" Chelsea asked, smiling. "We had to scramble to shop while Ben kept you busy in town. Here, open mine first!" And she pressed a small box into Penny's hand. "And hurry up, I want to show you the cake. It's gorgeous!"

Penny couldn't speak for the lump in her throat. But she leaned forward and gently kissed Chelsea's cheek, and hoped that one gesture could somehow convey the depth of what she was feeling.

∼

Ben thought he probably had the best family in the world. They made Penny feel she belonged—and she did, though she didn't remember how much a part of his family she had been. But he could see her relaxing, enjoying the celebration. He thought he was happier right now than he'd ever been in his life.

And then he saw Penny's eyes cloud over, and he followed her gaze. Kirsten stood in a corner, talking to Adam. It troubled Ben to see her here, set off that sense of foreboding in his gut—the one he'd been deliberately ignoring up to now. He hated that Penny didn't seem glad to see her onetime best friend. God, they'd been so close. And he'd been close to Kirsten, as well, as close as he was to his own sister. They'd been a foursome, he and Penny, Adam and Kirsten. If only Penny had her memories, she'd understand about this intimacy she seemed to sense between Kirsten and him. He'd picked up on that the last time he'd brought Kirsten's name up. It bothered him. Maybe in time....

He knew all too well there was another reason for that twist in his belly upon seeing Kirsten here. And likely another reason for the look on Penny's face when she glimpsed her. Kirsten had the answers. She knew how and why Penny had ended up in that clinic, and why he'd ended up grieving over the grave of a stranger. And he told himself he wanted those answers, and that Penny needed them. But that didn't alter the queasiness in his stomach when he thought about actually getting them.

He was curious now, though, to see Adam apparently having a civil conversation with the woman he claimed to hate. Penny was distracted for the moment. Jessi had drawn her into the dining room to show her that huge, beautiful sheet cake she'd had decorated for the occasion. So he sidled closer to where Adam and Kirsten stood, off by themselves.

"I was surprised you even wanted me here," Kirsten was saying.

"I invited you for Penny's sake," Adam told her. "Not for mine."

"And Penny's the only reason I came," she said. "Still...." She met Adam's eyes briefly, then looked at her feet. "It was good of you to call."

"I know you love her, Kirsten. Whatever you did, you did it

for Penny. I know that—and I think deep down, Ben does, too. Inviting you was the right thing to do." Adam kept averting his eyes, whenever she looked directly at him. But when she wasn't, he seemed unable to keep his gaze away from her face. "But no matter what your motives were, you did this family wrong."

"Adam, can't we put the past behind us? This hostility is just...just so useless. I can't change what I did. Not what I did for Penny—not what I did on our wedding day."

He lowered his head. "And I can't change the way I feel, Kirsten."

"I think you could...if you wanted to. Does hating me really give you such pleasure?"

"Yeah," he told her, his voice dripping sarcasm. "Thrills me to no end. Hell, I'm just getting good at it, I'd hate to quit now."

"You're a bastard, Adam Brand."

He shrugged. "My brother Garrett raised me too well to say what you are, Kirsten Armstrong."

"Cowan," she reminded him. "I'm married now, remember?"

Her barb hit home and drove deep. Ben saw his brother flinch with the impact. "I'm not likely to forget that."

Shaking her head in disgust, she turned, heading away from him. Ben caught her hand in his, and she stopped. She blinked as she looked up at him, and he thought maybe her eyes were a little bit damp.

"He's still hurting," Ben said softly. "Cut him some slack, okay?"

She turned her hand in Ben's, linking fingers with him, and managed a weak smile. "It's not like it matters."

"It does. Trust me, Kirsten, it does." He gave her hand a gentle squeeze. "Time's the only thing that's gonna help. You be patient, and he'll come around. You two obviously weren't meant to be together. You did what your heart told you, and he can't hate you for that forever."

"I did what I had to do," she muttered. But then she gave her head a shake. "But this is no time for the pile of garbage between Adam and me. It's a celebration. Ben, I'm so happy for you and Penny."

"I know you are, hon."

Kirsten leaned up and kissed Ben's cheek. When she stepped away, Penny was standing beside her, holding two small plates with a piece of cake on each one. Her eyes, when Ben met them, were cool, and maybe a little confused.

"Penny," Kirsten said, and she turned to plant a similar kiss on Penny's cheek, apparently unaware of any tension in the air. "You have no idea how often I've prayed for this. It's a miracle."

Penny only nodded, and her smile seemed to be made of glass. Fragile, and on the verge of shattering. "Thank you, Kirsten. I...I hope you can stay for a while. I think it's time we had that talk."

Kirsten sent Ben a look, and he thought there might have been a hint of panic in her eyes. But she drew a breath, faced Penny again and nodded firmly. "Yes, it is. I'll stay, Penny. There's a lot you need to know."

"I can see that." Penny handed Ben one of the pieces of cake, and gave Kirsten the other. Then, she turned to go back to the dining room.

CHAPTER TEN

The party lasted for hours, but at last, well after nightfall, the crowd started thinning out. Wes and Taylor had their horses to tend to at their place, Sky Dancer Ranch. Jessi and Lash had to take little Maria home and tuck her in for the night. And Chelsea managed to talk her own toddler into heading upstairs for his bath and bedtime story, though Bubba argued all the way to his room.

Eventually all that remained were Adam and Kirsten, Penny and Ben. And Ben knew the time had come for revelations, for truth. He was as afraid of hearing it as Kirsten seemed to be of telling it. And he didn't even know why. It was something in his gut that defied logic.

Adam brought freshly brewed coffee into the living room, while Ben knelt to build a fire in the fireplace, working around the two dogs who'd apparently collapsed in exhaustion. Too much running from guest to guest for attention and an occasional crumb of cake, he figured. Their swollen bellies were further evidence of that guess.

Blue lay in his usual position, head resting atop his forelegs, ears folded on the floor. Olive was not quite as conservative, though. She lay on her back, legs up. Gravity made her jowls pull backward, so her teeth were bared, and she was snoring like a chainsaw. Her chest rose from her body like a roasted turkey's. The sight of her would have made him smile under any other circumstances.

But not tonight.

He got the fire started, but doubted it would warm him. He thought maybe the chill in his bones had nothing to do with the temperature. He kept telling himself this was the happiest day of his life, and that he was a fool to be so apprehensive. The churning in his belly told him otherwise, no matter how little sense that made.

Penny sat in the rocking chair and took the steaming mug from Adam when he offered it. Kirsten paced like a caged lioness.

"It's time," Penny said softly. "Tell me what you know about what happened to me, Kirsten."

She stopped pacing, and her eyes widened just a little. "I thought we were going to talk alone."

Penny frowned at her, shaking her head. "No, of course not. Ben has as much right to know what really happened as I do. I want him to know."

"No, Penny, you don't." Kirsten's eyes held a warning as she stared hard at Penny. "Believe me, you really don't. We should talk alone."

Penny shot a startled glance from Kirsten to Ben, and back again. "What is that supposed to mean? Look, Kirsten, I have nothing to hide from my husband."

Drawing a deep sigh and shaking her head slowly, Kirsten said, "I guess it's your choice. But I think you should hear what I have to say first—then make up your mind, once you know what I have to tell you."

"It doesn't matter what you have to say," Penny told her. And then she got a funny look, a dark one Ben didn't recognize.

"Nothing matters, Kirsten, except that I am back now. I'm back reclaim my life, and knowing the truth is the only way I can do it. So will you just stop with the arguments and the innuendo and simply tell us what happened?"

Kirsten searched Penny's face for a moment, as if she was slightly confused, and maybe not quite sure what Penny was trying to say. But her words had definitely had the tone of a warning. She couldn't have missed that.

Finally Kirsten nodded, glancing nervously around the room as she took a seat in the overstuffed armchair closest to Penny's rocker. "Where's Garrett?"

"Playing taxi," Ben said. He leaned back against the mantel, crossing his arms over his chest. "A few of the guys got into the beer more than they should have during the party. He's driving them home."

"Why?" Adam cut in. "What's Garrett got to do with any of this?"

Kirsten met his eyes, and hers turned stony. "Because I'm not telling you a thing until your brother the sheriff gives me his word that I won't be arrested or charged with anything when I'm finished."

Adam's brows creased. "So you not only know about all this, but you were involved in it as well." He said it as if he was not the least bit surprised. "Rest assured, sweetheart, if there are grounds to arrest you, I'll do the honors myself. And I'm going to find out whether you tell me or not, so—"

"Shut the hell up, Adam," Ben said, straightening his stance and glaring at his brother. Fear had shone like glittering ice crystals in Kirsten's eyes before she'd hidden it. If she decided not to talk....

Ben went to where she was sitting, knelt down and took her hands in his. "You love her," he said gently. "Kirsten, please. I'm not gonna let anybody arrest you, I swear it. Just tell us. Penny needs to know—I need to know. What really happened that night?" He could feel Penny's eyes on him. But he didn't glance her way. His entire focus right now was on Kirsten, on convincing her to tell him what she knew.

Sniffling, brushing newborn tears from her cheeks with the backs of her hands, she finally nodded. "It was only because she loved you so much, Ben. You have to believe that. No matter what she did, it was—"

"What she did?" That knot in Ben's stomach drew painfully tighter.

"I had to help her. I had to. I was her best friend. I'd have cut off my arm for her, you know that, don't you?" She drew one hand away to drag it across her face. The tears left a red streak.

Ben nodded. His throat had gone bone dry. Penny leaned forward in the rocking chair. Adam remained standing, glowering at his onetime lover.

"Doc told her...how it was going to be when the end got close," Kirsten said, looking at Ben. "That she'd...that she'd slip into a coma that might last a very long time." She looked past Ben, meeting Penny's eyes. "It made you crazy, Penny. You were driving yourself nuts going over it all, again and again. Talking about how Ben would suffer, how he'd have to watch you lying there like a vegetable, wasting away. You said you couldn't do it to him." She closed her eyes. "I thought you were going to try suicide, just to save him from watching you die slowly that way. I was scared to death for you, Penny. The symptoms were getting stronger, more frequent, and you knew it wouldn't be much longer. You were so desperate not to put Ben through all of that...I just didn't know what you might do if I didn't help."

Penny nodded slowly. "I can see why you would have been afraid for me."

"So I wanted to help. I wanted to give you a way out."

Ben watched Kirsten, saw the torment in her eyes. "What did you do, Kirsten?"

"I...I helped," she said softly. She looked from Penny, to Ben, to Adam, and then lowered her eyes. "My...husband...has connections. I knew some of them were less than...scrupulous. He...suggested a name, a lawyer he'd worked with in the past, and I contacted the man. He...he was willing to help Penny and I...set up the accident."

Everyone was silent for a long moment. Adam looked stunned. He shook himself. "Hell, Kirsten, what kind of a man did you marry?"

"Not the kind I wanted to," she whispered, but Adam couldn't possibly have heard from where he stood.

Ben heard her, though. He also heard the hiss and crackle of his heart freezing over. "You're saying my wife..." he glanced at Penny, but only briefly. He couldn't look at her. Not now. "...faked her own death? Let me believe she'd crashed? Let me think she'd been trapped in a car that became a blast furnace—trapped there until her body was so charred it was...." His throat closed off. He had to close his eyes to try to shut out the memory, but even then the vision remained. It had torn him apart to see those blackened remains and believe them to be hers.

It was Penny who spoke then, her voice dull, lifeless. "Whose body is in my grave, Kirsten?"

"I don't know. The lawyer said it was an unclaimed body from a morgue out of state. I realize Garrett and the medical examiner have been trying to identify it, but I imagine they're wasting their time. I don't know how he got it here, or who it really was. A vagrant who'd died on the streets and wouldn't be missed, he told us. It didn't matter. He took your car and your wedding ring, and said he'd take care of everything. We never saw the body—or the accident." Kirsten turned to Ben. "We didn't know how it was going to be. I swear it, Ben. We never would have—"

"How did you think it would be?" he asked her. "Hell, Kirsten, how did you think they'd fool me into believing that corpse was my wife unless they burned the body beyond recognition?"

Kirsten shook her head. "We just...we just didn't think." She sighed. "Maybe we didn't want to think."

Anger welled up inside Ben like hot lava, bubbling dangerously near the surface, ready to boil over. "And the clinic?"

"The lawyer set that up, as well. He said it was a hospice, the best one in the world, set up specifically for people with HWS. He said she'd get the best of care there." She closed her eyes. "Penny was on a flight out of the country by the time her car went into that ravine and exploded."

Adam swore.

"It killed me to see you suffer, Ben. But it was for the best... or we thought it was at the time."

Ben only nodded, fury eating at him, gnawing in his belly like battery acid. Penny said nothing. What could she say? She'd deceived the man she'd claimed to love in the worst possible way. Denied him the chance to be with her when he'd needed to be with her most. Lied to him. Let him believe she was dead. God!

"When I tried to contact her later, to be sure she made it there all right," Kirsten went on, "the people at the clinic told me she'd slipped into a coma right after she'd arrived. They said she'd be dead within a month, and that we'd done the right thing. They told me not to contact her again, for her sake, and for yours, Ben. They said if I did, someone might find out. They told me to let her go. And I did...God help me, I did." She searched Penny's face, tears rolling down her own. "I'm so sorry, Penny."

Penny said nothing, just stared at her as if she wasn't quite sure what she was seeing, or hearing, or how to process this new information.

"I want the name of this lawyer," Ben said, containing his anger—just barely.

"So you can get him disbarred? No, Ben. I'm sorry, but I won't tell you who he is."

"She's protecting her own interests, Ben, you can bet on that," Adam snapped. "Dammit, Kirsten, how could you do this to my brother? My family? How much did you pay that sleazy mouthpiece to set all this up, anyway?"

Kirsten shook her head, got to her feet a little unsteadily. "I've told you everything I can, Ben," she said softly. "We were so close once...I hope someday you can forgive me. I truly thought I was doing what was best. For you, and for Penny. Truly."

Looking back at Penny, she said, "I'm glad, God, I'm so glad you're well again. And back home. I hope...I hope...." She bit her lip, tears flooding her eyes, and ran out of the house, leaving the front door wide open behind her.

A second later Ben heard Kirsten's car spinning its tires as it sped out the driveway, and Adam cussing under his breath, referring to Kirsten in less than flattering terms as he stood in the still open door, watching her go.

When Adam turned, his face was a mask of fury. But it softened when he looked at Penny, sitting as still and pale as a marble sculpture, and then at Ben. "Ben, listen...."

Ben held up a hand. "Take a walk or something, okay?"

Adam bit his lip, glanced Penny's way once more and finally nodded. "Okay. You two need to talk this out. But...just don't blow it, Ben. Not now—"

"Get out, Adam."

Nodding, Adam turned and left them alone.

Ben stood very still. The fire he'd started gained strength, licking up the logs, devouring them bit by bit. The way his wife's lie had destroyed him little by little over the years. And maybe now it was about to finish the job once and for all.

When he could manage it, he looked down at Penny, sitting motionless in the rocking chair. "How the hell could you do that to me?" he asked her.

"I don't know. I don't remember any of this, you know that." Her voice was lifeless.

He searched her face, feeling as if he was seeing her for the first time. "I thought you loved me. I thought no two people on the planet could ever be closer than we were. I thought there was nothing you couldn't share with me. God, Penny, was I that blind? Was I the only one who felt that way?"

"Ben, I—"

"I was, wasn't I? All those years, Penny, I thought...but I never really knew you at all, did I?" He turned toward the door, but Penny lunged after him, gripping his arm.

"Ben, wait. You can't just walk away—we have to talk about this."

"Don't touch me."

Her hand fell away. She lowered her head. "I thought," she whispered, "I thought...."

"Oh, come on, Penny. It's not like you're in love with me now, is it? You've been trying, I'll grant you that. But it's like playing house to you, isn't it? You had nowhere else to go, so you thought you'd play the devoted wife. But you never felt a thing. For all intents and purposes, I'm a man you met a few days ago. A stranger to you. So don't try to tell me you feel anything for me."

"You're wrong!"

"I'm only surprised it took me this long to realize it."

"But I do feel something for you.... Ben, wait!"

He didn't wait. He couldn't. He walked out, feeling as if his heart had been ripped from his chest and stomped on. He left her standing there, alone.

~

"He hates me now."

Several hours had passed since Ben had stalked out of the

house. No one seemed to know where he'd gone or what he might be doing. Moreover no one seemed to want to find out. Garrett and Elliot kept saying he needed some time alone. That everyone should just relax and let him be. Then they'd gone about their business, but Penny didn't fail to notice that their glances her way were chilly, or that their words were clipped. The warmth had left their eyes from the moment they had learned what she'd done. They were angry with her. Both of them. And they had every right to be. But they'd also had a right to know the truth. They'd mourned her bogus death—they deserved to know how she'd betrayed them.

Adam had seemed more understanding, but he hadn't returned to the ranch yet, either.

Chelsea seemed to be her only ally. She refilled Penny's teacup, and ran an encouraging hand over hers. Elliot and Garrett had finally gone upstairs, and the two women had retreated to the kitchen.

"He can't hate you for what you did back then. You don't even remember it," Chelsea said gently.

"That makes sense from a practical point of view." Penny sipped the tea, then set the pretty china cup carefully into its matching saucer. "But Ben's thinking from an emotional one at this point. I hurt him terribly."

"He's not thinking at all right now. Men never do when they're hurt. He's just feeling. But eventually he'll realize it and get control of his anger."

Penny shook her head. "He's angry at a woman who doesn't even exist anymore." Then she glanced out the nearest window at the darkness lying like a blanket over the ranch. "I'm worried about him."

"Then why don't you go to him?"

She blinked, glancing sharply at Chelsea. "Garrett and Elliot said to leave him alone. Besides, I don't even know where he is."

"Garrett and Elliot should mind their own business. If you

want to go to him, you should darned well do it. You're his wife."

Penny went still, shaken by the quiet, matter-of-fact way Chelsea dropped those words. As if they were as true and as natural as saying "It gets dark at night." It made her throat go dry and sandy. Made her head throb a little.

"It's true, Penny. You're his wife. You don't have your memory, but you still have your marriage, until and unless you or Ben decide to change that. You have every right to go to him, talk to him and insist he listen."

Slowly Penny nodded. "Maybe once," she whispered. "But I think I lost that right when I did what I did."

"You have to try."

"Do I?" Penny rubbed at her watery eyes. They were getting sore now from so many tears.

Chelsea shrugged. "Depends. Do you want to save your marriage? Maybe you'd rather just let him go. Maybe now that you have a long, healthy life to look forward to, you'd rather start over, fresh, without the past dragging you down."

Penny lowered her head. The thought of a long, healthy life without Ben...without this family...seemed more bleak than the prospect of an early death.

"You'll probably find him at the dojo," Chelsea said. She reached to the center of the table where her key chain lay, and gave it a shove. It slid to a stop in front of Penny. "You can take my car if you want."

Penny nodded and closed her hands around the keys.

"Wait a minute," Chelsea said. "You do remember how to drive, don't you?"

For the first time in what felt like a long time, Penny smiled. It felt weak and watery, but she managed it. "I did okay with the stolen Toyota, didn't I?"

"Yeah, outran the cops and everything. Do me a favor,

Penny? If you see a flashing light behind you, quell those urges of yours and just pull over."

"Promise," Penny said. She clenched her fist around the keys in her hand. "You're being awfully kind to me, Chelsea. I'm grateful."

"You're a Brand," Chelsea told her. "These guys are so fond of going on about how when one Brand gets into trouble, the rest are right there to help them out of it. I figure it applies to Brands by marriage as much as by birth." Chelsea winked. "You go get your man now, Penny."

And Penny went. But she was uncertain, far from confident and pretty much disgusted with her old self for pulling what she had on Ben. Although she could certainly see why she would have done it. She could also see why Ben was angry.

Just as Chelsea had predicted, Penny spotted Ben's pickup outside the dojo in town. She'd spied on him there before. And she couldn't help but remember coming here with him yesterday and watching him with all those small children. His haunted blue eyes had looked almost happy as he spoke to the kids.

She parked Chelsea's car and got out, then she stood there, staring at the red door, with the fierce dragon writhing brilliantly from top to bottom. Should she go in? Would it be an unforgivable intrusion? Maybe...maybe she should just look inside first, as she'd done before. Maybe she should make sure he wasn't meditating very deeply or whatever it was he did in there, before just bursting in unannounced.

She drew a breath and, feeling like a television sleuth, she crept around the side of the building, glancing up and down the sidewalk casually before ducking into the alley. There was a memory tickling at the edges of her consciousness, and her head began to pound harder.

She'd been in this alley before. Not when she'd first come back here and looked in on the man who believed her dead.

Before that. And the memory slipped up on her without warning.

~

Ben was acting awfully funny today, she thought, when he stood there digging up the dirt with his boot heel and asking if he could walk her home.

"We always walk home together, Ben," she told him, frowning. "What are you asking permission for?"

He looked at his toes. "I don't know."

He was fifteen then, and she'd gone from hero worship to full-blown adoration. Of course, she'd sooner be hog-tied and horsewhipped than admit it. He was her friend. He'd probably puke if she told him how she really felt.

Then he reached over and took her books, adding them to the stack he already carried.

"What'd you do that for?" she asked him, really curious now. "Ben, are you feeling okay?"

"Uh, yeah. Sure."

"You never carried my books before."

"Maybe I should've." He tucked the books under one arm, and casually grabbed hold of her hand.

Penny blinked at their joined hands in shock as they walked along like nothing unusual was happening. He was holding her hand. She closed her eyes and prayed her palm wouldn't start sweating! He'd never want to hold hands with her again.

She figured her heart was going a hundred miles an hour by the time they turned into the alley that ran between the feed store and the warehouse in town, a well-known shortcut they used every day. But today was different. The whole gang wasn't with them today, the way they usually were. And he was holding her hand.

And then he stopped walking, midway through the secluded,

dim alley, and he turned to face her. Penny stared up at him, so scared and excited and all wound up she thought she might die. Then he leaned close, still holding her hand, and he kissed her. A really gentle, slow, lingering kiss. She cursed her chapped lips and wondered if her breath was fresh...and then forgot everything except that place where his lips touched hers. Her eyes fell closed, and her heart melted into a warm, bubbling puddle.

Ben lifted his head away. He cleared his throat, and he looked right into her eyes and said, "I love you, Penny Lane."

~

"Oh, Ben," Penny whispered as the memory faded. But the feeling it invoked remained. That had been their first, innocent kiss. And the first time he'd ever said he loved her.

Ben had been wrong when he'd said she felt nothing for him. She did. She felt a great deal, more than she understood or could begin to explain. And maybe it was the memory of him making its way back into her conscious mind. Slowly but surely. The memory of loving him—that was alive inside her heart. It had been all along. And the more she remembered, the stronger it became.

Was it love she felt for him—or just the memory of love? Or were they one and the same?

She had to talk to him, had to make this all right somehow....

She moved up to the window, eager to see him for some reason she couldn't even name. And she peered through the glass.

Ben stood inside his dojo, holding a beautiful woman in his arms. She clung to him as if for her very life, and he held her back just as hard. His eyes were closed as he held her, and it was only an instant before Penny recognized the woman who'd claimed to have been her best friend. Kirsten Armstrong.

The sight of the two of them wrapped tight in one another's

arms, hidden away in the dojo after hours, hit Penny so hard she staggered backward until her back smacked into the building next door. She shouldn't jump to conclusions. She knew better, didn't she? Then again, she'd been away for a long time. Did she really think her husband had lived like a monk all that time? Could she have expected him to?

But the biggest question was why did she feel as if a knife had just been cleanly inserted between her ribs? Why did she feel hot lifeblood seeping away and leaving her as lifeless as if she'd just been hit by a truck?

Was it because that love she'd once felt for him was alive and real and not just a memory after all?

It was so confusing! But it was obvious she wasn't wanted there. Much less needed. She'd been worried about Ben. Well, Ben was safe. Kirsten was taking very good care of him.

~

He finally had his opportunity. Dr. Barlow had no idea how much Penny had told the Brands about him or his clinic. But it didn't matter what they knew. He'd moved everyone, hired a new staff, set himself up a new identity. It wasn't as if he hadn't been prepared for the day he'd have to move on. It wasn't as if it hadn't happened before.

They would never trace him now. But he needed Penny. Needed her desperately! She was the one success he'd achieved in all his years of research and study.

She was the only patient ever to recover.

He had to know why. And maybe, once he explained to her that she could help him cure hundreds of others, she'd be willing to come away with him. Maybe she'd understand that it didn't matter whether he was breaking the law, or using unapproved methods, or lying to the families of his subjects. Nothing mattered except the end result. Finding a cure.

He'd been watching her, following her, but everywhere she went that oversize cowboy was at her side. Until now.

He watched her go slipping into the alley, and he went to the car she'd left on the roadside. He tried the rear door, smiling to himself when he found it unlocked. Pulling the door closed quietly behind him, Dr. Barlow crouched down in the back seat and waited.

CHAPTER ELEVEN

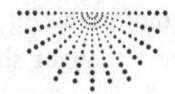

*B*en let Kirsten cling to him until her tears subsided. It turned out to be a long time, but it didn't much matter. He thought about his own pain and rage and the incredible feeling of betrayal. He had as much to work through as she did. Although, he thought, her demons were a hell of a lot more dangerous than his own. He might hurt, but at least he'd survive. She might not.

Finally he eased her away from him just a little bit, and searched her face. "I don't like this," he told her. "Not one bit. I think we should tell Garrett—"

"I'm handling it. My way. I want your promise you'll stay out of it, Ben."

Ben saw the determination in her eyes. She'd been one of his best friends before all this crap went down. She and Adam, and Ben and Penny had been inseparable for most of their lives. "If Adam knew—" he began.

"Adam can't know. Besides, now that I've seen this ugly side of him, I'm thinking I might be better off alone. He hates me, Ben. It wouldn't make a difference."

"But you're not alone. You're with that—"

"I'm where I have to be. Promise me you'll keep my secret, Ben. I only told you because…because I couldn't stand the way you were looking at me. I wanted you to know how much more there was to my decision to get Penny out of here. She was getting too close to the truth, Ben. If they'd have caught on, she might have died for real. And even though I knew she was dying anyway—I didn't want it to be like that. Not violently. Not horribly. But safe and comfortable in a place where she'd be cared for…a place where I thought she'd be cared for. I was wrong, Ben, and I'm sorry."

He nodded. "But Penny didn't know that she was in any danger," he said softly.

"No. Penny didn't know. She went along for one reason and one reason only. Because she loved you more than she loved living, Ben. More than anything else in the world. She couldn't bear the thought of you watching her waste away like that."

He lowered his head, shook it. "If she loved me, she'd have trusted me with the truth. She'd have known I'd want to be there for her."

"Ben—"

He held up a hand. "That part's between Penny and me. As for the rest of this cloak-and-dagger bull you've got yourself mixed up in—"

"It will all be over very soon. You'll keep my secret, won't you, Ben? You won't tell Adam why I really jilted him—why I had to marry Joseph Cowan?"

He searched her eyes, realizing now that the polish and the coolness were just a part of her elaborate act. The same old Kirsten was still there, inside. He could see her in those eyes. He nodded toward her designer handbag. "You carry a cell phone in there?"

"Yes."

"Put me on speed dial. I want your promise that you'll call at the first sign of trouble."

Kirsten nodded. "I promise."

Against his better judgment, Ben conceded. "Then I'll keep this to myself...for now."

"Thank you, Ben." She searched his face for a long moment "I'm sorry," she said. "I really am. I never wanted to cause you or Penny any more pain. Just the opposite, really. I just went about it all wrong."

"I know."

"You going to be all right?"

He averted his gaze and shrugged. "Only time's gonna tell me the answer to that one."

"Do you still love her?"

He lowered his head. "I reckon if I didn't, this wouldn't hurt so much."

Kirsten reached up to ruffle his hair. "When you remember all your hurt, Ben, do me a favor. Remember hers, too. She gave up everything—her home, her family, the love you two shared—just because she thought it would be easier on you that way." He said nothing and Kirsten sighed. "You'll get through this," she said.

He nodded, but secretly he wished to God he'd get through it soon. All his joy at finding Penny again, at learning she was well, cured, looking forward to a long, healthy life—all of that had turned to a heartache bigger than Texas. It was getting worse all the time. And part of him knew he probably shouldn't be angry with her for things she didn't remember. But knowing he shouldn't feel the emotion did nothing to actually keep him from feeling it. And Kirsten's rationalizations did nothing to ease it, either. How could Penny do this, and then expect him to believe she'd done it for his sake?

She'd deceived him, betrayed him, lied to him and pitched him headfirst into two long years of hellfire. Torture like nothing he'd ever known. Night after endless night of reliving that accident in his dreams. Seeing his beautiful wife trapped in a steel inferno, fists pounding impotently against the glass. He'd heard her anguished screams a thousand times, his imagination concocting the most horrible scenarios for the way in which she'd died. He'd seen her hair burning, her translucent skin melting, her tears boiling in his mind's masochistic eye.

When all the while the body that burned in that car had already been dead. And the woman he'd mourned to the point of madness had flown away without looking back.

And just how was he supposed to get over that?

"You're torturing yourself, Ben," Kirsten told him. "You have to let the past go, get rid of it, or it just keeps on hurting you."

"The way it does you, right?"

She bit her lip to prevent it, but the tears came again anyway, spilling over her cheeks. Ben held her, and though he loved Kirsten like a sister, he wished to God it was his wife in his arms right now. But he was beginning to wonder if he'd ever hold Penny this way again.

∽

Penny yanked the car door open, gritted her teeth, closed her eyes. "So what am I gonna do, run away and let her have him?"

A sigh of fury gusted out of her, and she slammed the car door hard. "No way in hell, not this time I'm not."

She whirled around in her tracks and stomped all the way back to the dojo. And she didn't take her time about it this time, didn't let her gaze linger on the ornate, exotic design on the door or let her mind dwell on the faint memory of how much her husband had loved her once. She was far too angry for any of that.

Instead she wrenched the door open, flicked on the light switch right beside it and stood there staring at the faithless pair as the door banged closed on its own, echoing from the walls of the hollow, gym-like room.

They both stiffened, pulling away from each other. And when they saw who it was standing there, they both began talking at once.

"Save it," Penny said.

And they both fell silent.

"So this is the husband whose heart I broke, and the best friend who's been praying for my return, is it?"

She walked forward slowly, her steps echoing from the ceiling. "Is it?" she asked again.

"Penny, this isn't what it looks like," Ben began. "There's nothing going on between me and Kirsten."

"Nothing but a few passionate embraces, you mean?"

He came forward, gripped Penny's shoulders and stared at her from harsh eyes. "You're being ridiculous."

"If you didn't want me back, Ben, why didn't you just say so? Why this big act, where you're the injured party and I'm the lying, scheming wife who did you wrong?"

"It was no act. You did me wrong and you know it."

"Bull." She jerked her shoulders, but his grip only tightened. "From the looks of things, Ben, I did you a huge favor."

"Dammit, Penny!"

Ignoring him, she shot a glance Kirsten's way. "So tell me, was I ever really a part of this plan at all? Or did you cook up the whole thing just to get me out of the way so you could move in on my husband?"

Kirsten's lowered head came up slowly. She was pale, her eyes round and wounded. "Penny...honey, you know better. I would never..."

"No wonder you didn't want me to suffer a lingering death. Better to get it over with, right? Just get me out of the way."

"No, Penny," she whispered, shaking her head. "No, you're wrong. God, you're so wrong."

"It looks it."

"But you are—"

"I need some money."

Ben blinked as if he was in shock. Kirsten only stared blankly.

"Adam says you married some kind of millionaire, Kirsten. Hell, you want my husband, my life, I ought to get something out of the deal. Enough to get so far away from here you'll never be bothered by my presence again. Tell me, Kirsten—tell Ben. How much is it worth to you to get rid of me?"

With everything in her, she willed Kirsten to confess, to lift the burden of what she had done from Penny's shoulders.

Ben suddenly clasped her closer, held her almost fiercely, pressing her face to his chest. His hand clenched and relaxed in her hair, and his arms closed around her so tightly she could barely breathe. "Stop it, Penny. God, just stop it. You're not going anywhere."

"The hell I'm not," she managed to say, though she was speaking with her face crushed to his chest. "But I'll be damned if I'm going anywhere broke."

"Penny—"

"Come on, Ben, it's not like you love me or anything."

He released her suddenly, blinking down at her and looking as shocked as if she'd just slapped him. "You know that's not true—"

"The hell I do. I only know what I see in front of me, Ben, and what I see is you and Kirsten all alone in the middle of the night in this dark hole, so close you couldn't fit a toothpick between you. If that's how you love me, Ben, then you can keep it. I don't need it."

She stepped away from him as he stared at her, saying nothing.

"I'm leaving," Kirsten said softly. "You two don't need me here for this. Penny…." She searched Penny's face for a moment, then shook her head and sighed in exasperation. "Hell, I don't know what to say to you. You're wrong. You're going to throw away the best thing that ever happened to you if you don't wake up."

She strode past them both and out the door.

When it banged closed again, they were alone. Penny's fury was spent, and now she only felt exhaustion. Emotional, physical, mental, bone-deep exhaustion. She paced away from Ben to where a soft mat lay on the floor, and then she sat down on it. She didn't want to leave. She wanted him to beg her to stay.

"What you saw here was nothing, Penny."

"Oh, hell, don't tell me it was nothing. Nothing doesn't look like that, Ben. I lost my memory, not my eyesight." She sat with her legs bent, elbows resting on her knees, head in her hands. "Besides, it doesn't matter, does it? It's over between us. It was over the minute you found out the truth."

Ben walked across the gym and stood looking down at her. "It was over," he whispered, "the minute you decided to lie to me the way you did."

She lifted her head very slowly. "It wasn't me. It was a woman I don't even remember, a stranger. That's who lied to you, Ben. And don't forget, will you, that if she hadn't done it, I wouldn't be alive right now."

He blinked as if those words hit him hard.

"But like I said, it doesn't matter. You can't love me because I'm not her. Yet you manage to hate me for her crimes."

Ben sat down slowly. "You are the same woman, Penny. You'll know that when you remember."

"I might never remember. And to tell you the truth, Ben, I'm not real sure I want to."

"What?"

Penny got slowly to her feet, pacing the gym in quick, agitated strides. "She sounds so weak to me. Giving up when she got sick, taking to her bed, running away." She stopped walking and faced Ben. "That's not me. I wouldn't do the things she did. When I came back here, I thought...I thought maybe you could learn to...." Pushing a hand through her hair, she turned in a slow circle. "But you don't even want to get to know the woman I am now, do you? You just want your wimpy, sickly, de-pendent wife back. Well, I'm sorry, Ben, but she's gone. I can't find her, no matter how I try. And I've just decided to give up the search."

He looked at her like she was speaking a foreign language. "If that's what you think I want, Penny—"

"It's what you think you want, Ben. And if you can't have it, you'll take Kirsten, because I'm just too poor a substitute for the sainted Penny you remember."

"No!" He reached for her, but she ducked his grasp and brushed tears from her eyes. "Penny, listen. Kirsten was just trying to explain why she helped you. She was just asking a dear friend to forgive her, that's all it was."

"Yeah? Well, tell me something, Ben. Did you do it? Did you forgive her?"

He stood where he was. Slowly he nodded.

"Then why the hell can't you forgive me?"

He shook his head slowly. "I don't know."

Penny stared at him for a long moment before she finally turned away. She walked out, battling tears all the way. And then she got into the car, slipped the key into the ignition and started the engine.

She should give up. She should go back to that ranch and pack up her dog and her clothes and get as far away from that big, dumb cowboy as she could go.

Penny closed her eyes and leaned her head against the steering wheel. Against her will, she recalled the joy she and Ben had shared yesterday. The thrill, the warmth, the closeness between them. The way it felt to make love to him.

She still loved him. She might not remember loving him in the past, but the feeling was still alive and well inside her. Maybe stronger than before. And it hurt that he didn't love her back. That's what she was running away from. The hurt. Not the man.

"I made him love me once," she whispered to herself. And somehow she knew she was twice the woman now as she had been then. "No, dammit, I'm not running away. I'm going to make him see me for who I am, not who I was. I'm going right back to that ranch and I'm going to win my husband back."

"No, darling," a deep voice whispered from behind her. Her heart jolted, and she opened her mouth to scream even as she saw the dark shape in her rearview mirror and felt a cold hand close over her mouth. "I'm afraid there's been a change of plans. You're not going back to that ranch after all. You're coming with me."

She twisted frantically, glanced once back toward the gym and even saw the front door opening. But Barlow reached past her to shift the car into gear, and she felt the sting of a hypodermic piercing her throat "Drive," he whispered, "unless you want me to depress the plunger...it'll be fast but lethal, I promise."

Swallowing hard against the pain and the fear welling up in her gut, she drove.

∼

"Dammit, Penny, wait!"

Ben slammed out the front door just in time to see her taillights fading. Looked like she'd borrowed Chelsea's car. Damn. He'd messed things up, but she hit him so hard and so fast and on so many levels he could barely keep up. He didn't know whether to try to explain about Kirsten, or to try to tell her how wrong she was about her assumptions. She always had jumped to conclusions quicker than a cricket on a hot griddle. But she was wrong. She was flat-out dead wrong.

She wasn't different from the Penny he'd adored all his life.

That same spunk, that same temper, that same fire in her eyes had always been there, along with an insatiable curiosity and a suspicious nature—those things had been a part of her all along. They'd only vanished when she'd been diagnosed with HWS. And dammit, he'd missed them! If Penny thought he preferred the sick and beaten woman she'd become over the true hellfire-and-brimstone woman who'd somehow been born again, she couldn't be more wrong.

He wanted her. The woman she was now—the girl she'd been before the illness. Memory or no memory. But he also wanted the pure and perfect love he'd thought they'd had. The love he'd believed in. And that love had been an illusion. It must have been. If it had been real, she'd have never been able to lie to him the way she had.

Or maybe he was being a pigheaded fool.

She still cared. And as he stood there watching Chelsea's car disappear into the night, he thought maybe she loved him, too. Because she'd seemed awfully upset to find him with Kirsten—far more upset than a woman who didn't care about him should be.

All right, he had to tell her. Talk to her. Tonight. She wasn't more than a minute ahead of him, and he'd catch up easily. He turned and ran to his pickup, and then he stopped and stood there cussing.

One of the front tires was utterly flat.

~

"Pull over, right here," Dr. Barlow instructed, and since the needle's point was still embedded in her neck, she did as he said.

Barlow nodded. "Good girl." Then he depressed the plunger. Penny screamed in stark horror as she felt the cool liquid spreading through her, chilling her neck and creeping lower. A wave of weakness swamped her, and when Barlow pulled the needle out she couldn't even lift a hand to rub the sting away.

He got out of the car, then opened her door and hauled her out, as well, pulling her up and over his shoulder. "Are you frightened, Penny? Do you think you're dying now?"

"P—please," she whispered. There were crickets chirping madly all around, and she was dizzy. He walked through deep grasses at the roadside, then knelt and lowered her into them. The tall stalks surrounded her and took on forestlike proportions looming overhead.

"You don't remember what it felt like to know you were dying, do you, Penny? Or maybe you do now. It's terrifying, isn't it?"

Darkness was creeping in on all sides. She had tunnel vision now. Only the tips of the tall grasses and the stars dotting the midnight blue sky directly above her were visible, until he leaned over, blotting out the beauty.

"This is what you were living with, Penny, when I took you in. This kind of fear. But I took that away from you. I cured you, Penny. I gave you back your life. No one else could have done that. You owe me, Penny. Don't you? Don't you?" He gripped her shoulders and shook them.

"Y-yes!"

"But you repay me by running away. Telling my secrets and forcing me to close the clinic and go into hiding. Like a criminal. You deserve to die, you know you do."

"No, please...."

He let go of her shoulders, and she fell backward, her body cushioned again by the deep grasses. "Don't worry. I lied. It was only a tranquilizer. You're not going to die, Penny. But you are going to come away with me. I'm starting a new clinic. And you, Penny, are going to be the center of my studies. The core of my research."

Fear gripped her, but even then her eyes kept falling closed. His words made them pop open again.

"You still don't understand, do you?" he asked her. "Penny, you're the only one. The only one ever to recover from HWS. I've found the cure, but the drug is only part of it. The rest is… hidden. Encoded, somewhere inside you." He smiled down at her, his face blurry and swimming before her eyes. "I'll find it, though. I'll find it, even if I have to take you apart to do it."

Her stomach turned, and she tried again to scream, but no sound emerged.

Dr. Barlow smiled and tipped his head skyward. "Just as I promised you I would, Mother. Just as I promised." Then he looked at Penny again. "That's it, you rest now. I'll come back for you as soon as I've returned the car you borrowed. Wouldn't want those nice Brands to worry, now, would we?"

He moved out of her range of vision, and she heard the grasses brushing his legs as he traipsed back to the car, then heard the engine as he drove away. They'd see him. Someone would see him when he left the car there. And they'd know. They'd come for her. And Ben, Ben must be on his way. He must have come after her…unless…unless he truly didn't care….

No. He did care. She knew he did. He was coming. But maybe not fast enough. She'd have to help, or he'd never be able to find her again. She'd leave something…a sign….

She couldn't stay awake much longer. She clutched at the first thing she thought of—the wristwatch Chelsea had given her as a gift at the party. It was a tremendous effort to tug it off, but she managed it, and then dropped it into the grass where she lay, and prayed Ben would find it there.

∾

Ben pulled into the driveway a half hour later, after changing the tire and driving back from town. He parked beside Chelsea's little car, relieved to see it there. At least he knew Penny had got home okay. He needed to talk to her. Didn't know what he was going to say exactly, but he knew they had to talk.

He sighed heavily and walked up the porch steps and through the screen door. The house was quiet, dark. Had that peaceful feel it only got when everyone inside was sound asleep, an event that didn't happen very often. Someone was usually awake. But it didn't feel as if anyone was up right now.

Blue lay on the floor next to the fireplace, and Olive was laid out beside him with her legs sticking straight out behind her like frog's legs. Both were sound asleep. That Stubby looked like a lumpy rug, stretched out as she was. Ben grinned and thought about showing Penny, but his smile froze and died slow. They wouldn't be sharing smiles or laughter...not until they got things settled between them.

Turning, Ben headed up the stairs to talk to her. But the sound of that screen door creaking stopped him, and he turned to see Garrett just coming inside.

Ben nodded hello and continued up another step.

"Hold up a minute, Ben." Garrett came farther into the room, pausing at the archway to the dining room and inclining his head when Ben turned to face him again. "We need to talk. In the kitchen."

"About what?" Ben asked. He was more eager to see Penny right now than to talk to his brother. He didn't like the idea of her falling asleep with this misguided idea that things could end between them just because she said it was over and he'd been stupid enough and angry enough and wounded enough to agree with her. It would never be over between them. She was as much a part of him as his own heart, and he was just that much a part of her. Or he had been once. And he would be again, dammit.

Garrett sent Ben an impatient look, swept his hat off his head and turned to march into the kitchen. He had his hat in one hand and a file folder in the other. Ben figured there was no sense arguing. It must be important, or Garrett wouldn't have been up and away from home so late anyway. It took major events to get him to work late these days. Had ever since he'd married Chelsea, in fact.

Ben came back down the stairs and followed his brother through the dining room and into the kitchen. He didn't pull out a chair, though. Instead he leaned back against the counter and crossed one boot over the other. Garrett slapped the folder onto the kitchen table. Then he hung his hat on the back of a chair and sat down. "You're gonna want to see this."

Ben stayed where he was. "What is it?"

"Information on Penny's Dr. Barlow. Turns out he isn't a doctor at all. At least, not anymore."

Suddenly interested, Ben straightened. "What do you mean, not anymore?"

"His license was taken away five years ago."

"What?" Ben lunged forward, yanking the file across the table and flipping it open to skim the contents. "Where does it say that? Garrett, where did you get all this?"

Garrett gently pulled the folder back and closed it. "Sit down, Ben. No sense you trying to translate it from legalese to English—I've already been over everything in there. Let me give you the gist of it in digest form, okay?"

Ben pulled out a chair and sat down. "I'm listening."

Garrett nodded. "Okay. To begin with, Gregory Barlow's real name is Barton, and he is a smart man. Probably a genius. The only child of an unwed mother, he sailed through high school, graduating three years early, and started college at sixteen. He was at the top of his class in med school, despite that he was also the youngest student there. About that time his mother was diagnosed with HWS—same disease Penny had."

Ben leaned forward in the chair. "And?"

Garrett shrugged. "The reports don't say what was going on

in Barlow's head, but it's a pretty easy guess. He was devastated. She was all he had, so they must have been close. He turned to full-time HWS research, and I don't think it would be too farfetched to assume he was hoping to find a cure before it was too late for his mother."

"But he didn't, did he, Garrett?"

Garrett shook his head sadly. He picked up the folder, tapping its edge on the table. "I've got documentation of hundred-plus-hour work weeks this guy put in nonstop for over two years. And the worse his mother got, the harder he worked. But the funding for the research got pulled, and the work was stopped. Officially, at least. It looks like Barlow was still working on his own." Lowering the folder, flipping it open, Garrett went on. "In 1984 he petitioned for permission to begin clinical trials with some new drug cocktail he'd developed, but permission was denied. The MHRA felt there was not enough data to begin using it on human subjects. Barlow's mother died in 1985, less than a year later."

Ben lowered his head. "You sound like you almost feel sorry for the guy."

"We both know what it's like to lose a mother, Ben."

"Yeah, and thanks to Barlow, I know what it's like to lose a wife, as well." Ben pushed away from the table and paced to the window, staring outside. "I can probably guess the rest."

"You probably can," Garrett said. "Barlow went ahead with the clinical trials anyway, but he did it undercover. Set up a hospice for HWS victims. People went there thinking they'd get the best of care up to the end. But instead of just caring for them, Barlow was experimenting on them. Injecting them with this new drug of his. The government caught on and shut him down, but he vanished. Turned up again running another clinic under another name, and when they shut that one down, he disappeared again."

Ben shook his head slowly. "He's unbalanced, isn't he?"

"That's the theory. And, Ben—" Garrett lowered his head "—Penny was right about Michele Kudrow."

"The nurse?" Ben asked.

Garrett nodded. "Autopsy showed she was drugged. So much of it in her bloodstream, she couldn't possibly have been conscious when she allegedly slit her wrists."

Ben felt the blood drain from his face. They'd been taking all of Penny's theories so lightly, just the way they always had.

"She's safe here, Ben. No one's going to get to her here."

"We gotta get this guy, Garrett."

"We will. Meanwhile I don't want you taking your eyes off your wife. Got it?"

"You can bet on it."

Garrett walked Ben into the living room, and Ben turned to head toward the stairs, glancing fondly at that comical dog again as he passed her. Then he paused, and his blood ran cold. He lifted his gaze. "Garrett, why is Olive sleeping down here?"

Garrett shrugged. Then he frowned.

"Olive sleeps with Penny. Every time Penny lays down in bed, that dog...." Ben said.

"Damn."

Ben took the steps two at a time, and burst into his bedroom wide-eyed. But it took only a glimpse to know that Penny wasn't there, and the bed was still made. No one had been in it. He ran to the bathroom, but it was empty, as well.

Garrett came up behind him. "She's not in Jessi's room, either." Then he went back into the hall to pound on Adam's door, and then Elliot's.

"I don't get it," Ben muttered as his brothers came awake, staggering into the hall. "The car is here. She must have come back."

"What's going on?" Elliot demanded.

"Something's happened to Penny, hasn't it?" Adam swore

when Ben nodded at him, then ducked into his room to throw on some clothes.

"Go check the car out, Ben. We'll meet you out front," Garrett said as they trotted down the stairs together. Then he fumbled in his pocket for his key chain, and crouched in front of the locked gun cabinet in the living room.

Ben hurried out the door into the darkness. He cupped his hands and called Penny's name, but heard only his own lonely echo on the wind. Adam was beside him before he even made it to the car. His shirt untucked, and belt hanging loose.

"You okay, Ben?"

Ben shook his head and reached for the driver's door. "She was angry," he muttered, half to himself as he opened the door and leaned inside. The overhead light came on. "She saw me and Kirsten at the dojo and—"

Adam's hand clasped his shoulder and yanked him out of the car again, so that he spun around and his back slammed against the side of the vehicle. "Saw you and Kirsten doing what?"

"What do you think?" Ben shouted.

Adam's face reddened, and he glared at Ben, his hands bunching Ben's shirt at the neck.

"I swear, Ben, if you—"

Ben looked at Adam, then looked down at Adam's hands on his shirt. "You know better. I'm your brother."

Adam's face froze for just a second before it fell in shame. He let go of Ben's shirt and lowered his head. "I'm sorry. You're right, I know better. I don't know what the hell is the matter with me."

"I do," Ben said. "But right now I want to find my wife, so we'll talk later." And he turned to lean into the car again.

"So Kirsten came to see you at the dojo. Penny saw you together and jumped to the wrong conclusion," Adam said slowly. "But do you really think that's why she left?"

Ben went still as he noticed the tiny droplets staining the

upholstered headrest. He touched the spots with his fingertip, and found them still damp. "No," he said softly. "I don't think that's why she left." He straightened and turned to face his brother. "Adam, there's blood in the car."

Adam swore and leaned in to see for himself. Ben felt sick, dizzy. "He couldn't have taken her far," he said. "I would have been right behind her if not for that damned flat— Oh, God," he muttered. "The flat, it was no accident. Couldn't have been."

"So he had time," Adam said, still searching inside Chelsea's car. "He could have dropped the car here and taken her somewhere else. Everyone was probably in bed." Adam was in the back seat now. "Or maybe he dropped her somewhere else and brought the car back," he said, then he got out.

"She'd have run."

"Maybe not." Adam held up the hypodermic he'd found in the back seat, and Ben's heart went icy cold.

"He won't hurt her," Ben said softly. "How could he hurt her? He saved her life. He cured her. Why the hell would he hurt her now?" He kept saying those things over and over again. But in his mind's eye he was imagining the nurse, Michele Kudrow, brutally murdered in her own home. And he knew damned well that Penny was in danger.

He'd promised to protect her. Always. And once again the means to do it had been wrenched from his hands.

"No," he whispered. "Not this time."

CHAPTER TWELVE

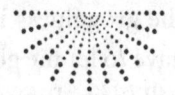

*P*enny opened her eyes slowly. And for just a second her mind played the strangest trick on her, and she thought she was only just now waking from the coma and that all the rest had been a dream.

Only, if it had been, she wouldn't have known she'd been in a coma, would she?

Confusion blurred her thoughts, as well as her vision. She felt drunk. Light-headed. And somewhere between giggling and crying. And then she thought of Ben, and the crying seemed more desirable. So she did. He didn't love her. He hadn't come after her. She'd wanted him to, but he hadn't.

No. She couldn't believe that. Maybe he hadn't come because he couldn't. God, what if Barlow had hurt Ben?

"There, now, it's not as bad as all that," the doctor said from somewhere in this...this room. For the first time she wondered where she was, and her tears came to an abrupt halt at the sound of his voice. She looked again at the room around her, and her mind seemed to grasp that she wasn't at the ranch she'd begun to think of as home. She was in some different place. A place she didn't recognize.

And the man of her nightmares sat in a chair opposite her bed, just watching her.

"It's coming back to you now, is it?"

She blinked. "I...you drugged me. You kidnapped me.

"Unpleasant, all of it, but necessary, I promise you. No need to worry, though. The trauma of all this will soon be a thing of the past, Penny. You'll remember none of it soon enough."

She sat up, battling the grogginess in her brain. "Let me go. Dr. Barlow, please, you have to let me go."

"How much did you tell them, Penny?" He got to his feet and crossed the room to stand over her bed. "Not that it matters really. You're mine again now. And even if they know exactly who has taken you and why, they won't be able to find you."

He adjusted a bag that hung from a pole, and Penny felt her pulse quicken as she saw it there, and traced its tubing to the spot where it disappeared into her arm. "What...what is that?"

"Saline solution," he replied calmly. "Harmless. It's only here in preparation for the Senitrate. I'll inject that right into this IV the moment it arrives, and once you've had it you won't be so uncooperative, I promise. Had to have it shipped from London, you know. But it should be here this afternoon, and then we can be on our way."

She shook her head. "I don't understand. What is it, this... Senitrate? Why do you want to give it to me?"

Dr. Barlow frowned at her. "You haven't answered my question, Penny. And it's imperative you do. Soon you won't remember how much you told those Brands, so you'd best tell me now. What do they know?"

"Nothing!" she blurted. "They've been trying to find out... where I was and why, but...but I couldn't remember and so I—"

He shook his head. "Now you're lying to me."

"No. It's the truth." She sat up slightly in the bed. "Why can't you let me go? I'll never tell anyone a thing about you or what you're doing. I swear—"

"Your tranquilizer seems to be wearing off, doesn't it? Well, now, we can't have that." He pulled a prepared hypodermic from his deep pockets.

"No!" She pulled away, but he gripped her arm and drove the needle into her. She cried out in pain—briefly. The pain faded fast, along with her consciousness.

"Not as good as Senitrate," she heard him mutter. "But it will do."

∽

The rain began just after 4:00 a.m. It came in torrents, and it matched Ben's mood perfectly. He'd lost her. All over again he'd lost her.

Worse than that, he'd let her leave the dojo last night without telling her how he felt about her. And dammit, that just wasn't acceptable. But he'd find her again.

His horse was as wet as he was, but uncomplaining as he rode along between Adam and Jessi into a sodden bit of a scrub lot just off the main road.

"Right about here," Ben said loudly, speaking into the wind. "One of the locals told Garrett there was a car pulled over here for a few minutes last night. It might have been Barlow with Penny."

"Is that all we have?" Adam asked, huddling more tightly into his raincoat. "It could have been anyone. I can't believe no one saw anything more concrete!"

"Garrett's got Texas Rangers all over town asking questions," Ben told his brother, though he understood the frustration. But if Adam thought he had the market cornered on worry, he was dead wrong. "He's doing the best he can."

Jessi ignored them both to climb out of the saddle and hunker down in the soaking-wet grass. Ben and Adam looked at her, then at each other. If there was a sign left in all this rain,

Jessi would find it. They both got down, as well, and, crouching low, examined the ground, inch by inch.

"Here!" Jessi yelled.

Ben's heart jolted in his chest, and for a moment he was certain he'd see his wife's body when he ran to where Jessi knelt in the tall grass. But he didn't. He didn't really see much of anything. Except a few broken blades.

"This is where he walked in from the road. You see?"

Ben knelt down and looked back toward the road where she pointed. And in a moment a pattern seemed to solidify in the grass. Trodden places formed a path. He turned the other way, but Jessi was way ahead of him, following where it led.

"Looks like only one person, though," she was saying. "Maybe it wasn't them...." Her words trailed off as she came to a stop.

Ben caught up, and then he saw why. This place where the grass was all flattened was much larger. As if someone had been lying down on it.

The ramifications shook him to the core, but he refused to believe what he was thinking. "It could have been a deer," he said, though he knew his voice lacked conviction. "Or a couple of deer...they just bedded down here for the night, is all."

Jessi got down on hands and knees. "She didn't go any farther than this. It's like he brought her in and left her lying here, then came back for her and took her somewhere else."

"That's when he returned the car," Adam said. He looked at Ben, his eyes full of sympathy. "She must have been drugged. That needle we found...."

"You can't even be sure this isn't just an animal trail!" Ben closed his eyes, not wanting to think of Penny, helpless in some insane bastard's arms. Alone. He'd promised to protect her, dammit!

"Ben...."

He looked down to see his sister holding up a small wristwatch. He shook his head. "It's not hers—"

"Yes, it is, Ben," Jessi said softly, getting to her feet. "Chelsea gave it to her at the party. I know, I helped her pick it out. She's leaving us clues, Ben, don't you see it? She must have been okay if she was still with it enough to think of taking off the watch."

Ben lowered his head. "I should have never let her leave the dojo. I should have stopped her. Damn, I don't know what I was doing, letting myself get so wrapped up in my own pain that I put her at risk. And then the flat tire—"

"We both know that flat tire was no accident," Adam said softly. "He planned this all out. Left her here, then took Chelsea's car back home, probably hoping we wouldn't even realize Penny was missing until morning. Then he came back here and…." Adam stopped and frowned hard.

"There had to have been another car," Jessi said. "He must have left one somewhere between here and the ranch." She looked up at the rainy sky, shook her head in disgust. "There might still be some tracks, but not for long. Come on."

Taking Ben's arm, she dragged him back toward the road. When they reached it, Garrett's pickup was just rolling to a stop, headlights and wipers at full power. He got out, pulling up the hood of his yellow raincoat. Doc clambered out the passenger side, using his black umbrella like a shield, and Ben wondered why Garrett had dragged the poor man all the way out here.

"Find anything?" Garrett asked.

Jessi nodded. "Her watch," she said, holding it up.

Garrett took it from her. "Why don't you and Adam show me where you found this, while Doc here has a talk with Ben?"

Jessi nodded, and the three took off. Ben looked at Doc, shivering and wet, and reached past him to open the truck's door. "Get back in, Doc," he said. "We can talk just as well where it's dry."

Nodding hard, Doc climbed back inside, folding and shaking

the umbrella. When Ben was settled in the other side and the heater was blasting at full power, Doc said, "I have the results of Penny's blood work, Ben."

Ben braced himself, squared his shoulders and met Doc's dark eyes. "The HWS?"

"There is no trace. She's cured, my friend. It is nothing short of a miracle. This Dr. Barlow...he is a genius."

"He's also a criminal," Ben said.

"This I know." Doc lowered his head. "And I suspected it to be the case even before Garrett told me about Penny's disappearance. Ben, something else showed up in the blood tests. I thought of it when Penny talked about these headaches of hers. But I had to be sure."

"Sure of what?" He watched Doc's face, fearing more bad news.

"There were traces of a drug called Senitrate in her bloodstream. It...it is a drug that has been banned in most countries. It was written about in all the medical journals not long ago. Something certain government researchers developed for use in the military."

Ben frowned as he took this in. "What does it do? Cure HWS?"

"No," Doc said, shaking his head. "We still do not know how Barlow managed that." Drawing a deep breath, Doc went on. "Senitrate, it induces amnesia. If given in high enough doses, the effect can be permanent."

He could have struck Ben and hurt him less. "Are you saying that animal deliberately took away her memory?"

Doc nodded. "No doubt he began administering the Senitrate as soon as she came out of the coma. If she remembered you, Ben, she'd have never stayed with him. And if she is one of the few—perhaps even the only patient—he's ever cured successfully, then he'd want to keep her in his care. Study her,"

"Study her? Jeeze, Doc, this is my wife, not some lab rat."

Doc nodded, patting Ben's arm repeatedly. "I know. I know, I'm only telling you what I've learned. And, Ben, if he has her now and can get access to more of the Senitrate...." Again he averted his eyes.

Ben gripped Doc's arm. "He could erase her memory all over again?"

The older man nodded shakily. "I'm afraid so."

"No." Ben pounded his hands on the steering wheel. "No, dammit!" He wrenched the door open and got out, running down the muddy road in the pouring rain until his lungs burned and his heart thundered in his chest. Stopping, breathless, he flung his head back and shouted her name into the storm-tossed sky, making it a cry to the heavens, to the gods if they were listening. And when his breath ran out and the sound of his anguish was swallowed up by the storm, he dropped to his knees in the mud, lowered his head and whispered, "God, Penny, where are you?"

A heavy hand came down on his shoulder. Garrett's hand. "Doc told me on the way over here...about the drug."

Ben nodded. "I can't lose her again. Dammit, Garrett, I can't."

"You won't," Garrett promised.

Ben shook his head slowly, looking at the ground. "We don't even have a clue which direction they went. They could be anywhere by now."

"Penny's a handful when she gets her dander up," Garrett said. He gripped Ben's arm and helped him to his feet. "Or she was, when she was younger. And she seems more like the kid she was these days, than the woman she grew into. He'd have one hell of a time taking her far without her drawing notice somehow or another. You know that."

Ben nodded slowly. "I know that. It's taken me a while to see it. I've been trying to treat her like the helpless, sick woman I lost. When all the time she's been someone else."

"Yeah. A hellion."

Ben managed a sad smile that died quickly. "That's why the bastard is shooting her full of drugs to keep her still."

"Right. But dragging a half-conscious woman around in public would attract just as much notice as hauling a fighting one, don't you think? To say nothing about getting her onto a jet bound for Europe."

Ben lifted his gaze, searched Garrett's face. "What are you thinking?"

"I'm thinking he wouldn't bother risking it. Not when he has a supplier out there somewhere for this Senitrate that Doc was talking about. I'm thinking he'd hole up somewhere nearby, keep her quiet and then give her the drug to erase her memory again. After that he could feed her some bull story, and she'd probably believe him. Go where he told her to without fighting him or having to be tranquilized at all."

Ben listened, but he knew Garrett was only trying to give him some kind of hope to cling to, thin though it was. "That's a pretty wild theory, Garrett. I could come up with a dozen others that have as much basis in fact, including Penny being abducted by aliens."

"I have a hunch, though," Garrett said.

Ben shook his head. "Does it matter? We still don't know where he's hiding out with her. Hell, he might have had the drug with him, might have given it to her already."

"Maybe. But if he didn't have any on him, he'd have to get it. And frankly I don't think he'd have risked coming into the country carrying a banned drug. Why would he? He didn't even know if he'd find her or not."

Ben's head came up. "And if he didn't bring any, he'll have to get some shipped to him."

"That's right, and he won't risk having it sent to wherever he's staying, in case the drug is discovered. They'd have cops all over the place if it was discovered."

"So he'd use…what, a P.O. box?"

"And a fake name. I got a judge to sign a warrant, and we've got Rangers checking in with every post office in three counties, Ben. Any suspicious packages addressed to new P.O. box customers with overseas return addresses will be checked. I doubt there will be that many in this part of Texas."

"And if we do find the Senitrate?"

"Put it in the post-office box, stake out the place and wait. When he comes for it, we'll follow him back to wherever he's holding Penny."

Ben sighed deeply. "It's a long shot."

"It's not the only oar I have in the water, Ben. I've got guys going to hotels flashing photos at the clerks, road-blocks and APB's, but I think the Senitrate is our best lead."

Ben nodded. "God, I hope so. We have to find her, Garrett. He can't give her any more of that poison." Ben bit his lip when he felt it trembling. "I can't lose her again."

"I know, Ben. I know."

~

Penny drifted in and out of a drug-induced stupor. Every time she woke, he gave her another shot. So she told herself to pretend she was still out, and prayed she'd remember when she next came to.

And she did. As consciousness slowly returned the next time, she heard her own voice warning her to be still, and she heeded it, even though it was several groggy moments before she remembered why. Then she saw him, sleeping in the second of the twin beds in the room. A hotel room, she guessed. She tried to sit up, and couldn't. Damn. He was asleep. It would be the perfect time to make a run for it.

But she couldn't. She needed to wait for her strength to seep back into her body. But in the meantime....

She reached very quietly to the stand beside the bed. If this was a hotel, there would be a notepad and a pen there. Yes. There were both. She drew them quietly toward her.

Dr. Barlow kept saying she would forget everything again, very soon. If that was true...then there were a few things she needed to get down on paper...things she wanted to remember. So she wrote, in the dark, with a trembling, weak hand. She wrote about the things that mattered most to her, and prayed she'd see these notes again if her memory vanished once more.

She'd only been writing for an hour when Barlow stirred, and she had to act quickly. She stuffed the notepad beneath the mattress, and then lay very still.

But it didn't matter. He glanced at his watch, and injected her again. Nonetheless she'd fooled him. And if he was going by his watch, and drugging her at regular intervals, that meant she would wake again before the next injection.

And maybe next time she'd find an opportunity to escape.

Hours—many hours, she suspected—later, she woke again. Sunlight streamed through the hotel windows and splashed over her face. She opened her eyes to slits, and tried to see the room around her without moving her head too much and giving herself away. She could hear Dr. Barlow moving around. Pouring something into a glass, swallowing it. The sounds made her painfully aware of the dryness in her own throat. But she forcibly ignored it, and closed her eyes again when his footsteps came nearer.

"How's the patient doing?" He lifted her wrist, took her pulse, dropped it again, and she let it fall limply to the bed. "Good. Now, you lucky girl, your Senitrate should be here. Guaranteed delivery by noon, you know." He patted her cheek, stinging little slaps no doubt intended to assure him that she was truly unconscious. She never flinched.

"I won't be long," he told her. "And since you seem to have become so devoted to a husband you don't even remember, I believe I've decided that after I erase your memory this time, I'll tell you that you're my wife. You'll stay with me then, won't you, Penny?" He laughed as he walked to the door. "Just think of it. I can create an entire life for you, and you'll believe every word of it. Oh, why didn't I think of it sooner?"

The door opened, closed again. Penny lay very still and listened. She could still hear him breathing. If that wasn't the oldest trick in the book, she didn't know what was. She lay there as limp and lifeless as a rag doll. The second time the door closed, it was for real.

She opened her eyes first, just to make sure. Then she sat up in the bed, dizzy and weak, but so determined she figured the entire U.S. Marine Corps couldn't stop her. She missed her husband, even if he didn't know enough to love her the way he ought to just yet. And she missed her bulldog, dammit. How was she supposed to sleep, tranquilizers or not, without Olive's warm little body curled up close on one side of her?

And Ben's big strong body pressed tight to the other side?

Her heart skipped a beat when she thought of him. Dammit, she wasn't going to give up without a fight, and it might very well be the fight of her life.

She put her feet on the floor and looked around the room. Everything swayed and loomed in and out of focus. Where was the phone? There had to be a phone somewhere, didn't there?

There it was, way over there on the stand by the other bed. She caught hold of the headboard, pulled herself to her feet... and fell to her knees. Okay, fine, she couldn't walk. She'd crawl.

Inch by inch she made her way across the room to where the telephone was. Gripping the stand, she tried to pull herself up again, but the stand tipped and the phone crashed to the floor.

Penny grimaced at the noise. Then she sat very still, looking around, listening, half expecting Barlow to come running any second. But he didn't. And she could reach the phone now.

She picked it up, pushed the nine, then the one, then the one again.

But nothing happened.

Blinking in confusion, Penny tried again. Then she rattled the cutoff, but still nothing. No dial tone, nothing. Finally she traced the wire coming out the back of the phone, and saw where it had been cut in half at the middle.

"No," she whispered.

She had no choice now. She had to get out of here. But first....

She had to take precautions. Give Ben some way to find her, in case she didn't make it. As hard as she had to fight to stay awake, she knew with a sickening certainty that she might well pass out before she ever made it to the lobby, and it didn't take a huge imagination to see how Dr. Barlow might find her right there upon his return. He certainly wouldn't leave her alone for very long.

Frantically she looked around the room. Okay, first her paper. She crawled to the bed, tore the top few sheets—the ones she'd filled with her thoughts—from the notepad she'd hidden there, and then stuffed them back underneath for safekeeping. She scribbled a fast, sloppy note on the pad, then tore that sheet free and jammed it into her pocket. Then she scribbled another, and dragged herself to the window. It was an effort to open the thing, but she managed, and then tossed the entire pad out, praying someone would pick it up and see her plea for help.

Almost as an afterthought, she dragged the extra blanket from the foot of the bed, and tossed that out, as well, closing the window on one corner so it flopped in the wind like a flag. But only until it became too soaked with rain to do so anymore. Then it hung limply, plastered to the side of the building, and she thought it must be all but invisible from below. Still, she left it there, and drew the curtains closed so Barlow wouldn't see it right away.

She dragged herself into the bathroom, pulled herself to her feet by gripping the edges of the sink. A message. She'd leave a message, just in case. Lipstick, if only she had some lipstick. Soap. Soap would work. She gripped the tiny bar with the Holiday Inn wrapper on it, and struggled to peel the paper away. Then, bracing one hand on the sink for support, she scraped the soap across the mirror with a shaky hand. "Call police. Kidnapped. Penny Brand."

Her body shook with the effort of remaining upright so long. But it was done. If she couldn't get away, maybe someone would see this before Barlow did. A maid. Maybe she'd call for help.

Now. Time to go. She'd thought she might get stronger, but she hadn't. In fact the dizziness was swamping her more than it had before. Damn those tranquilizers....

Wait. The tranquilizers. She should get rid of them.

She searched her foggy mind, and recalled Dr. Barlow bending low...on the far side of the bed opposite the one she'd been in. A cabinet. She saw it now, and made her way with excruciating effort across the room to it.

Dropping to her knees, she opened the door. And there she saw several tiny glass vials of the drug he'd been giving her. Anger surged. How dare that bastard do this to her? With one swipe of her hand, the tiny bottles all clattered to the floor. And Penny pulled herself upright, and stomped them to bits.

There. Let the bastard drug her now.

And let him try keeping her captive without the help of his evil little injections, she thought with venom. She'd get out of here. She had too much at stake to lose it all to a madman, even if he was the one responsible for saving her life.

Penny leaned on furniture and slowly made her way to the door. It took time, but she did it. She twisted the knob and pulled the door open. There was a hallway, and closed doors with numbers on each one. And there was a man coming around the corner at the far end. Another guest—help at last!

Penny lifted a hand toward him, managed to cry out. "Help me. Please, help me…"

His head came up fast. Then he ran closer, and her blurred vision cleared, and she saw his face.

"No…." she whispered as Barlow closed his hands around her arms. "No!"

Not gently, he shoved her back through the door. Penny managed to tear the ring from her finger as she struggled against him. She dropped it on the carpeted hall before Barlow got her back into the room. Her prison. And she could only wait, and pray he hadn't brought the Senitrate back with him.

∼

They had a lead on the drug, and Ben was frustrated with the way the police were handling it. DEA had been brought in, and their agents were all over the small El Paso post office the package had been addressed to. Ben and his brothers had been pushed aside, told to stay out of the way, despite Garrett's attempts to intervene. The closest they could get to the post office was the coffee shop across the street. Ben sat there in a booth with Adam, watching. There was little else to do right then.

"Barlow would have to be an idiot to walk into that place," Adam said, leaning close.

He was right, Ben knew. Anyone who'd seen the docile area the day before would know something was up. No less than ten dark-colored sedans lined the street. Unmarked cars, they called them, though the police antennas were obvious to anyone looking. And the men sitting inside the cars watching the post-office door almost unblinkingly were not exactly inconspicuous.

"I can't just sit here, Adam. I have to do something."

"There's nothing to do."

Ben shook his head. "She's here, in this damned town, somewhere."

"But where?" Adam asked, staring out the window.

Ben shook his head. "If Barlow spots the cops, he'll move her. Maybe even decide it's too risky to keep her…alive."

"Ben, don't think that way."

Ben lowered his head, closed his eyes. "I'm getting out of here." He shoved his chair back. Its legs made loud scraping sounds on the floor as he got to his feet.

"To go where? You don't even know where to begin looking, Ben."

"I have to try. It's Penny, for God's sake. She's fighting for her life, dammit, and she's doing it alone." He turned toward the door, but his brother came behind him, not about to let him alone.

"You're beating yourself over the head with guilt, aren't you?"

Ben whirled to face him. "Of course I am! How can I not be? I let her think it was over, Adam, just to soothe my wounded pride. I let her walk out of that dojo when I should have been on my knees begging her to stay, and to hell with what she did or didn't do in the past! God gave me a miracle, and I threw it away. I love her, Adam." He lowered his head, his face contorting in agony. "God, I love her." He got himself under control, lifted his head again. "I'm going out there, and I'm damned well going to find her." He waited for Adam to argue some more.

Adam said, "I'm going with you."

CHAPTER THIRTEEN

"**I** should have guessed you'd try something like this!" Barlow's voice was loud and angry, and Penny hit the bed hard when he shoved her toward it.

She said nothing when he loomed over her. But when he reached for another vial of the tranquilizer and saw them all smashed to bits, he looked even more furious. "Damn you! I saved your life!" His eyes narrowed. "Maybe you'd prefer death to life, though. Is that it, Penny? Is that why you're so ungrateful? Do you want to die?"

"You saved my life," she whispered. "And then you stole it from me. You lied to me, told me I had no one when—"

His hand lashed out to slap her face, and the impact knocked her backward on the bed. Then he went silent, staring at her with dead eyes. "We've worked far too hard. I won't let you do this to her!"

And that frightened Penny more than the blow had done. "Do...what...to whom?"

"You're trying to destroy her, aren't you? Well, I won't let you, do you understand? I won't let you!"

"Dr. Barlow," she whispered, "who in the world are you talking about?"

"We're getting out of here," he said. "If you weren't so valuable to my research, Penny, believe me I would leave you behind, just as dead as you would have been if you'd never come to me. But I can't do that. And I can't get the Senitrate." He shook his head sadly. "Believe me when I tell you, this would have been so much easier on you if I could." Hands shaking, he pulled a pack of cigarettes from his pocked, shook one free, and lit it, tossing the matchbook onto the nightstand and puffing smoke into the air.

She'd never seen him smoke before, but then, he wouldn't in a clinical setting. In a hotel room, apparently, he had no such reservations. He said he couldn't get the Senitrate. She wanted to ask why, but thought it best to keep quiet. He paced away from her, and Penny scooped the matches from the stand beside her bed and buried them in her pocket. Her face stung, but her head was a bit clearer. Maybe his slap in the face had done more good than harm. She thought she might even be able to stand up without wobbling, maybe even walk now.

"We can take the elevator directly to the garage where I've parked," he said, thinking aloud. "With luck we'll run into no one on the way."

"Wh-where are we going?"

"Away from here. Where there won't be police surrounding the post office waiting for me to show up. Eventually, love, I'll take you back to England with me, but until you're...cooperative—"

"You don't have to drug me," she said quickly. "I'll go along, I swear it."

He smiled grimly at her. "No, you won't. We both know that, don't we, Penny? But you will, once you have enough of the drug in your bloodstream. You'll be as meek as a lamb if I tell you to be."

"Don't be so sure," she told him, glaring. "I wasn't last time, was I?"

His brows rose. "Which is why the dosage will be higher this time, Penny. Much, much higher. I'll make sure the effects are permanent this time."

His words sent a chill through her blood. "Why are you doing this to me?" she asked, her voice less hostile than before. It trembled instead. Her heart was breaking, she realized. She'd only just found love, and he was going to take it from her all over again.

"To save lives, Penny. Don't you realize what you are? You're the first patient ever to recover fully from HWS. And it was my treatment that cured you. For years I've worked for this. I won't let you rob me of it now."

She shook her head slowly, seeing for the first time the glint of madness in his eyes. "But you have the cure. You did it—you...you did what no other scientist has been able to do so far. Why do you need me?"

"I have the cure, yes, Penny, but I've explained this to you before. It's failed for other patients. It failed...it failed for my mother."

She caught her breath, and thought perhaps she was finally beginning to understand. "You...you lost your mother."

"Oh, no," he whispered. "She's still with me, Penny. Guiding me, telling me what I have to do. I promised her I'd end HWS forever, and that's a promise I intend to keep."

Penny swallowed hard. So the "she" he'd been ranting about was his dead mother...and he still spoke to her. And she to him. She closed her eyes, wondering if things could get any worse.

"On you," Dr. Barlow went on, "the treatment worked, and there has to be a reason for that. Something in your body chemistry. You should be honored, Penny, to be given an opportunity like this—to save lives, to cure an incurable disease. You'll go down in medical history."

She shivered and he reached for her. "Come, it's time we left. They're getting too close to us here."

She drew back in fear, and he paused, studied her with bunched brows. "You still don't understand how important this is, do you?"

Shaking his head sadly, he pulled a gun from somewhere beneath his jacket. He pointed it at her. Penny stared at the perfectly round black barrel, and felt her knees go weak all over again.

"I told you this would have been easier for you with the tranquilizer. But you've ruined that. And now I'll have to shoot you, Penny, if you don't do exactly as I say. If you don't think I will carry out that threat, Penny, you will be in for a surprise. Because I will. And unfortunately the same fate will befall anyone who gets in our way. Now up, on your feet, come on."

Swallowing hard, Penny got up.

∽

Adam and Ben had stopped at a dozen hotels in El Paso, talked to the clerks, shown them Penny's photo. And so far nothing had panned out. Ben was afraid Barlow had already fled, taking Penny with him, and God knew how he'd find her again.

At least Barlow didn't have the Senitrate. Ben clung to that with everything in him as he paced the sidewalk toward the Holiday Inn, Adam at his side.

Adam stopped walking, tugged on Ben's sleeve.

"What?" Ben looked at Adam, saw him craning his neck and then followed his gaze. "What the hell...?"

"Looks like somebody stuck a blanket out the window."

Ben went stiff. "It's a signal. It's Penny!" He ran forward, but Adam was beside him in an instant, gripping his arm, stopping him. His foot came down on a notepad some slob had dropped, and he kicked it aside impatiently.

"Ben, slow down. Let's do this right. Call the police and wait for them before we—"

"And have them show up en masse, ready for a shoot-out? Dammit, Adam, we don't want to turn this thing into a standoff. Barlow could panic. He could hurt her." The thought made him sick to his stomach. "I'm going up there."

Adam looked at Ben, and finally nodded. Then he glanced upward again. "Fourth floor, corner room. Come on."

Together they ran to the entrance. Adam seemed inclined to stop at the desk, but Ben had no such inclination. They'd never give him a key for the asking, and he didn't have time to go into explanations. He took the stairs two at a time, and after a moment of indecision, Adam came running after him. He knew they drew curious glances, and figured the desk clerk was probably calling security right now. He didn't care.

At the fourth-floor landing, he burst into the hall, turned in the direction he knew the room to be and ran all the way to the room at the corner. Then he stood outside the door, terrified of what he might find beyond it.

Adam caught up, reached past him and tried the knob. Useless, Ben knew, without a key. Adam glanced up at him with a quick shake of his head. "You want to knock?"

Ben looked at the floor. A glimmer caught his eye, and he knelt, gathering the tiny golden ring into his hands.

Penny's wedding ring. He closed his palm tightly around that ring and straightened. "Yeah," he said. "You bet I'm gonna knock. Step aside, Adam."

Adam grimaced, but stepped out of the way. Ben drew a breath, let it out and then delivered the most powerful kick he knew how to perform, shouting as he did so.

The door crashed open, banging into the wall on the other side. Ben leaped into the room, ready to do battle.

It was empty. A rumpled bed gave him nightmarish chills. The lamp lay broken on the floor beside an over-turned stand.

When he moved closer, his boots crunched over shattered glass, and he bent to pick up a piece of a vial with the label still on it.

Adam was already checking the closet, then the bathroom.

"They're gone," Ben whispered. "Dammit, he's already taken her somewhere else."

"She's not making it easy on him, though," Adam said from the bathroom.

Ben noted the cut telephone cord. The bastard wasn't making it easy on Penny, either. But she was trying. Damn, but she was trying. He walked into the bathroom, and Adam pointed at the mirror. Ben read Penny's plea for help written in soap on the glass.

"She's something else, that wife of yours," Adam said. Then he glanced at the bit of glass Ben clutched in his hand. "What's that?"

"Drug vials. Tranquilizer, I think. He doesn't have the Senitrate, Adam, but he's keeping her sedated."

"That would explain the handwriting. It's shaky."

Ben closed his eyes. "Shaky or not, she managed to leave a note. Smashed his cache of dope to bits, and put up a flag to let us know where she was. Left her ring in the hall…" Ben drew a shuddering breath.

"And she'll keep on doing it, Ben. We're going to find her."

There were footsteps in the hall. "Just what do you gentlemen think you're doing?"

Ben turned to see a man in a suit, probably the manager, looking aghast at the trashed room. "My brother will explain," he said. "Where's the parking lot?"

"But—you…you don't think I'm going to let you walk away from this mess, surely? Someone is going to have to pay for all the—"

Ben gripped the man's shirtfront and lifted him off his feet. "I don't think you heard me. I asked, where is the parking lot?"

"In the b-back! And there's a garage—below."

Ben released the fellow, tipped his hat. "Thank you kindly." Then he left, while Adam blurted explanations.

Again Ben took the stairs, too impatient to wait for the elevator. All the way down his steps echoed in the empty stairwell. Halfway down, he kicked something that skittered down a few more steps. Frowning, he picked up a part of a torn up matchbook. The letter P had been hastily, sloppily scrawled on the inside.

"Well I'll be..." He stuffed the matches into his pocket and ran the rest of the way down, pushed the bar on the door and flung it open, then stepped into the cavernous underbelly of the hotel. Shiny cars lined the place, colorless in the darkness. Ben didn't know which way to turn, where to look. Until he spotted another piece of matchbook off to the right. "Good girl, Penny," he whispered. "Lead the way, honey, I'm coming for you."

He walked, skimming the rows of cars, scanning the floor for another clue. And he found it. The rest of the matchbook, resting in an empty parking space. For a moment his heart fell. Dammit, they'd already got out of here. But then he heard a voice, and turned. A parking attendant stood in a small booth near the exit sign, holding a telephone to his ear. Ben glanced at the vacant spot again. Level 1, slot 14. He ran toward the little booth, gripping the sides' of it with both hands. "I need your help. What car was parked in slot 14, over there?"

The young man had an earring in his nose, and he rubbed it, frowning. "What? Why you wanna know that? Look, I'm not supposed to—"

"A woman's been kidnapped, dammit. And she was in that car! Now tell me."

The boy's eyes widened, but then he lowered his head. "Sorry, man. We don't keep track of what car's in what spot. Only check to see if they're registered or not."

Ben gritted his teeth in frustration.

"Was the woman sick or something?" the kid asked.

Ben's head came up fast. "Why do you ask?"

"Well, it's just that a guy did leave here with a woman just a few minutes ago. I wouldn't have noticed, except she looked sick. Sort of leaning on the door, kinda limp and—I'd have thought she was drunk, you know, but it's sorta early in the day."

"Not drunk, drugged. What do you remember about the car?"

The kid grinned. "Black Chevy Cavalier."

Ben frowned, instantly suspicious.

The kid shrugged. "My dad bought one just like it last year."

For the first time Ben felt hope. "Thanks, kid. You've been a big help."

"Oh, heck, I can do better. If you know what room they were in, I can get you the plate number."

Ben gaped, gave his head a shake. "Room 410. And if you'll let me use that phone, I might just name my first-born after you."

The kid handed Ben the phone, and flipped open his logbook. While Ben dialed Garrett's mobile number, the boy wrote the plate number on a piece of scrap paper and pushed it into Ben's hand. Ben glanced down. Under the number it said, "Reginald Kenneth."

Ben frowned at the kid.

"My name, for your firstborn."

"Reginald?"

The boy nodded. "Mom was a big Elton John fan."

∽

Garrett answered his phone.

The hotel room was swarming with cops and forensics teams. Reginald was ensconced with one officer, and looked to be feeling pretty pleased with himself as he answered the man's endless questions.

Ben paced.

"Easy. We're going to find her," Garrett told him, slapping his shoulder.

"I want to be out there, looking, not in here answering questions."

"Look, we've got roadblocks, we've got choppers, we've got the damned plate number and a description of the car. They're not going to get far. And as soon as we spot them, I'll take you to her myself. You got my word on that."

Ben shook his head. "Suppose Barlow turns this into a high-speed chase? They could crash. She could end up dead." He closed his eyes, thinking how ironic it would be to lose Penny in exactly the same manner he thought he'd lost her two long years ago.

"We're not going to risk Penny's life, Ben."

"Suppose he pulls a gun, uses her as a hostage, demands we let him leave with her?"

"Will you quit thinking the worst?" Garrett shook his head, and pressed a handful of sheets taken from a hotel notepad into Ben's hand. "Here, read this, it'll take your mind off things."

Frowning, Ben took the sheets and glanced down to see a wobbly semblance of Penny's handwriting slanting across the page. "What is this?"

"Looks like she knew what he was planning. She wanted to write things down, things she wanted to remember. She must have done it when he wasn't watching too close. We found these sheets stuffed under the mattress."

Ben's breath escaped him in a rush, and he glanced down at the notes.

To whoever finds this note: it belongs to Penny Brand. She might not be around anymore, but she'll be back. Please, make sure she gets this. It might be her only link to the life that was taken away from her...again.

Below that there was a line or two about every member of his family. He read them all. How Chelsea had been kinder to her than a sister, and how Jessi had taken to her dog.

And that's another thing. The dog, don't forget about her. Olive. She loves me so much, and she'll love me even if I can't remember her. I know she will. She's my best friend. She doesn't care what stupid mistakes I've made.

If only Ben could love me like that.

Ben paused, blinked a hot moisture from his eyes, and read on.

I mustn't forget Ben. There's so much about him that I want to remember. The way his eyes light up when he works with the little kids at his dojo. The way he moves like a dancer when he works out at dawn. I watched him once, and I was swept away. I think I knew, right then, that he was the one—the only one—but I knew it in my heart, not my mind. I have to remember to trust those kinds of things. My heart will remember him, even if my mind can't. I know it will. But mostly I have to remember that he's my husband. And I love him. I loved him before, and parts of that are coming back to me now. But even if I never remembered the past, I would have fallen in love with him all over again. And if I forget again, I know it won't matter. My heart will never forget him. And in my heart, in that deep place that never truly forgets anything, I know he's the only man I could ever love. Dr. Barlow and his drugs can take away my memory, my life, my past. But nothing can ever take that love away from me.

I hurt Ben, though. Deceived him and caused him a lot of pain. That's something I need to remember. Because no matter what happens, I'm going to find my way back to him. And when I do, I'll have to fight to win him back. I'm going to make him love me again. If I don't, my life won't be complete. Not ever. Not without him.

Ben's hands were shaking when he finished. Garrett gently

took the sheets from him. "I have to keep these for now. Evidence, you know. But I thought you ought to see them first."

Nodding, Ben swallowed the lump in his throat. "I've been a complete idiot."

Garrett pursed his lips, nodded. "That you have, little brother."

"She thinks I don't love her anymore." He covered his face with his hand. How could he have let her think that, even for a moment, even in anger?

"You'll just have to tell her otherwise, then. When you see her."

A radio crackled to life, and one of the police officers replied, then rushed over to Garrett. "They've spotted the car."

Ben's heart pounded harder.

"Where?" Garrett demanded.

"Chopper pilot said it looks like they're heading for the border," the officer replied. "But they're not far from here."

Garrett turned toward the door.

"Sheriff Brand, we have cars en route, and they'll make it there long before you can."

"Don't be so sure about that," Garrett said.

Ben thought he could beat them on foot at this point.

CHAPTER FOURTEEN

*H*er head was clearing more and more now that Dr. Barlow had no drugs to force on her. And as it cleared, Penny was thinking of ways to escape. Grab the wheel? He was only holding it with one hand, after all.

But that was because he still held the gun in the other, and he kept it pointing toward her all the while. It scared her, that looming, dark barrel.

If she yanked the wheel, they could crash into a tree. She'd probably be killed, as fast as he was driving. But if worse came to worst, she'd do it. Better to take the chance than to risk returning to being a woman without a life, without a past.

Without Ben.

She reached to the side to take hold of her seat belt, and pulled it forward.

"What are you doing!"

She jumped, startled at his shout. He was nervous. And that made her nervous, as well. "Just fastening my seat belt. Your driving scares me."

Then she paused. Maybe wrenching the door open and jumping from the car would be a better option. In which case the seat belt would be a detriment. Of course, he was driving too fast to make that a viable solution, either, but he might slow down for a curve or something. If she was very lucky.

She could bash him on the head, she supposed. But he was still holding that damned gun on her. He'd probably panic and pull the trigger.

Damn. What would Nancy Drew have done in a case like this? Mentally she recalled the plots of every Nancy Drew mystery she'd read as a child. Surely Nancy had escaped from a moving vehicle and a gun-toting madman at least once in her long crime-fighting career.

Then she blinked...and realized that she remembered reading those stories. Every last one of them.

She closed her eyes, searched her mind...my God, she remembered her parents. Her throat swelled shut, and her eyes brimmed with tears. She remembered her wedding day. How bittersweet it had been, because by then she and Ben had both known she was dying.

But he'd loved her anyway. He'd looked into her eyes with so much love it had made her cry, and softly vowed to be with her to the end, to take care of her no matter what.

And she'd denied him the chance to live up to those vows, even knowing how much they had meant to him.

"My God," she whispered. "My God, I remember...."

But she'd completely forgotten, for just a moment, about the man at her side. His head turned sharply toward her. "Enjoy it while you can, Penny. You'll forget all of it soon, I promise you that."

It was more than anger that surged in her this time. It was pure, undiluted fury. She had it back! All of it. He wasn't going to take it away from her again.

"The hell I will!" She gripped the steering wheel and jerked it toward her with all her might. The gun exploded; the car reeled crazily and crashed. Glass shattered and metal crunched as the vehicle came to a sudden, immediate stop in a cloud of dust. She was hurled forward only to smash into something hard and be flung back into her seat again. Her head screamed with pain.

When Penny blinked her eyes open, she couldn't see for the blood streaming into them.

∽

Garrett drove. Ben was glad of it, because the way his hands were shaking, he'd have likely killed them all before they caught up to Barlow's car. And he couldn't have driven any faster than his brother was doing. Garrett pushed the pickup's oversize engine hard, and more than once he'd taken a curve on two wheels instead of four. Adam held on for dear life while Ben prayed in silence.

Then the radio crackled to life.

"Shots fired! Shots fired! Suspect car just veered off the road, Sheriff! It looks bad."

Garrett grabbed the handset. "How far?"

"Two miles from your position. I've already called for an ambulance. We're closing in."

"So are we," Garrett muttered, and replaced the small handset. He pressed down harder on the gas, and the pickup's nose lifted like a jet getting ready for takeoff. Garrett undid the snap on his holster.

In a little over a minute the truck screeched to a sideways halt in the middle of the road, and Ben leaped out practically before it came to a stop. Officers surrounded the black Chevy, moving in carefully, and way too slowly in Ben's opinion. They shouted things like "Exit the vehicle with your hands up," but they were getting no response from Barlow.

The car embraced a telephone pole, its nose crumpled, windshield shattered. Steam boiled from under the hood, hissing in the cool rain.

Penny was in that car!

Ben shoved the pair of cops nearest him aside, and ran forward.

"Dammit, Brand, get away from there!" someone shouted, but he ignored the order, ran to the car and wrenched the passenger door open.

Penny lay with her head resting on the dashboard. So still. His heart skipped a beat as he reached for her, but he paused when the man beside her moved, lifting his hand—and Ben only had a second to realize that hand held a gun.

"Drop it!"

Garrett's firm voice came from the driver's side as that door was yanked open and his own gun appeared, barrel pressed to Barlow's head. "Now."

The doctor's face was cut and bleeding. He didn't look too steady. Barlow's hand shook, but he let the gun fall to the seat and lowered his head. "I'm a doctor," he muttered. "I can save lives, don't you understand? My work can't be stopped—it's too important...."

Garrett pulled the man from the car, and several others closed in around him. Ben heard sirens. The ambulances, he hoped. Gently he touched Penny's hair, but his hand came away bloody. "Penny," he whispered. "Honey, hold on. For God's sake, hold on."

"Ben?"

Slowly she lifted her head, looked up into his eyes. "I love you, Ben," she whispered. And then she lay down again, unconscious.

God, he hoped she was only unconscious.

The sirens screamed closer, and in seconds Ben found himself pushed aside by paramedics with heavy cases and caring eyes. He didn't go far. His brothers surrounded him. All of them. The entire family had been in El Paso awaiting news, and they'd flocked to the scene the moment they'd heard what was happening. Jessi wrapped her arms around him and held him hard. All of them kept muttering that Penny would be all right, but he wasn't so sure. Maybe he was being punished for failing to appreciate the gift he'd been given. Maybe she'd die now because he'd thrown his miracle away. How many people were granted two in a single lifetime, after all?

No. She couldn't die. She had to be all right. She had to be.

He couldn't see her, with the medics leaning over her. Minutes ticked by like hours. But finally they stepped aside, one gently holding her arms, and Penny stepped out of the car, wobbly, but standing. Ben rushed forward even as they eased her down onto a stretcher.

"Penny?"

"Relax," one of the medics told him with a smile. "All that blood is from a cut on her forehead. She'll need a few stitches, might have a concussion, but other than that, I think she's fine."

"Fine hell," Penny muttered. "My neck hurts."

The medic laughed. "Whiplash," he told her. "Hell, you oughtta sue the guy."

Penny frowned up at him. "Since when are stitches, concussions and whiplash funny to you people?"

"Since we thought you'd been shot," Ben said softly. He knelt down beside the stretcher, clasped Penny's hand in his. "You're gonna be okay."

She nodded, then grimaced and rubbed her neck. The medic bent over her from the other side, washing the blood from her face and putting a temporary bandage over the cut in her head. "Yeah," she told him. "I'm going to be more than okay. And there's something else, too, Ben. My memory—"

"It doesn't matter." Leaning closer, he gently kissed her lips. "If you never remember, Penny, it doesn't matter. I've been a fool."

"But, Ben, I—"

"No, listen. Please, honey. I've done nothing but think of all the things I should have told you, worrying that I'd never have the chance. But I have the chance now, so let me tell you. Please." Ben looked at her, so glad to see her alive and in one piece he could barely think straight.

She nodded, eyes wide and searching.

"I was wrong," he whispered. "Feeling sorry for myself, and blaming you for all the pain. When I should have been thanking my lucky stars you'd come back to me...that I'd been given another chance with you." He swallowed hard, clasping both her hands in his. "Penny, you did what you did for me. I've been wondering if I might not have done the same thing if I'd been the one sick. Dying. I know I would have wanted to spare you the pain of watching me waste away slowly. You did it out of love. All that pain I've been in since I lost you—you're the one who took it away. You brought me back, honey. I swear, since you've been gone, I've been as dead inside as I thought you were."

He drew her hands to his mouth and kissed them.

"I've waited...wished to hear these things for so long, Ben," she whispered.

"I know. I should have told you. I've been so blind. Penny, you have to believe there's never been anything but friendship between Kirsten and me. I haven't so much as touched another woman since you left."

She blinked up at him. "You haven't?"

"How could I? I loved you." He stroked her hands, then her face. "I still love you."

Closing her eyes, she asked him, "Even if I never remember?"

"Even if you never remember," he told her.

Her eyes opened, and she smiled, though her lips trembled. "I'm glad. But, Ben...I remember," she told him. "It's all coming back to me. All of it. Everything we had. Our wedding day...."

He squeezed his eyes tight to prevent his tears from spilling over, lowered his head and pressed her hands to his brow.

"But...but it's not going to change me, Ben. I'll never be that weak, dependent, sick wife who left you two years ago."

He brought his head up slowly. "That woman never would have survived this," he told her. "But you did. You and your girl-detective ploys. You led us right to you, Penny. You know that?"

"I don't care about that."

The medics started to wheel her toward the waiting ambulance. But she held up a hand, and they stopped. "Please, give us just one more minute."

The men in white exchanged glances, nodded and moved away to where Barlow sat, handcuffed, in the grass on the other side of the car.

Penny licked her lips. "I need to know, Ben...can you ever... can you love me as much? I mean, me—the woman I am now. Not the one I was before...before all this. Because if you can't, then you might as well tell me now. I know it might take time, but—"

"Shh." Ben pressed a gentle finger to her lips. "The woman you are...honey, don't you know that's who I fell in love with in the first place?"

She frowned in confusion.

"Penny, this is you. This is who you always were. That disease...that's what turned you into someone else. You were diagnosed so young...you never had a chance to become the woman you were supposed to be. Instead you grew into a patient...a terminal patient."

She bit her lip. "I know. I was...I was hopeless. Already dead inside, I think."

"It took me a while, honey, but I see it now. You're not different. You're exactly who you would have been if that damned HWS had never happened. The adult version of the girl you were before we found out. I loved that girl. I kept on loving her when she got sick. I still love her. I love her more than ever."

"Do you mean that?"

Tears were flooding her eyes, and a smile teased her lips. Ben leaned close, kissed her tenderly. "I mean it, Penny." He searched her face, drinking in her beauty and thinking he must be the luckiest man in the world.

"Then it's complete," she whispered. "I have my life back…all of it."

Ben smiled down at her. "We have our life back," he corrected her gently. "And what a life it's going to be."

"I love you, Ben. I love you—and I never stopped. Not really."

Ben closed his eyes and drank in the sound of those precious words he'd thought he'd never hear again. Then he reached into his pocket and pulled out her wedding band. "Promise me," he said as he slipped it onto her finger where it belonged, "you're never going to take this off again."

"I won't," she told him. "Not ever."

EPILOGUE

Six weeks later

Penny sat on the porch swing thumbing through the text-book for the course she'd be taking at the university this fall. Private Investigations 101. Olive lay in the huge doggy bed Ben had bought for her, nursing her four bulldog pups, all of whom resembled piglets more than they did puppies at this point. Jessi had to deliver them by cesarean section, a turn of events she'd assured Penny was not uncommon in bulldogs. The pups' heads tended to be huge.

Penny smiled and thanked the fates that she had such a wonderful family.

Ben came out to sit in the swing beside her. He patted Olive on the head as he passed, then slipped his big arm around Penny's shoulders and gently kissed her cheek. "Here," he said. "Put the professional-snooping book down for a second, and take a look at this."

She glanced at the newspaper he held, then dropped her

book and took it from him. The sensational headline screamed Mad Doctor Provides Keys To Curing Rare Disease.

"Is this true?" Penny asked as her gaze eagerly skimmed the lines of text.

"Sure is. Barlow turned over all his research," Ben told her. "He's cooperating fully from the psych hospital where they put him."

"That's wonderful!"

"Paper says that with a bit of fine tuning, his treatment program is going to eradicate HWS for good."

Penny sighed. "Thank God. You know, the man is a genius. He just...he just cared too much, I think. Losing his mother when he was so close to finding a cure...it just pushed him over the edge."

"I wanted to kill him," Ben said softly. "But I'm grateful to him at the same time."

"I know. It's odd, isn't it?"

Ben nodded, kissed her again, then leaned back on the swing as Penny snuggled closer to him.

"Ben?"

"Mmm?"

"You remember that collection of Nancy Drew books I had?"

He smiled lazily as she tipped her head to look up at him. "How could I forget? You insisted on moving them in with you when we got married. They took up half the space in the bedroom closet."

She laughed. "Don't you dare complain about Nancy. Her methods saved my butt."

"Who's complaining? Nancy should be sainted."

Olive lifted her head. "Mrruff."

"See? Even Stubby agrees," Ben said.

Penny stroked Ben's chest and closed her eyes. "Are they still there?"

"The books?"

She nodded.

Ben's hand ran gently over her hair. "Do you think I could bring myself to get rid of anything that was yours, sweetheart?"

"Then you kept them?" she asked.

"Yeah. They're the reason that top shelf in the closet is buckling in the middle. Why?"

She drew a deep breath, sat up and took his hand in hers. Gently she pressed his palm to her belly. "I thought our baby might enjoy reading them someday."

"Sure, someday when we—" He stopped talking, sat up straighter and gaped at her. Olive did likewise, tilting her head to one side and cocking her ears. "Are you saying...we're having...?"

Penny nodded. "We're having a baby, Ben."

Ben leaped to his feet, hollering at the top of his lungs until a half-dozen Brands spilled out of the house to see what was causing such a commotion. He scooped Penny out of the swing, right up into his arms, and kissed her long and hard as Olive jumped out of her bed and danced excitedly around his feet. The four pups peered out, blinking fuzzily and wondering where their lunch had gone.

"What in the Sam Hill is going on out here?" Adam asked, looking from Ben to Penny and back again.

"I'm gonna be a daddy, that's what!" Ben shouted, and his face practically glowed as he gazed down at Penny. "I'm gonna be a daddy."

"Hallelujah!" Adam shouted, yanking off his hat and slapping his thigh with it.

"Hot damn!" Garrett yelled, hugging his wife.

"Congratulations!" Chelsea said, sniffling.

"We're gonna need a bigger house," Elliot observed thoughtfully. But then he grinned ear to ear and let out an earsplitting "Yee-haw! I gotta call Jessi! And Wes, Wes is gonna want to know about this!"

Olive jumped and spun in circles and barked with unconcealed excitement. Even old Blue came to the front door to check out the revelry, peering through the screen with his brows raised in question.

Penny gazed at the smiling faces of all those Brands, and felt them sharing her joy. Chelsea was crying already, for heaven's sake.

Then she faced her husband once more. "If it's a girl," she said, "I want to name her Nancy."

Ben frowned for just a second. "Well, then I surely hope she's a girl."

"Why?"

"'Cause if she's a boy, we're gonna have to name her Reginald."

Penny tilted her head to one side. "Reginald?"

All the other Brands frowned at Ben and chorused, "Reginald?"

Ben shrugged. "It's a long story."

Then he smiled down at his wife again, and Penny rested her head on his shoulder and knew she was home. Surrounded by love, no matter where she looked. She'd never leave this place, or these people. The family she'd nearly lost, the man even amnesia couldn't make her forget, the love of her life, a love that could not be defeated or erased, no matter what.

Tears in her eyes, she looked deeply into his and saw dampness there, as well. And it touched her soul. "I'm so happy," she whispered.

"And I'm gonna make sure you always are, Penny. Just this happy. Always."

-THE END-
Continue reading for an excerpt from
THE LONE COWBOY

THE LONE COWBOY

PROLOGUE

SILVER CITY, NEW YORK 1985

The broadsword missed his neck by mere inches, flashing by so close Marcus actually felt it.

Caine smiled. His face craggy, rugged. Fifty-two, and the lines in his face showing every day of it. But he moved like a twenty-year-old, and his cobalt blue eyes sparkled with the mischievous charm of a schoolboy.

He lunged forward, thrusting the sword upward, but Marcus dodged the blade and brought his own down atop it. When Caine's weapon clattered to the floor, the older man smiled. "First time you've disarmed me, boy. Either I'm getting older or you're getting better." He tugged at the front of his sweat-damp, sleeveless T-shirt.

Marcus didn't relax. The old man was full of tricks. He resisted the urge to swipe away a trickle running down the center of his own bare chest and stayed focused.

Caine turned as if to walk away, only to whirl again, quarterstaff in hand. He spun the thing like a windmill, passing it from one hand to the other as he came closer.

Marcus tossed the broadsword down and picked up a staff of his own from the racks of weapons lining the gym walls. For a time they circled each other, and then they sprang, and the echoes of wood crashing against wood filled the room to deafening levels.

Caine's staff broke Marcus's in two. Marcus gave a mocking bow. "One for one," he said. "Care for some hand-to-hand combat?"

"Not this time." Caine pulled a gun, a small black revolver, and pointed it at Marcus.

Marcus froze. He froze just the way he had nine years ago. And for an instant, he could hear it all again. The rapid pattering fire of the automatic. His mother's anguished scream.

She'd screamed a name. A name he couldn't remember, like so many other things about his childhood. But he remembered that day. Just before Christmas. His little sister, Sara, all excited because they were going to their cousins' ranch in Texas as they did almost every Christmas. His little sister, Sara. And his mother and his father. Dead. All of them.

Marcus hated Christmas.

The sounds faded, and eventually the smell of gunpowder did, as well. Not real. Memories. Faded, half-formed, but part of his past. Marcus lifted his chin.

"I don't train with guns. You know that."

"And I understand it, Marcus. Better than you know. In nine years, I've never pushed the issue."

"So why are you pointing that filthy thing at me now?"

Caine shrugged, lifting one eyebrow and cocking his head as he did. "You're nineteen, Marcus, and you can call yourself an expert in just about any form of combat I can think of. All except one."

"And that's good enough. I'll never use a gun. Hell, I'll probably never use any of this stuff you're always teaching me. Sometimes I wonder why you bother—"

"I have my reasons. Besides, knowledge is power."

"You've certainly seen to it I'm powerful, then." Caine had taught him everything. Marcus was fluent in seven languages, could do complex calculations in his head, knew the names of the leading lawmakers of every country in the world and could draw maps of most of those countries. He had never known why he had to know all these things. It had never occurred to him to ask until very recently. It always just... was. "But I'll never use a gun," he finally said.

"Don't use one, then. But learn to defend yourself against those who do." Both brows rose this time, accompanied by a slight nod as if to say, "Make sense?"

"All right. What do I do?"

"Use your feet. It's unexpected, fast and effective. However, accuracy is vital. You miss, you don't get another chance. Spinning back kick or a simple crescent. Just hit the target. Ready?"

Marcus nodded. Caine lowered the gun, then quickly lifted it again. Marcus spun, kicked and missed by six inches.

"Bang. You're dead. Try again."

Sighing, Marcus complied. He'd always complied with Caine's wishes. Devoured Caine's instructions. Caine was all he had. All he'd had since that Christmas nine years ago, when the older man had come upon a ten-year-old boy wandering the dark streets in shock. Unable to speak, barely able to remember his own name. Marcus didn't know what would have happened to him without Caine. He supposed if he could love anyone, he'd love the old man. But since he couldn't, didn't even want to, he simply called it fondness. Caring.

On the tenth try, Marcus hit the gun and sent it sailing from Caine's hand. The man smiled and slapped Marcus's back, the closest thing to physical affection he'd ever demonstrated. He's a loner, Marcus thought. Like me. Two of a kind.

"Good boy."

There was a tap at the double doors. They opened, and Graham stepped in. Impeccable black suit, black shirt underneath. Nehru collar, no tie. Unlike Caine's, Graham's face was ageless. He could be Caine's age or twenty years older. It was impossible to tell. Silver hair, contrasting with dark brows. Lean, but still muscular. Fit. Marcus had never been exactly sure what Graham did besides provide sarcasm and take care of the two of them. He'd seen the older man working in the room downstairs with all the computer equipment once or twice, but he wasn't supposed to go down there, so he'd never asked. On the surface, Graham acted like a butler, but that was some kind of scam. He was no gentleman's gentleman.

"The morning paper, Caine," Graham said, very butler-like but with a twinkle of mirth in his eyes. As if it were some inside joke.

"Couldn't it wait until breakfast? We're starved."

"Oh," Graham said, and sniffed. "I hope there's ample time for a shower first."

Caine looked at Marcus. "I think he just said we stink."

"We do," Marcus said, and took the paper from Graham, curious. He read the front-page headline, shook his head, rolled his eyes. "It's that urban-legend garbage they keep playing up. 'The Guardian Strikes Again.' God, what a crock."

"Utter nonsense," Graham said.

"Absolutely," Caine added. "Read it to us, Marcus." He slung a towel around his neck and led the way out of the gym, heading for the showers. Graham followed.

Marcus brought up the rear, reading aloud as he walked.

∽

"**SILVER CITY LIQUOR** Emporium was the scene of an attempted robbery last night. Witnesses claim two men wearing ski masks and wielding shotguns burst in demanding cash. The attempt was foiled by a man dressed all in black, wearing a long dark coat and a wide-brimmed fedora pulled low to shadow his face. This man—who matches other crime-scene descriptions of Silver City's legendary Guardian—quickly disarmed the suspects with no more than his bare hands. 'He just flew into action,' Tim Gaines, the cashier on duty, said. 'And the next thing we knew, the two creeps were on the floor whimpering and the big guy stood there ejecting the shells from their guns.'

Police arrived to find the suspects bound, gagged and disarmed. The unnamed hero simply vanished into the night. 'It was him,' Gaines told reporters. 'It was the Guardian, I know it was. I just wish there were some way I could thank him.'

So if you're out there reading this, Guardian, Tim Gaines sends his thanks. And so do all the citizens of Silver City."

∽

MARCUS FOLDED THE paper and handed it to Graham. They stood in the dressing room where the showers were now. Caine was already cranking on the water and stepping into a shower stall out of sight

"Sensationalism, pure and simple. That and a few scared, confused witnesses." Marcus reached into another stall to turn on the water.

"You're quite right, I'm sure," Graham said. Then he turned to go, clearing his throat as he did so.

Marcus popped his head out of the shower stall to look after him. For a second there, he thought Graham's overblown throat clearing had been disguising a laugh.

Nah.

∽

MARCUS HAD BEEN wanting to go out into the world by himself for a while now. It wasn't that he wanted anything to do with people. He didn't. He liked things just the way they were. It was safe behind the gilded gates of Caine's estate. He didn't have to deal with anyone—no complicated relationship skills to master. Just the lessons.

But he was curious. He didn't want to take part, he just wanted to...observe.

Of course, Caine forbade this, though Marcus never knew why. Not that it mattered. He'd always been fairly strong willed, and though he'd never disobeyed Caine before, he did this time.

He slipped out, after dark.

It was winter in Silver City. Christmas season in full swing. Snow danced through the night sky and dusted the sidewalks and cars. And Marcus walked, trying to ignore it. It was tough, though. Carols blasted from speakers attached to every lamp-post. The shop windows were lined with colored bulbs and pine trees were decorated so heavily their boughs drooped under the weight. People ran past him with red and green foil shopping bags and gaily wrapped packages.

He hated Christmas.

He hadn't always. The nightmare had happened just before Christmas though, and he'd never enjoy the holiday again. Besides, he could barely remember the Christmases before that tragic one. Just vague bits and pieces. Some cousins. That ranch in Texas. Riding horses. Something about a porch swing his little sister would never leave alone.

He gave his head a shake and continued walking. He wasn't a part of this, he realized. He was different. Like some alien walking among earthlings. He didn't belong. He was no more like the people around him than he was like the snow-dusted sidewalk under his feet He didn't interact. Didn't connect or communicate. He just observed. Detached, but interested in spite of himself.

This became his ritual, his secret, his...hobby, if you wanted to call it that. This observing.

Until one night, when he came upon something he couldn't watch dispassionately.

It began with a scream that seemed to split Marcus right down the center of his being. So like his mother's scream. And again he was ten years old, impotent to help her, so frightened he was unable to even try.

But then he saw the men—young men, several wielding blades—crowding closer to a woman whose back was pressed to the far wall in a dead-end alley, and he snapped out of the momentary flashback.

The old rage, though, remained. The same rage he'd felt years ago and been unable to act on. Now he didn't think, he just moved. The terror-stricken woman huddled, wide-eyed, while Marcus kicked the hell out of her would-be attackers. Six of them. Four went down, two ran off.

Marcus stood there a moment, slightly amazed. He'd frankly expected to get his ass kicked. It was the first time he really understood just how powerful he was compared to other men. They couldn't fight their way out of a shoe box. He wasn't even winded. All thanks to Caine.

Shaking his head, Marcus turned to the woman and took a step toward her. But she suddenly shifted her gaze and pointed past him, babbling something incoherent.

Marcus sensed the movement, started to turn, caught what was happening from the corner of his eye. One of the men he'd put down was getting up. He had a gun and was lifting it, aiming it at Marcus.

Marcus spun the way Caine had taught him, but he knew there was no time. Then two things happened at once.

The gun went off.

And a man dressed in black, wearing a fedora with an

unusually large rim, lunged out of the shadows and into the path of the bullet.

The man in black jerked, then crumpled to the ground. Marcus finished his motion, kicked the assailant, sent the gun sailing, kicked the man again and knocked him cold. Then he bent over the fallen hero.

"My God," Marcus whispered. "You're real. It's true. You're...the Guardian."

The hat brim bobbed with the man's weak nod. "That's right, Marcus. I am."

Marcus felt his heart stop in his chest at the familiar voice. "Caine?" Gently, he lifted away the hat. It was. His own mentor—the Guardian. "B-but...how? Why?"

Caine's face contorted in pain. "Take me home, son. There's a lot you need to know. Not much time, I'm afraid."

"But—"

"Take me home, Marcus. Take me home."

∽

"I WASN'T THE FIRST."

Marcus sat beside the bed. The doctor had come and gone by now but he'd said there wasn't a thing he could do. The strongest man Marcus had ever known was dying. And yet Marcus thought he'd never really known Caine at all.

"The first took me in when my parents were killed. He trained me, raised me. When he retired, I stepped up to take his place as Silver City's Guardian."

"Why?"

Caine wasn't in pain. Thank God. The doctor had given him something to take the edge off. But he'd refused to be overly sedated. Said he had things to say, things to see to, before he went.

Caine shrugged then, in that way he had, not just with his

shoulders but with one eyebrow and a slight cocking of his head. "Had a score to settle. Criminals took away my life. I wanted payback. But it was more than that, Marcus. Some men...just aren't cut out for that other kind of life. I liked the solitude, the protection of secrecy. The anonymity. It was..."

"Safe," Marcus said.

Caine nodded. "I was on my way to help your family that day, Marcus."

Marcus's head came up, and he supposed he looked startled.

"Graham...he has ways of finding out things. Computers, connections. He got a tip about the hit, and I was on my way. But I was too late. By the time I got there it was over. I was devastated. My first failure, and I felt solely responsible for your family being killed. I wandered in the night, alone, miserable, and then I spotted you. And I knew immediately who you were."

Marcus nodded.

"It was meant to be, I think. I took you in, trained you. Now...now it's your turn, Marcus."

"My turn?" He stared at Caine with wide eyes.

"Everything I have is yours now. My wealth. The estate." He nodded at the rack near the door. "The coat and the hat. The identity."

"B-but...I'm not ready."

"Yes, Marcus, you are. Graham will help you."

"I can't..." Marcus shook his head, terror filling him. He could never fill Caine's shoes. Never. Caine was the greatest man he'd ever known. How could he even try to live up to such a legacy?

"I'm counting on you Marcus. It's my dying wish. Promise me you'll carry on in my place."

Marcus closed his eyes, lowered his head. "All right. I promise. I'll do my best, Caine."

"I know you will, son. I know you will."

Look for The Lone Cowboy

**Don't miss any of the books in
The Texas Brands Series**

The Littlest Cowboy
The Baddest Virgin in Texas
Badlands, Bad Boy
Long Gone Lonesome Blues
The Lone Cowboy
Lone Star Lonely
The Outlaw Bride
Texas Angel
Texas Homecoming

ALSO AVAILABLE

The McIntyre Men
Oklahoma Christmas Blues
Oklahoma Moonshine
Oklahoma Starshine
Shine On Oklahoma
Baby By Christmas
Oklahoma Sunshine

The Oklahoma Brands
The Brands who Came for Christmas
Brand-New Heartache
Secrets and Lies
A Mommy For Christmas
One Magic Summer
Sweet Vidalia Brand

ABOUT THE AUTHOR

New York Times bestselling author Maggie Shayne has published more than 50 novels and 23 novellas. She has written for 7 publishers and 2 soap operas, has racked up 15 Rita Award nominations and actually, finally, won the damn thing in 2005.

Maggie lives in a beautiful, century old, happily haunted farmhouse named "Serenity" in the wildest wilds of Cortland County, NY, with her soul-mate, Lance. They share a pair of English Mastiffs, Dozer & Daisy, and a little English Bulldog, Niblet, and the wise guardian and guru of them all, the feline Glory, who keeps the dogs firmly in their places. Maggie's a Wiccan high priestess (legal clergy even) and an avid follower of the Law of Attraction.

Find Maggie at http://maggieshayne.com

        facebook.com/maggieshayneauthor
        twitter.com#!/maggieshayne
        instagram.com/maggieshayne
        bookbub.com/authors/maggie-shayne